GRADY WHILL

AND THE TEMPLETON CODEX

A SUPERHERO HIGH SCHOOL ADVENTURE

CAROLE P. ROMAN

978-1-950080-43-4 Paperback

978-1-950080-04-5 Hardcover

Chelshire, Inc.

Photo credit Owen Kassimir

"What lies behind us and what lies before us are tiny matters compared to what lies within us." Henry Stanley Haskins

For Dad and Mom —my first heroes

Carole P. Roman

PROLOGUE

SCARFACE MOUNTAIN – PRESENT DAY

THERE WHILL BE BLOOD

A BARELY COOLED LUMP of lava hardened under my feet. One of my sneakers was stuck between two small rocks in the solidifying mess. I stared at my foot in disbelief. Instinct told me I should be a human torch, my legs nothing more than toasted stumps. I glanced up, my heart beating wildly. We were trapped on the side of the mountain facing our school, separated by a burning sea of molten rocks.

The world around me steamed, the lava staining the sky burnt orange. Trees swallowed by molten rock looked like skeletal hands emerging from a grave that glowed beneath the blackened crust. I saw heat waves shimmering from the earth but felt none of its intensity. I pulled fiercely, feeling my ankle twist. Aarush steadied me as I nearly toppled over. He was shirtless, his back slick with sweat and covered with scrapes. His fingers worked feverishly to free my foot.

Overhead two helicopter-sized pterodactyls circled the craggy summit. The wind from their leathery wings buffeted the two of us. I think the air they circulated stopped the patches of lava from cooking us alive, but what do I know?

"We better get moving, Grady. Leave your sneaker. We are risking getting burned by staying too long in one spot." The ever-practical Aarush reasoned as he pulled the velcro releasing my foot. I wobbled, then fell to one knee.

"Do you think they're real?" I hollered to my friend over the noise, pointing upward.

"I'm not sure," Aarush responded with a shake of his head. "Right now I can't tell the difference between fantasy and reality." The answer to that question was resolved when one of the predatory birds spiraled downward in a dive. "We have to go that way!" He waved to the lee side of the mountain, where small brush fires dotted the hillside. "The lava appears to be traveling in the other direction." His hands moved to push glasses up on his nose, only to realize they were long gone, lost in our escape.

"Look out!" Aarush hunched down as the wind from the pterodactyl's wings fanned the area around us. "Oh yes, I'd say they're real!"

Flames shot up as the aptly named Scarface Mountain erupted like a Fourth of July Fireworks show.

"It's not even a volcano!" Aarush shouted, his voice cracking. I could hardly hear him over the buzzing and hissing spewing from the hollow cone. I looked at his face, wondering if this was a good time to tell him he didn't look like he was on the spectrum. Displays of emotion didn't come easily to him.

"Really?" I shouted. "You think that matters now?"

The earth shook, breaking the surface around us. Stones bobbed like buoys in a burning river. The ground collapsed cracking open a chasm, the sulfuric smell of rotting eggs assailed my nostrils. We both fell onto the soil sliding down Scarface's rocky incline. I closed my eyes, the world spinning by with dizzying speed.

I heard Aarush scream. "Tuck your head and elbows!"

It seemed like the natural thing to do. Covering my head, I pulled up my knees allowing my arms and flank to take the worst of the beating while I prayed the lava stayed on the other side of the hill.

Trees uprooted and debris loosened as if someone had upended the mountain like a salt shaker. We rolled, our clothes catching on torn roots. Branches lashed my face. the musty scent filled my nostrils until I thought I would choke. I didn't know if it was the beating I was taking or the smell. Either way, tears coursed down my face.

Aarush rushed past me. Sharp rocks dug into my skin, scraping me raw. The rapid descent and the spinning scenery made my gorge rise. All I saw was a blurred green landscape as if water had diluted a painting leaving everything indistinct, smudged.

My chest tightened as it did when I became skittish, my breathing turning into a wheeze. "Breathe!" My inner-voice ordered. The air was sucked out rather than in, no matter how I tried I couldn't get my lungs to cooperate. Snatches of the breathing exercises flitted through my memory like a disjointed movie. Try as I might, I couldn't get my mind and body to work together.

I couldn't focus beyond the fact that I was sure I was about to die. Someone must have been watching over us as we made our descent. It was a miracle that neither of us ended up a splattered mess against a boulder.

I clutched at the racing ground trying to find a loose root to grab. My rubbery legs were soon too numb to be of any use.

Breathe in, breathe out. I closed my eyes, concentrating on my strained airways, trying to implement the training Miss Garcia had pounded into my head. No luck. My world narrowed to a tiny pinprick as I struggled for oxygen.

I heard a splash as I landed in a babbling brook a minute later. Maybe that was Aarush babbling. I was too winded to know the difference.

Cold water stole what little breath was left in my battered body, soaking through my school uniform, making it stick to my backside. The material was supposed to be impervious to water. It was obvious it had to be sent back for product testing. Apparently the special material failed under extraordinary circumstances. The cloth acted like a sponge becoming waterlogged and weighted on my body.

I noticed with no small amount of relief that it was cold and we hadn't landed in a sea of burning lava.

"Where's the lava?" I croaked.

"It went down the front side of the mountain," Aarush gasped.

I splashed around in the water as I tried to rise. Even though it was no deeper than a few inches, my body felt leaden.

We had to get moving.

My muscles refused to work no matter how hard I coaxed them. I was a patchwork of stinging abrasions, and I tasted iron in my mouth where I'd bitten my tongue. Rolling over, I crawled on my stomach to the edge of the water. I lay onto the bank where I tried to catch my breath. Blood dripped into my eye from a cut over my brow making my vision fuzzy.

My left hand appeared to be stuck. I fumbled with my right hand to find my inhaler they'd given me at school, blindly bringing it to my lips to take a blessed puff. It worked faster than any inhaler I used at home. The medicine filled my throat, traveling into my airways opening my chest like bellows.

Relief. Pure relief. It worked. My airways expanded. I wasn't so positive about the rest of my body. I tugged my left arm, but it wouldn't move.

Someone groaned. I'm pretty sure it wasn't me. I had to get up and help Aarush. Taking another deep breath, I crushed the crazy thoughts galloping in my head and focused on what to do next.

On a shaking elbow, I propped myself up to find a pair of finely polished boots planted on top of my hand. The foot pressed down, gently at first, then with a bit of force, enough so small pieces of gravel embedded in my flesh. I pressed my mouth into a firm line, refusing to utter a sound. The tips of my ears burned. I knew they were bright red; I could feel their heat. It matched the warmth of the ring I wore around my neck.

The sound of a deep voice snickering sent chills down my spine. It grew into booming laughter that filled the ravine, the sound of it reminding me how much I hated that kind of thing.

I peered up. The bright sun blotted out my captor's face. I didn't need to see it to know who was above me. I recognized the voice.

The prehistoric birds made one last circle over us. I watched, stupefied, as they banked toward the setting sun.

"At last!" he shouted to the sky like a triumphant combatant.

At last? I thought. *Who speaks like that?* A chuckle escaped my lips before I could stop it. *Is that the best you can do?* I wanted to ask. I pulled my hand, trying to extricate myself.

Oddly enough, he let me. I rolled onto my back and considered the goliath looming over me. His jutting chin obstructed my view of his face. As if he knew what I was thinking, he looked down so I could see the dark pits that served as eyes. Hunched like a Neanderthal, he towered over me, an evil smile revealing oversized teeth. They could have been tombstones they were so big. His jawline hardened into granite as I watched him.

You think I'm kidding? I watched his skin tone change as his flesh tightened into living and breathing stone—impossible, magical, living and breathing stone.

"Now what?" he asked, his voice echoing in the small newly created canyon.

Good question, I wanted to say, but having felt the power of those solid fists, I felt it prudent not to volunteer anything. We had a good, long stare that seemed to go on forever.

Like me, you're probably wondering how I got here. Long story.

My name is Grady Whill, and a little over twelve months ago, I was an average kind of guy in a mediocre middle school with a brilliant but nerdy best friend.

Aarush moaned.

Yep, that's him.

CHAPTER 1

WHERE THERE'S A WHILL –

TWELVE MONTHS EARLIER

"THERE'S NO WAY I'm going to get in." I crumpled the pamphlet in my hand and tossed it toward the trash can. It bounced off Gerald Thurson's half-eaten bologna sandwich to land on the floor in a colorful puddle of orange juice. The paper soaked up the liquid, darkening, the vibrant pictures dulled as if it were being burned.

Someone pounded into my back, knocking me against the garbage can so that both of us fell over in a tangle of gangly limbs.

"Hey!" My forearm automatically shot backward, almost connecting with the soft cheek of Aarush Patel. "What the heck, Aarush?" We landed on the lunchroom floor. I raised my hand with a sticky wad of gum now attached to it.

Aarush was on his back, propped up by his bony elbows,

his glasses lying crooked on his large nose. "Elwood pushed me." Aarush rolled his eyes at the retreating back of the middle-school quarterback. "Ugh. This place. I wish I could get into—"

"Don't even say it." I stood, then reached down to haul him up. I brushed off the remnants of the bologna sandwich from Aarush's khaki pants. "You're going to have to be careful when you go past Ivan's house on your way home. You look like Processed Meat Man."

"Ivan's house?"

I gave him an arch look, one eyebrow almost reaching my hairline. It was a hidden talent, and I had spent hours perfecting it. It worked great when I needed to make a point. In this case it was about Ivan's pit bull, Marcie.

Aarush blew a gust of air from his mouth and with a nod confirmed, "Marcie."

He rubbed vainly at the glob of mayo on his knee. "Maybe the mayonnaise will disguise the meat odor." Aarush spoke mostly in a monotone. I don't think anyone had ever heard him raise his voice an octave much above a whisper. Right now, he was obsessing about the mayo stain. I knew it would bother him for the rest of the day to the point that he would miss the conversations going on around him.

Not that anybody is too eager to talk to him anyway. Aarush did just fine for most of elementary school until some aide let it slip that he was on the spectrum, then slowly kids drifted away. Playdates and parties became rare for him.

I guess parents thought it might be catching, like he'd cough and you could get infected with autism.

I'd known Aarush almost my whole life. He wasn't diagnosed until he was eight. The day after the doctors informed his parents, he still looked and acted the same to me.

"Leave it." I shook my head. He was smearing the stain down his leg, his hands scrubbing and making it worse. He did that when he was upset. It was as if he didn't have a shutoff valve.

Sound receded and I knew he was attracting attention. Next would come the taunts. Onlookers made everything worse.

"We'll take the long way home, Aarush," I told him from the side of my mouth so no one would hear me. "Stop. It's okay."

With a sigh, Aarush picked off a piece of half-eaten meat glued to his plaid shirt.

"That's better than Potato Chip Man," I offered, trying my best to sidetrack him. Aarush was a hard person to distract.

Aarush's top lips tilted in what passed as an Aarush smile. I brushed off a cluster of chips onto the floor that was embedded in my shirt at the shoulder.

Aarush was the most serious kid I'd ever met, yet when he smiled, I have to tell you, his face transformed. It might have been slight, but it was there. His dark eyes lit up with merriment, as if he knew a joke and was sharing it with you. I couldn't understand why no one else could see it.

They called him Robot Boy or a lot of other less complimentary names. Aarush always took it in stride as if it didn't bother him. I always wondered though if deep down inside, it did. I know it bothered me. Over the years, more than one of my old friends melted away, as if I had to choose between him and them. For me, there was no contest. Anyone who'd make you pick one friend over another is not worth investing your time.

Not for nothing, he had been my best friend since pre-K,

and he played a killer game of *Super Dude*, our favorite video game. Super Dude was the epitome of all superheroes, impervious to nuclear events, and managed to save the mythical folks of Silicon City without breaking a sweat. I don't like to admit it, but he had a few chinks in his armor, Master Disaster being his major Achilles heel. But what's a superhero without a nemesis? Pretty boring, I'd say.

I heard laughter, looked up to find the school jock, Elwood Bledsoe, and his group of followers, as they pushed past us kicking the garbage that had fallen from the trash can into the center of the room, turning the small pile of refuse into a more noticeable mess. If Master Disaster was Super Dude's enemy, Elwood Bledsoe was mine. You could say we had a history. My hands curled into fists, but I kept them hidden at my sides.

Elwood set his court up at the corner table. He was surrounded by the popular kids. He sat on the tabletop, breaking almost every lunchroom rule. The lunchroom aide, Mr. Mason, lounged behind him, his back to the wall, clearly ignoring Elwood's violation.

Mr. Mason was hired to watch us in the lunchroom and during recess. I was taller than him already and probably outweighed him by a few pounds. He wasn't a teacher, but some sort of all-around aide the school brought in to help with security, and other odd jobs needed throughout the day. Right now, he was manning the lunchroom making sure we didn't revolt from the crappy snack food they'd recently brought in. He had a poor excuse for a mustache that clung to his thin upper lip. His long hair was combed over his small head and tucked behind two of the biggest ears I'd ever seen outside of a circus tent. Those ears, I had learned, had very selective hearing. Mr. Mason rocked on his black sneakers, his beady eyes watching me.

"I'd like to—" I started. I was sick of Mr. Mason, Elwood Bledsoe, and school in general.

"Like to what?" Aarush interrupted me. "You can't win." He held up his hands, ticking off each point with his fingers. He could be analytical at the most inconvenient times. At least he had stopped fixating about the grease stain on his pants leg.

Only right now, I wanted nothing more than to retaliate against the bully. Adrenaline coursed through my body, but Aarush's voice persisted. "One, he's the school star, beloved by everyone. Two, he's massive. He could crush Super Dude with those ham-sized hands."

"He couldn't crush Super Dude," I said, horrified at the mere thought, interrupting him. I didn't care if I was rude. Aarush Patel was the nicest guy in the whole school, but that was sacrilege. "No way. Super Dude wouldn't even waste time on a creep like Elwood Bledsoe."

"Would too," Aarush shot back quickly, watching for my reaction. He was distracting me, just as I had done before to him, and we both knew it.

I shook my head. "I'm not doing this with you, Aarush."

"Won't matter. You will lose this argument." Aarush stopped speaking. He spied a wadded-up ball of paper on the floor. "What's this?" He reached down to grab it.

"Leave it." I kicked it under the table.

Aarush snatched it up. "That's the application. You were supposed to bring it home. Your uncle has to fill it out. I can't go there without you."

"Go without me? Aarush, wake up, bro. We are never getting into the Temple. No way, no how." Temple was Templeton

Academy for those of us on a first-name basis with the best and newest school in the universe. Getting in was the dream of almost everyone I knew.

"Of course we are going to Templeton Acedemy." Aarush's voice was reasonable, as if being one of five hundred hand-picked special students to attend the most exclusive high school in the world were possible.

"Besides"—I waved my hand—"my uncle can't afford—"

"Tuition is free," Aarush stated.

"And there's the extra supplies I would have to buy. I'll be going to Middlebury High with the rest of this riffraff." I gestured at the packed lunchroom. We still had a good part of the school year to go before graduation.

"There will be grants." Aarush was nothing if not insistent. He placed his books on the table and gave me his full attention. "I could ask my father." He smoothed out the application in the middle of the brochure.

"No. I'm not taking charity." Both of Aarush's parents were doctors. Money was never an issue. I was an orphan, living with my father's brother, who was barely old enough to take care of himself, never mind me.

I never revealed my past to just anyone. I hated pity. My parents died when I was an infant, leaving me to the care of my grandparents. Don't get all moony-eyed; it wasn't bad. You can't miss people you don't remember, and Grandpa and Mema were great grandparents—I mean, not great-grandparents; they were my grandparents. You get it, right? They were nice people. Sadly, illness took one, and the after-effects of a stroke took the other.

Uncle Leo, the son they had late in their lives, was now my guardian. While he hadn't seen thirty yet, he hadn't quite gotten the maturity memo. Sometimes he was overwhelmed with the idea of *me*. He was a shock jock at the local radio station and worked long hours. I think I got paid more than he did with the hour and a half I spent at the supermarket bagging groceries.

"Between friends is never charity." Aarush was organizing trash in size order that students had left on the table.

"Not going to happen." I shook my head, then looked at him. "It's enough, Aarush. The garbage is neat now. Throw it out."

I took an empty milk carton and tossed it toward the trash can. It bounced on the rim and, to the dismay of my audience, landed on the floor. There were a few jeers and some choice words, all relatively harmless.

A whistle blew. "Whill!" Mr. Mason, it seemed, had noticed my failed attempt at basketball. "That's littering. Pick it up." He stomped over, pointing to the crushed milk container, the whistle dangling from a chain around his neck. "In fact, make sure you two are back here at three. You can sweep the entire room."

"We didn't make the mess," I protested.

He came close to my face, his mustache quivering. "You threw the carton." He pointed to the milk container next to the trash that had fallen earlier. "So you made the mess."

"Oh, come on. It's just one container. We don't have to sweep the whole room," I complained as I reached down to toss it in the garbage can. "Besides, I have to go to work. I'll lose my job."

"Be here at three," he said through clenched teeth.

I could hear Elwood hooting a chant, his friends echoing him. "Clean it up! Clean it up! Clean it up!" The first bell rang, cutting off their cheer.

Mr. Mason smiled good-naturedly at them, sharing their fun at our expense and waved them out of the lunchroom.

I snatched the brochure off the table while Aarush cleared the rest of the junk. The paper was wet and cold, but it burned in my hand. I threw it toward the garbage without looking backward. I didn't see Aarush catch it in midair or see him stuff it in his book bag, nor would I expect him to intercept it. Aarush Patel couldn't catch a cold, much less a paper missile.

The second bell rang, letting us know we had to head toward science or suffer another disciplinary action.

CHAPTER 2

MY FIRST DANGEROUS ENCOUNTER

I DON'T WANT TO bore you with class. It's bad enough one of us has to go; no reason we all have to suffer. Suffice it to say the only person having a good time was Aarush.

He was in his element with the elements. This was the Aarush most people saw, someone focused on his subject. While he was a great listener in class, he failed miserably with conversations. It appeared that he didn't relate to the stuff that's important to everybody else. I never found him that way, though. Most people said he couldn't do small talk. I say it's because they never bothered to listen to him. We had lots of great conversations, so maybe the problem was with them rather than Aarush.

Aarush was really interesting. He had laser vision that saw right through the crap. Maybe it was his monotone voice or lack of reaction. He reminded me of Spock—you know, from *Star Trek*—which made me feel like Captain Kirk. Most people don't know what I'm talking about either. That's what happens when the uncle who is raising you is stuck in the eighties watching reruns of the sixties on the Sci-Fi Channel.

In our house it was either *Star Trek* or anything with a zombie. Zombies make me want to puke. Give me a superhero any day. Uncle Leo is, however, king of the remote, and what worked while my grandparents were alive doesn't work now. My uncle reigns supreme over our household like the king from *Game of Thrones*.

History class followed science, where we learned a whole lot of useless information about stuff that happened in the past. I mean, does it really matter what happened five hundred years ago? What's that got to do with today, I'd like to know? At least Mrs. Farber was nice to look at.

Three classes later, Aarush met me at the entrance to the lunchroom. Mr. Mason was waiting, two brooms in hand.

"Lucky for you the custodian cleaned up most of it," he sneered. "I left the remnants from the last study hall." He was referring to the students who met there during free periods for extra studying.

His smirk made me push the broom hard on the floor, smearing crushed snack bars and fruit roll-ups. Aarush worked meticulously on his side of the room. He hung the chairs upside down on the tables and swept methodically, leaving the linoleum spotless.

"Whill." Mason's gravelly voice grated on my nerves. "Look at the job your friend *Rain Man* is doing." He was, of course referring to an autistic character from a movie I'd watched with my uncle.

I didn't even think. "That's it!" I threw down the broom handle, which cracked when it impacted the floor.

Aarush ran over and placed himself between me and the aide, who was now squaring off on the other side. "I don't care." Aarush blocked me.

"You're barely on the spectrum," I said, my voice raw. Aarush simply gave me one of his looks, stopping me in my tracks. *Don't pay attention*, I could almost hear him say it. The air rushed out of me like a deflating balloon. I sighed and grumbled, "At least you won't end up babysitting kids in the cafeteria during lunchtime when you graduate from an Ivy League school." I said it to Aarush knowing Mason was within earshot.

"Stop." Aarush shook his head, looking over his shoulder at the aide. "His opinion of me doesn't mean anything."

Mr. Mason placed his walkie-talkie down and picked up the broken broom as though he was going to use it as a weapon. "You're going to answer for this, Whilly." He held it up close to my face. I eyed him back trying not to flinch.

"There are rules about calling people names," I said. I glanced at the discarded walkie-talkie and added, "You can't do anything to us."

He seemed to wrestle with something, and the moment broke. I guess he must have second thoughts about corporal punishment. I mean, we're in eighth grade in a suburban bubble, not some reform school from one of those old boring English novels.

He grabbed the two-way radio and stalked to the door. "Think so?" he sneered, snapping off the lights, leaving us in the darkened room.

I stood in the shadows, my heart fluttering, my cheeks

flush with anger. Now, not only do I have to deal with Bledsoe, but some creepy school security guy too. Where's a superhero when you need one?

"I'm going to report you!" I shouted out, but it sounded hollow. "Should we say something?" I asked Aarush.

"Nothing happened. All he's going to do is respond that you were obnoxious to him, and he left us alone in here."

"I wasn't!" I burst out then added, "He threatened us."

Aarush shrugged. "Not really. He picked up the broom. He wasn't going to do anything with it."

I looked at him sharply. "How do you know that?"

Aarush nodded once. "He's a bully and a coward. He stretches his authority only to the point that he won't get caught. Observe him, next time. You'll see what I mean."

I replayed everything in my mind, but couldn't wrap my head around what Aarush said.

"Let's go," I told Aarush.

"The long way home," he reminded me, grabbing his bag.

"Any way we go is the long way home," I muttered, disgusted with the school, the other kids, and my life.

We walked home in the late March afternoon. It was chilly enough for jackets, but real men that we were, we didn't wear them. They were squashed in our backpacks.

Aarush sniffed the air. "It will rain soon."

I looked at the clear azure sky, then back to my serious friend. I nodded, trusting him. I've learned not to doubt him. If Aarush says there'll be rain, then you can bet money there'll be rain.

I was in a funk. Selection to Templeton would start soon, and I wasn't anywhere on their radar. I knew I had better give up the dream and accept I'd be spending the next few years here. If only I could get into Templeton Academy. The mysterious Dr. Clifford Templeton and his daughter, Valencia, had founded a new center of learning that supposedly was going to separate the wheat from the chaff. In other words, only select people went there. I bet there were no bullies in the handpicked, elite student body.

My backpack was slung over my shoulder. Aarush kept up a running commentary about some stuff we were learning about DNA. I nodded as I listened, stopping him once or twice to explain something. I was having some trouble distinguishing between the two types of nucleic acids.

An insistent horn broke through my thoughts. I looked up to see a black Explorer pulling alongside.

"Tell the geek to shut up." Elwood Bledsoe had his arm out the passenger window, and to anyone observing this tableau, it would have seemed we were having a friendly chat.

"Hey, you're parked illegally," Aarush called out. "You have to move the car." He squinted to see who was driving, but the windows were darkened.

Elwood snickered, then said in a stage whisper, "Call the cops, *Rooshy*. I bet you memorized their number."

Aarush seemed impervious to the remarks. That Aarush—he had a bulletproof personality. Insults dropped off him like ammunition off a superhero.

"Piss off, Smellwood." I kept my head down.

"Don't call me that," he ground out. "I am Bledsoe." He pointed a finger to his chest.

I opened my mouth to comment about being famous enough to be known by one name seemed a bit ego-driven, but he interrupted me before I could speak.

"You'd better watch how you speak to me. I'm moving out of this dump and won't have to put up with morons like you."

"Shut up," I said.

We used to be friends, Elwood and I. I can't put my finger on what happened, but by fifth grade I'd stopped hanging out with him. We'd grown apart. His idea of fun and mine didn't go together. I couldn't find joy in tripping somebody or giving monumental wedgies, leaving a guy in music class singing like a soprano. I guess as he got meaner, I stopped wanting to hang out with him. He had an ill-concealed hatred of Aarush that made me uncomfortable.

"Thanks for the mess in the lunchroom. I probably lost my job because of you."

"You're such a loser, Grady." He rattled a shiny paper out the window. "Hey, Aarush," he shouted. "I made it. I made early admission to the Temple."

The world receded for a moment. *Elwood Bledsoe made Templeton?* I could feel my heart drop to my knees. My stomach flip-flopped leaving me breathless enough to reach for my asthma inhaler. I willed the feeling away. There was simply no justice in this world.

Aarush stopped dead in his tracks. "What?" He adjusted his glasses and walked quickly over to the car door. "You did not. The names haven't been released yet." He peered at the sheet of wrinkled silver paper. "I don't believe it. You have incredible luck." He reached out to touch the missive. Elwood snatched it back.

"It's probably a fake," I said hoping my voice sounded steady. There had been a rash of forged acceptance letters circulating. I saw a site online where you could buy one for six hundred dollars. For another two-fifty, they had a fake reporter deliver it to you in front of people to make it look real.

Elwood waved the gray envelope from the window. "See? It's addressed to me: Mr. Elwood Bledsoe. It's the real deal."

Aarush backed away, lost in thought.

"Watch this," Elwood told the driver in the next seat.

I heard a soft voice respond. I couldn't make out what was said. I knew the voice, though. It was Lindsay Carruthers, the prettiest girl in the high school. She was the head cheerleader. Aarush was crazy about her. I mean, who could blame him?

Elwood rattled the paper before Aarush's stunned face. Aarush's body tightened until he stood straighter than a soldier. He seemed oblivious to anybody watching him. He was going all distant and hyper-focused on us. *Oh no*, I thought, *Aarush is going to hate himself later.* Even if he didn't, I was mortified enough for us both. I leaned forward to grab his arm.

Elwood kept taunting him. "It's not luck, jerk. It's strength. Raw, unadulterated strength that got me in. Oh yeah, and my superior intellect." Elwood drew out the words proudly.

"Superior-" I started, but snapped my mouth shut when I saw Aarush's expression.

Aarush walked backward five precise steps, pivoted on his heel, and turned in a tight square, his face devoid of emotion, mumbling to himself. I placed my body between Aarush and the SUV to no avail. Everybody in the world could see Aarush going all weird on us.

"Well, congrats. Gotta go," I said walking backward hoping to steer Aarush from their line of sight.

I shook with rage.

This was cruel. You'd have to have been blind to miss Aarush's face whenever he saw Lindsay. He was near to drooling. Right now, he was skipping over mindless drooling by going into a catatonic meltdown.

I watched Elwood preen. He understood how to press Aarush's buttons. He knew Aarush was desperate to be accepted into the new school. *Heck*, we all were.

Templeton Academy was a groundbreaking concept. The school was built in a secret location, cut off from all outside influence. Dr. Clifford Templeton was assembling the greatest minds in the world for a school so special, they claimed they would transform the student body into a class of people with highly advanced abilities. It was the stuff of dreams! Just what those capabilities were, was not explained. It could be anything, but our imaginations went into high gear.

Templeton boasted his team of educators could harness undeveloped talent and train anybody to use their hidden potential to overcome nature. The sky was the limit according to chatter on the internet. All sorts of exciting things were being hinted. The entire concept was mind-blowing. Then, there was the mysterious Codex, a newly discovered ancient artifact that was filled with secrets that made the whole thing possible. There was just enough mystery to keep us all titillated for more information. Anytime there was a press release, we talked about it for days.

"He just started recruiting." Aarush appeared puzzled, as if he were coming out of a deep sleep. He stopped his circling. "Templeton is only taking people—"

"I know who Templeton is signing up, and make no mistake, I was recruited. Face it, Aarush, no matter how connected your parents are, you are not going to make it."

I watched Aarush digest the information. People who didn't know him wouldn't have noticed the slight slump in his shoulders or his worried expression. Admittedly, it was barely there, but I saw it. His bony shoulder blades stuck out like wings, making small dents in his plaid shirt.

"Your father went to school with Templeton." I placed a reassuring hand on his shoulder. "You have a better chance than most."

"So do you." He looked up hopefully.

Elwood's triumphant laugh made me turn in disgust. That laugh. It bounced off the houses like an echo chamber. *How does he manage to do that?* I wondered.

"Come on," I said.

I hated when Elwood laughed, as if he were superior in some way. So what if he was the fastest quarterback in the nation or had a face like he belonged on a *CW* network vampire television show? Tall, skinny people with asthma may have some hidden potential too.

I grabbed Aarush's arm before he could begin his aimless circling and walked purposefully away from the truck.

"Wait!" Elwood called loudly, his taunting voice grating on my nerves. "Don't you want to read my acceptance letter, Aarush? *Ah-ah-rooosh!*" He drew the name out so that we heard him after we turned the corner sooner than we'd planned.

"Crap." I stopped to stare at the street sign.

Aarush's head snapped up. He had followed me blindly, not aware of our direction.

"Look. We're on Chestnut Avenue." I pointed to the green street sign as I eyeballed the deserted street. In my haste to get away from Elwood, we'd ended up in the exact place I wanted to avoid for fear of being mauled.

"Marcie," Aarush said gravely, pushing up the glasses that had slid down his long nose.

"Marcie," I confirmed.

"More like Cerberus."

"What?" I scratched my head. Aarush was always coming out with statements like that.

"The three-headed dog that guards the gates of Hades. Don't you remember?"

As if on cue, we heard the deep-throated barking of a large dog. It came from down the street, the sound ricocheting off the buildings so it was amplified as if a pack of animals were coming for us.

"Run!" I cried, grabbing Aarush's backpack and dragging him as fast as my feet could go.

We raced up the nearest lawn, churning up clods of grass and dirt. Aarush was a sloppy runner, his movements spastic. He looked like a loping dog himself. He moved as if in slow motion. I yanked his schoolbag, half dragging, half carrying him across the once-manicured lawn.

The hound from hell was hot on our tracks. I twisted and saw it dripping chains of saliva from its huge maw.

Marcie was one ugly dog. Her coat was splattered with reddish hair, looking as if she were fresh from her last kill. She was all coiled muscle, with thick legs that ended in paws like mallets. We gawked at her, my knees shaking. She slid to a stop, panting, her eyes widening with...*could that be joy?*

"Move!" I screamed, but it came out in a hoarse whisper. I had no air in my starved lungs. My heart raced like a jackhammer.

Never the most athletic, Aarush fumbled. I caught him up and hauled him to Old Man Ivan's backyard through a small hole in the fence. We heard the sound of fabric ripping as I pushed Aarush through the opening. His bulky backpack snagged on the rolled-up chain link.

"Leave it," I urged him.

"No." He tugged. "All my notes are in here."

"I'll give you mine," I said frantically.

Aarush stopped long enough to look me in the eye, his face full of pity, his glasses crooked. "You can't be serious."

"Aarush, this is not the time!"

I was wheezing already. I grabbed my inhaler and took in two quick puffs, freeing the tightness in my lungs. I was always surprised by the air rushing into the constricted space and the relief that followed.

"Hey, you kids!" The old guy came out, spitting remnants of whatever he had been eating as he yelled at us. He waved his hand at us and I could make out a half-eaten sandwich. "You're ruining my daffodils."

The massive liver-colored pit bull shook her head violently as if coming out of a stupor. She wore a black leather collar studded with sharpened spikes that gleamed in the late afternoon sunlight. She reared back, then surged forward, tearing up the turf with her great paws. Her eyes rolled in her massive head. Her bark, I thought, was as throaty as my great-aunt Marilyn, who drank gin and smoked tons of cigarettes.

"I wonder if her bark is worse than her bite," Aarush said, watching her intently, analyzing the dog.

"My daffodils!" Old man Ivan flailed his arms, chunks of turkey flying from the sandwich.

Marcie skidded to a dead stop, her nostrils twitching. She turned in a curious circle, the tiny nub of her tail darting from the right side to the left. She sniffed the ground, then trotted to Ivan and vacuumed up the turkey, her powerful jaws not stopping to chew.

"Interesting," Aarush commented. "We should pack meat if we want to go this way again."

"Move out of the way," I told Aarush.

I got on my back and gave his bag a solid kick, dislodging it. Aarush bent over and pulled me through the fence. We ran, laughing at our narrow escape, until we reached the modern monstrosity that Aarush called home.

CHAPTER 3

CHUTES CAN BE LADDERS

*A*ARUSH LIVED IN a smart home, as opposed to my stupid home. It performed all kinds of tricks. His parents have tons of money and could have lived on the other side of Middlebury but chose to bring up Aarush near people rather than down a two-mile driveway. They wanted him to play on the sidewalk with neighbors, walk to school, and ride his bike to the park.

But life had changed in our little neighborhood. Nobody played outside anymore, not with all the video games available. People had playdates; everything had to be arranged. If your parents didn't socialize or you were just a bit off, then nothing was ever planned. You fell into the crack where you were basically ignored or became fodder for the bullies. Aarush didn't care. He was impervious to their taunts. I wondered how much he really was on the spectrum or if he played up certain aspects to avoid having to deal with those kinds of kids.

As I said before, I had met Aarush in pre-K. His parents didn't mind that I was an orphan, and Mema, my grandma, had never met a kid she didn't like. I enjoyed his peaceful nature, and his mom was...well, she was a pediatrician and happy to have somebody, anybody, play with her son.

She is beautiful. Dr. Patel—his mother, not his father—is the prettiest woman in the world. Not that Dr. Patel, his father, is not a nice guy, but who notices anything when Dr. Patel, Aarush's mother, comes into the room? I realized early on that their names may present a problem if I was to be friendly with Aarush, so I devised a brilliant plan to identify the good doctors.

I started calling his mom Mrs. Dr. Patel, and his father Mr. Dr. Patel after that. They thought it was cute and it kind of stuck, however, I don't like to do it in public.

Anyway, Mrs. Dr. Patel works about five minutes from home. His dad is a bigshot at Dream Weaver Industries in the next town. He's the head of research or something like that and travels a lot. They do stuff with computers. Mr. Dr. Patel tried to explain it to me once, but I never got much beyond thermodynamics.

Gita runs the house. Gita is his mom's third cousin and takes care of Aarush like a doting grandma. She reminds me a bit of my grandmother. It's not unusual to feel that lump of longing in my throat when I'm around her.

Gita can usually be found in the kitchen. The house had the warm smell of curry. Today, the stove was on with lots of pots steaming.

"Aarush!" Gita cried out when we fell through the door.

"What did you do to your pants again?" She spoke with that lilting accent that somehow reminded me of music.

"Nothing, Gita." He brushed off her fussing when she examined his torn trouser leg.

"Was it that *Bledsloo* boy?"

We both laughed at the way she said Elwood Bledsoe's name.

"No. Marcie," Aarush informed her.

"A girl did this to you?" She reared back, looking incredulous.

Aarush cracked a rare smile. "In a manner of speaking."

"Dreadful…this is dreadful. I hope you didn't hit her back, though. I will have to call her mother, I see." Gita clucked her tongue a bit.

Aarush grabbed a *nankhatai* cookie, which is a sort of butter cookie, from a plate on the table. He tossed one to me. "I don't think you will be able to call her mother. She's a mean, old dog." Aarush's voice was as deadpan as ever.

This time I cracked up at Gita's reaction, spitting bits of cookie everywhere. Gita rushed back into the room, her face flushed. Her mouth was moving rapidly as she cried out her response in Hindi. Believe me, I have spent a lot of time in Aarush's house and know a few words. I couldn't recognize anything she said. Finally in English, she said, "That's no way to talk about another person, Aarush!"

"Marcie's a dog, Gita. A real dog," Aarush explained patiently. "Which means her mother is a dog, too."

However, the older woman was having nothing of it. She went on and on, slamming drawers, placing things on the table with a lot more force than necessary. "Well, I never!" she huffed. "Go change those pants, and I will see what I can do with them."

Apparently, she was still annoyed. She swiped the cookies from the table and left them on the counter before we could take another. We beat a hasty retreat to Aarush's room on the second floor.

Aarush's room was one of many cubes that comprised the Patel house. The entire dwelling was divided into different-sized glass, wood, and aluminum boxes, as if a giant had been playing with blocks and set them down on the lot. The ground floor had a bunch of rectangles comprising the living room, dining room, kitchen, Mr. Dr. Patel's study, a room where Gita grew herbs, and presumably her private room as well. From the outside, the house looked like corrugated metal with big glass picture windows.

Aarush's room hung suspended over the living room in a marvel of modern architecture. He had a million-dollar view of the Long Island Sound. Dr. and Dr. Patel had a room another level up with another study, this one for Aarush's mom. Mr. Dr. Patel had designed the house. I'd seen it do all sorts of crazy things when buttons were pressed. Shades retracted from skylights I never noticed, walls of drapes vanished in a blink, opening to picture windows strategically placed for the best view. They even had an observatory upstairs to look at the stars through a giant telescope.

While I understood Aarush wanted to attend Templeton, I couldn't figure how he was going to give up what he had here. Aarush's room was the size of my entire home. One wall was taken up by a game system built into a wall unit. His bed appeared only when he pressed a button.

As I said, the house did all kinds of neat things. Walls changed into furniture or could move sideways and transform into a doorway. It was like a giant puzzle. Every time I was there, I discovered something new. Aarush seemed mildly bored with it all.

Aarush ran into an alcove and changed his pants. They disappeared down a chute that snapped open when he pressed a panel on the wall.

"That's new," I said with interest.

"Laundry chute. Gita is having trouble climbing the steps. Trash chute is over there." Aarush waved airily at another door in the wall near his *PlayStation*.

"Where's it go?" I asked, peering down into the darkness.

Aarush shrugged. "Laundry room, I suppose. Gita will be on the receiving end." He pressed a button. Her angry chatter filled the speaker. "Contact." Aarush smiled that slow, lop-sided grin that few people saw. It made me smile too.

We heard something slam through the speaker, and we both laughed this time. "Can she hear you?"

"Not unless I want her to." He raised his eyebrow in a way similar to how I did it, only both his brows shot up to his dark hairline, making him look surprised. I didn't have the heart to tell him he was doing it wrong.

I looked out the vast window in his room at the low clouds hanging over the gunmetal water of the sound.

Aarush came to stand next to me. "There'll be rain soon."

"Yeah." I considered the wind whipping the waves on the ocean, making the bay look choppy. Aarush's prediction was coming true. I didn't relish walking home in that. "I have to leave."

"Aw," Aarush complained. "I wanted to play *Super Dude: Infinite Enemies*." He pressed a button on his remote and a large screen lit up with the newest version of our game. "I'll be Master Disaster." He was upping the ante, making it hard to leave. He took out two smaller controls with brightly colored buttons on them. "Besides, it looks like it's going to rain. You could stay here. We'll fill out your application together." He reached into his bag, which was on the floor next to him, and pulled out the sodden mess that was once all my hopes and dreams. "Gita will make dinner."

"Forget it, Aarush." I picked up my backpack. His house suddenly seemed as cold and dreary as outdoors. Hollow anguish settled into the pit of my stomach. I was going to be alone.

Aarush, like my nemesis Elwood Bledsoe, would be leaving soon, moving to the secret Temple campus to discover hidden talents and develop them into formidable powers while I bagged tuna fish for the next three years and hoped I could get a scholarship for college. My breath hitched while I shredded the skin on my lower lip. It couldn't be helped. Elwood had strength; Aarush had connections as well as a brilliant mind; I had nothing.

I felt jealousy creep in, lodging heavily in my chest. I fought the feeling, resenting the fact that it was even there. I didn't want to be envious of my best friend.

Forcing a smile, I refused to acknowledge the leaden feeling of despair stealing into the room and leaving an oppressive heaviness, obliterating all light.

Suddenly, I missed the cluttered mess of the cozy home I shared with my uncle. I looked around at the carpeted floors, the ice-colored walls. "Nah. I think I'll head for home. I have to call work and explain why I missed my shift."

"You're too young to be working," Aarush said simply.

I shrugged. Technically, I was too young. It was a pet gripe of his. He didn't understand why I joined the school-work program. Aarush had never wanted for anything. My job kept the shampoo and toothpaste flowing in my modest household. When they offered the program, both my uncle and I thought it would be a minor windfall to help with the household expenses.

Aarush looked at me with a hopeful expression. "Stay, Grady and we'll take care of this," he wheedled. He held out the wad of paper in his hand. It was the brochure with the application on the inside. I ignored the paper. Instead, I wrote a quick text to my manager, explaining why I missed work. This made it possible for me to avoid eye contact with Aarush.

"Grady," he repeated drawing out my name so it sounded like *Graaaady.*

Words clogged my throat. I simply shook my head and walked toward the door. I had filled it out several times, but every time I finished it somehow never made it to the mail. I had left more than one application in my backpack carrying it around until they fell apart. Uncle Leo shrugged with indifference and made it perfectly clear he didn't think the school was a good idea. I forgot exactly what he said, but something like *not for us,* whatever that means. I brought it up more than a few times, but he would clam up faster than a peregrine falcon, which is the fastest animal in the sky, according to Aarush, so after the fourth attempt, I gave up.

Uncle Leo's young to be in the parenting role, and as I have no one else to help plead my case, in the end, it is easier to let it go. Still, it rankled, I wanted to be thought of as good enough to be included. I mean, who doesn't like to think that they are special?

It was, however, a lost cause, and much as I enjoyed vain attempts like tempting the fate of pissing off nasty numbers like the lunchroom aide, the odds of me making it into the school and then convincing Uncle Leo to let me go, was just too much of a hurtle.

I stopped and looked at the wall, remembering the trash chute near the entertainment center. I reached over to snatch the papers, pressed the knob on the chute, then tossed the brochure down the dark tunnel to wherever the Patels sent their garbage.

"Nooo!" Aarush tried to grab it. "Why did you do that? My father—"

"Your father can't help me."

"No," he interrupted me.

"It's okay," I told him. I paused and added. "It's nothing new for me."

I felt like I should explain what was comfortable for me. I don't know what I'd have done if things ever turned out differently. I didn't think I could actually handle getting something I wanted. "You will get into the Temple, and I'll be happy for you." I felt that by saying it, maybe it would get easier to accept.

I put my hand on the polished bar that served as a doorknob to his room, ready to leave. Aarush waved goodbye as I trotted down the steps past the kitchen. Gita smiled at me, her good humor restored.

I grabbed a cookie on the counter as I left, never noticing the wet papers spread across the kitchen counter, drying under a rotating fan. I was later to learn that all the chutes in the house led to Gita.

CHAPTER 4

UNTOUCHABLE SUBJECTS

*I*T DIDN'T TAKE long to get home. I had to admit I was tired.

I dropped my schoolbag by the front door and called out for Uncle Leo, who didn't answer back. I deducted that he wasn't home yet.

I boiled water, dumped in a pound of macaroni, sliced up some cheese, and waited for the pasta to rise to the top. With Mema's old slotted spoon, I sampled a few of the elbows. Crunchy. They weren't done yet. I wish I'd known how Mrs. Berry made mac and cheese. She delivered buckets of it when my grandparents had died the previous year. We froze it and lived on a variety of casseroles for months, but then the food stopped coming. Everybody went back to their lives, including Uncle Leo and me.

Uncle Leo had switched his shift to the morning so he'd

be home at night even though I told him I was old enough to take care of myself. My uncle had shrugged those sloping shoulders of his and flipped his life around to accommodate mine. He never complained even though I knew that by changing his time slot, he'd lost his nightly radio show as well as his fans and took on boring stuff like traffic and events taking place around town—cookie bake-offs and dog talent shows. For a guy who made our bread and butter talking on the radio, at home he didn't have much to say.

The only good thing to come out of it was Joni, his special "friend." If he heard me calling her that, though, it would piss him off. I don't know why it was so hard to admit he'd finally gotten a girlfriend.

The water boiled over. The pasta went to that soft mushy place of a couple minutes too long. I sighed. After draining the water, I poured bacon bits into the pot with the cheese, hoping the added flavor of fake soyish pork would make up for overcooked pasta.

The door slammed, and I heard one set of footsteps.

"Squirt?" Uncle Leo called.

I rolled my eyes. I was almost as tall as Uncle Leo. Another growth spurt would have me topping him pretty soon.

"You're alone," I said without looking up.

My uncle came into the kitchen, his long brown hair tied back in a ponytail. He stretched, his bones cracking. He looked at me, his head tilted in an unspoken question.

"Superpowers. I can see through walls," I said, explaining how I'd deduced he was solo tonight.

"Hah. Just like your father," he laughed.

Wait, really? My father. That's a first, I thought. Usually an untouchable subject. It was a rare event when Uncle Leo shared an interesting tidbit about my dad.

"Tell me more," I said without looking up. I didn't think I wanted him to see the longing in my face

"Yeah." He opened a drawer, grabbed a soup spoon, and started eating the macaroni straight from the pot. I pulled over a stool and dug in with the serving spoon. "Ugh. You overcooked the macaroni, again."

"My father?" I prompted him.

"Yeah, well, your dad had this innate ability to see what I was doing when I wasn't even in the same room," Uncle Leo said, though all his attention was on the pasta. "I wonder if more cheese can save this." He dumped a handful of shredded parmesan cheese from a can I had left on the counter.

"Really?" I tried not to get too excited. "He would be in, like, one room and knew what you were doing in...what... the kitchen?"

Uncle Leo paused thoughtfully. "It used to scare the crap out of me. He knew when I was into his stuff and was on me in a flash. Mom...you know, Mema...said it was because of his superpowers. Dork that I was, I believed it too."

"You think he was born with them?" All I could think was, *Could they have been passed down, and how can I use them to get into Templeton?*

Uncle Leo barked a laugh. "Grady, your dad was twelve years older than me. He knew what I was doing 'cause I was an inquisitive little sucker like you were when you were young." He chuckled to himself, apparently lost in a memory of me messing with his belongings as a baby. "Don't tell me you're still angling to get into that stupid school."

I lowered my head, my cheeks flaming. It wasn't shame,

maybe a little anger. "I don't know what you have against Templeton," I replied.

"Don't want to talk about it," he retorted, and the subject was closed just like that.

Clamming up about stuff ran in the family. After the accident that took my parents, the story was that Grandpa had forbidden mentioning them in the house again. I guess Uncle Leo was following his lead. Not that that made any difference to me...about my parents, not the school. I was just a few months old when they died. Still, sometimes I imagined I could catch a whiff of a scent so soft, so ethereal, it made my eyes sting for something I didn't know I yearned.

The hair rose on the back of my neck when you know someone is watching you. I jumped when Joni's voice broke the quiet.

"Aren't you going to save anything for me?" Joni stood in outraged indignation in the doorway. She was short and stocky, her pink hair clipped almost to her scalp under a knitted cap. She wore a small round stone in the crease of her nose that I knew would have set Grandpa off something fierce. She had the quality and exuberance of the ex-gymnast that she was. I swear, it always looked like she was going to leap into the room.

Uncle Leo hooked a stool with his gangly leg and pulled it toward the counter. "Find a spoon and dig in."

As usual, Joni vaulted into the seat. Making herself comfortable, she grabbed a utensil and chowed down with us.

"I thought you said you were alone." I looked up, a little horrified at Uncle Leo, the red in my cheeks now stained with embarrassment. I handed Joni the glass of water she pointed at.

"No, *you* said I was alone. I didn't answer." Uncle Leo smiled, taking the sting out. My uncle was a teaser; not mean spirited—everything was a joke. I guess that was how he'd developed his radio personality. "Besides, there's no such thing as superpowers, Grady."

Joni volunteered to wash the dishes. I was happy to escape to my room and do my homework. I checked my messages on my phone. My manager had called and left a message, it seemed I hadn't lost my job, as he felt detention was a reasonable excuse.

I settled onto my bed, math homework done, and started my science assignment. I glanced at my alarm clock, my gaze resting on a framed photo next to it. Mema had framed the small Polaroid and placed it beside my bed despite Grandpa's edict. I picked up the scratched chrome frame and examined my father's expression. His mullet bracketed a narrow face with wire-rimmed glasses. My parents were sitting casually on a couch I didn't recognize in a room I didn't know. It looked messy. The background had stacks of books—a dorm room, maybe?

They had met at school. Love at first sight, Uncle Leo told me once. They were together from the first day to the last, graduating, then getting married and having *moi*.

Dad's family became hers. "Your mother had no one," Mema once responded when I asked who my mom's parents were. They died when she was young.

In the photo, my mother was leaning her head on my dad's shoulder. Her long, dark hair covered half of his hand, which was wrapped around her arm. They were smiling, their faces rosy with mirth at some shared joke.

I had looked at that picture every day of my life. It was the first thing I saw when I opened my eyes in the morning. It was like a piece of a puzzle that completed my room, the part that reflected me. It was as much a part of my make-up as my hand or arm. I slid my lids closed, then opened them slowly, knowing the picture would be there just like the *Spinal Tap* poster that was my sole inheritance from them.

I placed it back on the night table and rubbed the flat part of my chest, feeling a weight of sadness like a wet blanket. Wherever the sentiment had originated, I wished it would go back. Those types of emotions made me uncomfortable.

CHAPTER 5

FIND MY POWER

I'D LIKE TO say that life improved, but I'd be telling you
a lie. Elwood Bledsoe continued to bully Aarush. While
Aarush constantly cautioned me to rein in my reaction to him,
I could not. It landed me in two more detentions, and the last
one finally cost me my job at the supermarket where I bagged
groceries.

"You're coming for dinner," Aarush informed me one
afternoon.

I shook my head. "Can't."

Aarush neatly packed his brown bag with unfinished food
and said, "You have to come over. You're not working. Tonight
they are announcing the winners of the *Find My Power Essay*
on television. Devon Neely has to win. Imagine losing your
sight and learning— "

"Aarush, they'll never accept a blind kid."

"They took that girl Lydia," he blurted.

They had indeed.

"She's not blind," he retorted.

I raised my eyebrow. She hardly looked like someone people expected to make it into the Temple. All I could recall was she seemed most unremarkable. Most of the kids who were accepted had a rare talent. They could run the fastest or do math without a pen or paper. I couldn't remember what made her special.

The show was one avenue to get into the school. Kids were voted in by the audience watching the program, like a singing competition. The other was being recommended by the president of the country, or someone equally extraordinary, like an ambassador, or the Pope. Had to count me out on that one, I didn't run in those circles. And of course, there was simply catching the eye of Dr. Templeton or his daughter, Valencia, in the millions of applications that were sent from all over the world.

The girl highlighted on last week's show, Lydia Cullen, resembled a quiet little mouse. Her essay was forgettable, her squeaky voice grating, yet she appealed to the public enough to be voted in along with her twin brother, Forrest.

The *Find My Power* television show featured students in heart-warming segments where they talked about themselves. It felt staged. It made me not want to go to Templeton...well, *almost.*

An applicant had to write an essay that was read by famous actors. Every big name in Hollywood was clamoring to be on the show. It made me wonder if a kid was really winning, or was it an A-list movie star reading the essay that made it special? To be fair, the night Kiki Williams performed, I even voted. I couldn't remember the content of the essay if my life depended on it, though.

There were ten essays per show. They flashed pictures of the kid, where they lived, and their families. Then the actor or actress came out onto the darkened stage and read the essay. Some of them were really moving. Others were funny. Mostly the students on the show were plain extraordinary. These kids did amazing things: collected money for worthy causes, overcame great obstacles, had some brilliant talent. It was jaw-dropping to watch.

At the end of the program, numbers were flashed, and the audience had to text in their favorite contestant. The winners were announced in a half-hour program the next day. Each week, two lucky students gained admittance to Templeton Academy.

Oh, it was quite a spectacle. They'd be in a section with all the other hopeful students. Everybody received a light gray envelope, which they opened at the same time. They must have rehearsed it a lot. I was amazed no one messed it up. Most discovered a printed white page with a standard rejection. There were a lot of disappointed sounds coming from the audience. Two lucky kids found a sheet of shiny silver paper. It was a special ticket to the Port of Miami, where these talented students would embark for the secret location of the school. You wouldn't believe the sound of the audience cheering when the kids revealed the shiny paper.

Aarush's essay had been eliminated early on. I have to admit he didn't photograph well, and some C-list actor didn't impress as his representative performer. I said he should write and demand the guy who played Super Dude in the movie. Aarush disagreed.

I had to say, that kid had moxie. He still thought he was

getting in. He watched the show each week with avid fascination, cheering when each student succeeded. Me, I'd stopped watching when my essay was returned without making it on air. I got the standard rejection note and threw it out before Uncle Leo got home. They didn't even spell my name right. It was one of those moments you want to forget.

I was miserable. Every day there was another online article somewhere in the country about a student making it into Templeton Academy. It was on the nightly news. Traveling reporters crisscrossed the country doing stories about a basketball player in Chicago or a science whiz in Florida beating the odds to receive the gray envelope with the reveal of the silver ticket inside.

News about the school leaked out. It would be a shortened school year, but no holidays, or contact with families at home gave me a solid argument that it wasn't the enchanted wonderland Aarush was making it out to be. It mollified me enough not to live in a constant state of longing and disappointment. Still, despite these hardships, most kids wanted to go. Being accepted meant there was something special about you. *Who wouldn't want to be told that?*

Our school made a big deal with an assembly detailing Elwood's outstanding school career. It made me want to throw up. He was given a one-of-a-kind jacket with the school name on it to remember us. His football jersey with the number 14 was permanently retired. It was as if he farted gold dust the way they carried on about him, and now, for sure, he could do no wrong.

He became our resident celebrity with an actual reality show in tow. The camera crew followed by his father appeared out of nowhere the day after he went public with his admittance. It seems they were paying his family a substantial sum of money to document his final months before he left for Templeton.

I didn't have to read the school newspaper to know everyone at Middlebury Middle School felt honored, as if Templeton had chosen the entire school instead of just Elwood Bledsoe. Most of the major magazines did a feature on him that included several of the teachers. It was as though his admittance reflected their superior abilities as educators. I still wasn't sure how he made it in.

Once Elwood had this new entourage, I steered as far away from him as I could. Lunch was torture, so I started skipping mealtimes and staying in the lab. Mr. Felix let Aarush and me hole up there in exchange for cleaning the place up. It wasn't as though I had anything else to do. I even longed for my job at the grocery store.

Truth be told, I missed the forty bucks a week I made at the supermarket. Uncle Leo's a nice guy, but getting money out of him was tough. As I said earlier, I couldn't blame him. He made a pitiful wage. I kept calling my old manager to see if they'd take me back. I was nothing if not hopeful that a spot would open up as Easter drew near and they'd need my expertise with stacking canned goods for the holiday rush.

Still, there was something relaxing in putting away hot plates and storing bunsen burners in the lab. I also got an impromptu chemistry lesson because Aarush had an annoying habit of repeating the uses of all the equipment.

I worked hard to avoid Elwood Bledsoe's new group. I could hear them a mile away with Elwood's booming voice bragging about his exploits on the football field. You'd think he was running for president of the United States the way he greeted the kids in the hallway.

The teachers were useless, more charmed by the cameras and the crew than by Elwood, I think. We all had to sign consent forms, in case we were caught in the shot they were filming. Anyone who didn't agree was banished to the library for the time the cameras were in the class, but I saw some of the shows. Mostly the camera was on Elwood, anyway. Holy crap, you should have seen Mrs. Farber the day they filmed her segment. I'd never seen her wear anything like *that* before, let me tell you. I wouldn't have minded doing the Texas two-step in front of the camera if she'd worn that outfit again.

Every time I rounded a corner, Elwood appeared, the producer, director, and two camera crew members following his every move. Upon an Elwood sighting, I would duck back to where I came from and try an alternate route.

I turned around just at the same moment Leander Phillips decided to upchuck the three pizzas he'd shared with Casey Dennis. I guess competitive eating didn't go down well with him. It was an epic performance of "I Can't Stop the Vomit," and he managed to spray not only the entire hallway but also the walls, lockers, and, from the looks of the dripping light fixture, the ceiling too.

I had no choice but to move forward. The back hallway now resembled the ninth level of hell. People were dropping like flies, the groans of sympathy vomiting echoing in the area.

Lowering my head, I tried to walk past them without getting caught in the camera's wide net but found myself blocked by a line of human flesh. Looking up, I saw Elwood's toothy grin. I knew that look, he was up to no good. I wondered if the film crew was pressuring him for more material, like his ratings weren't high enough, or something. Make no mistake, Elwood Bledsoe had something up his sleeve.

I feinted toward the left to dart around him. He blocked my way, his new school jacket obscuring everything in my path. He placed a hand casually on the locker to my right as if it were a barricade.

"Right here," he told the cameras, the bright lights glinting off his straight blonde hair. "Right here we have one of Middlebury's finest—Grady Whill, average in everything he attempts to do."

A crowd closed in around us. This, I'm sure, was certainly, more entertaining than the hall of vomit behind us.

I could feel the tension in the space. It buzzed as information was spread. That was the student's grapevine for you. A thousand fingers texted our confrontation onto social media.

I was restarting my old job that day at the supermarket. Just as I hoped, my manager had indeed called and rehired me back. I didn't need detention, so I tried to force my stubborn mouth into some semblance of a smile. "I don't want to fight with you." My voice was low.

A fuzzy black mic shaped like my grandmother's old slipper was shoved into my face. I pushed it away with my forearm. The guy resisted, and I have to admit, it probably bruised my arm. *There has to be some sort of law against this*, I thought.

"Oh, tough guy Grady." Elwood spoke expansively, sharing our conversation with the crowd of students pressing in on us.

"What? Could you repeat that? Did you hear that?" the director shouted.

Elwood laughed in that irritating way of his. "He doesn't want to fight. There's not going to be a fight. I don't believe in fighting." He mugged for the camera, his voice dripping sincerity. He placed one hand on his heart. "I've been getting ready for Templeton. I want to show you what I've learned."

I heard Aarush before I saw him. He was pushing his way through the crowd. "Let me in. Excuse me." Finally an exasperated, "Move already."

"It's your little friend. Maybe he wants to start a fight. I should alert the proper authorities." Elwood knew exactly how to get me. "You can't hide out in the lab today, Whill," he said in an undertone only I could hear.

I heard a commotion. I looked up, and relief washed through my body. The principal's bald head was cutting through the mass of students like a shark in the ocean. Mr. Thompson had a smile pasted on his face. His voice seemed higher than normal. It wasn't until I realized his jerky movements were all for the camera that I understood he too was starstruck.

"Boys, boys. No need for a confrontation."

All innocence, Elwood put on a fairly reasonable performance of wounded contrition, while I was caught wrestling with the mic being shoved in my face.

"Certainly, you can handle this like gentlemen," Mr. Thompson said, his voice a little too loud.

"A duel, perhaps?" Elwood supplied.

A duel? Are you kidding me? My jaw dropped. *What the heck is he talking about?*

Mr. Thompson laughed so heartily that he ended on a choking wheeze. "You kids. You're one funny guy, Elwood," he added with great fondness. "I suggest an arm-wrestling match. Certainly you can settle your dispute fairly."

"A noble solution." Elwood nodded gravely. He smiled for the camera. I swear his teeth actually sparkled. The principal beamed at him, his hand on Elwood's shoulder. I noticed Elwood's father press in and swallow hard when I saw Mr. Thompson wink at him.

I had the distinct impression that this was planned. Much as I wanted to bolt, I couldn't. This had somehow turned into an affair of honor. They were forcing me to see this to its conclusion.

"I have just the place," Mr. Thompson said, his head shining from the overheating lights of the crew. He grinned for the cameras. I realized that he too subscribed to some superior tooth-whitening product. His smile blinded me.

Elwood, Elwood's dad, and Mr. Thompson chatted away for the camera. Apparently, my consent for the duel wasn't an important part of the negotiation. I was swept away in the tide of humanity as Elwood, the production crew, Mr. Thompson, and a throbbing horde of students moved into the lunchroom.

Elwood walked purposely to the center of the room. He kicked away a few chairs, then hooked one with his muscular leg and straddled it. He placed his elbow on the tabletop, wiggled his fingers, then grinned up at me. The flash of his smile lit up the room.

"What are you waiting for, Whill?" He nodded to the seat opposite him.

I thought about leaving, picking up by backpack and refusing to be filmed, *I really did*. My eyes scanned the bobbing heads of the student body. Everyone was there. I'd be branded a coward. Pick your battles, I told myself, loser or coward. Either way, I was screwed.

The room erupted into chanting. "Elwood! Elwood!" The director walked through the mob of kids, his arms raised in the air, urging them to shout the name louder. When the camera panned them, their cheers became a roar.

Everybody's an actor.

Mr. Thompson stood at the head of the table. I placed my book bag on the surface, then, with a sigh of resignation, took the chair opposite Elwood. Aarush stood behind me. I swear, if he'd started to massage my shoulders like in an old *Rocky* movie, I'd have strangled him.

Instead, he leaned close to me and whispered, "It doesn't look good. He's got muscle on his side." Aarush was in his babbling mode. "It's clear he's been working out. His biceps brachii and pronator teres are rock solid. However, your flexor carpi ulnaris are well developed."

"What?"

Aarush turned his palms out, then flexed his fingers widely. "From gaming. Your forearms and fingers are strong too. You can beat him. It's simple physics."

"Are you crazy?" I asked in a harsh whisper. "He's going to crush me." Sweat beaded on my forehead.

Aarush's response was drowned out by the chanting crowd.

"Settle down everybody. Settle down. Elwood Bledsoe" –Mr. Thompson smiled warmly at him, and they seemed to enjoy a weird little bonding moment—"and Grady Whill are having a friendly dispute."

We are? Did we even have a dispute? Was wanting to walk past a former friend considered grounds for a *friendly* dispute?

I wanted to interrupt, but the principal was having an *Oscar* moment with the camera. Hand on heart, he was spouting how much he loved his students and was proud of the fact we had developed peaceful ways to settle our differences. He smiled for the cameras with a devilish smirk that I guess his wife must have told him made him look charming.

"Place your right foot forward. You wrestle with your right arm. Your weight will shift from your front foot to your back foot," Aarush, apparently the Don King of arm wrestling, was droning on in my ear.

"Stop it!" I said and waved him away. "Sit down over here." I pointed to a chair on my right.

"Remember what I said about keeping your upper arm close to your body. All it is is simple physics."

"Aarush, I don't know what you are talking about."

"Grady." Aarush looked at me with his eyebrows so far up, they disappeared under his hairline. He looked like a cartoon character.

A laugh bubbled up in me, threatening to erupt. I forced it down to the pit of my stomach. I didn't have time for hysteria.

"Grady," Aarush said calmly. "Think of what Gandhi said: 'Strength does not come from physical capacity. It comes from an indomitable will.' You can do this if you believe you can."

I did a double-take from Aarush's slight form to Elwood's hulking body opposite me. I was going to be obliterated. "Yeah, sure, dude. Right, Gandhi."

I bellied up to the table, and placed my elbow on the Formica.

Elwood used this moment to acknowledge his adoring fans. He made a fist, then stretched his fingers dramatically. He positioned his feet and placed his arm on his side of the table.

This was taking forever, and I was about out of patience. I leaned over the surface to grip his hand. I knew at once it was a mistake. Aarush's moan of dismay was my first clue, the second the dawning realization I should have kept my arm closer to my torso.

Now Elwood had two advantages. He was bigger than me, and his body and arm strength would overpower my thinner arm in no time, despite my well-developed flexor carpi ulnaris muscles.

Our hands slapped together like a clap of thunder. The room went deathly quiet.

"You're going down," Elwood said for only me. He even looked strange. All I saw were the whites of his eyes through his slitted lids. Let me tell you, that was pretty unnerving by itself. My belly sank to my knees, which at this point were shaking pretty badly.

I could have thrown the match, but found I didn't want to. Gritting my teeth, I fought my trembling muscles, willing them to lock and surprise everyone by beating the bully. *After all, that's the way it happens in the movies.*

Clenching my mouth, I concentrated on not having my elbow slide on the slick surface of the table. My feet moved. They couldn't seem to root to the floor the way Elwood's did. He was standing so still, I fought the urge to tap him. He appeared as if carved from stone.

Mr. Thompson raised his hands and shouted, "On my count! One, two, three...go!"

I dug in my heels, knowing it was a losing battle from the start. I could see Elwood literally had the upper hand.

Elwood had maneuvered his arm close to his body and was pulling me into his tight embrace. I was not only off-balance, but he had curled his thumb so that he held the upper part of my palm and I was grappling with the lower half of his.

He glanced up, flashing those white teeth of his at me. "We could have been friends," he said for my ears only. "You chose him over ..."—he jerked my arm almost out of its socket and smashed my knuckles on the hard surface of the table—"...me."

His gaze met mine. He was filled with anger. He gave a loud grunt and raised both his hands in the air. The crowd went nuts. He looked like a gorilla.

Of course, good sport that I was, I shook hands with him. The blood came back into my numb knuckles as he squeezed it in an iron grip. Elwood waved to the crowd, enabling me to duck down, grab my bag, and beat a hasty retreat from the lunchroom.

Aarush followed me, his head shaking. "You didn't have to lose. You think it's about—"

"Forget it Aarush. He outweighs me by at least forty pounds."

"Size is no indication of strength. Don't you remember my report about the crayfish in Australia?"

"What?" I looked back at him. I walked as fast as I could to get away from the school. "No." I didn't want to talk about it.

Two kids walked past. "Hey, Whill," one of them called. "Wanna arm wrestle?" They laughed, and I could hear the word *loser* drift across the schoolyard.

"It's a matter of cryptic asymmetry," Aarush went on, oblivious to my clipped tones.

"I thought you said it was physics," I shot back. I was simmering with shame and anger. I wanted to get as far from the school as I could.

"Well, that too." Aarush was thoughtful. "The asymmetries of a limb performance sometimes don't match up with limb size."

"I don't know what you are talking about." I picked up my pace, hoping Aarush would be too breathless to speak. It seemed as if I had had absolutely no luck today.

"The crayfish," Aarush patiently explained. He doubled his pace to catch up to me. "They have one limb or claw that's larger than the other. You would think that the ones with a larger claw would be stronger than, say, a smaller one, but what scientists discovered was sometimes these larger pincers were made up of lower-quality muscles and are not as strong as the crayfish with smaller pincers."

"Well, let me assure you, Elwood Bledsoe's pincer was very strong."

"You're not listening to me. Just because someone is bigger, they project the illusion of more strength. You have the same amount of power as Elwood. All you had to do was use your brain."

"Like you do?" I asked sarcastically and instantly regretted it. I was taking out my humiliation on Aarush. He didn't deserve it. He had done nothing but show loyalty and support. It seemed I had a lot of regrets today, the first being the thought that I had any ability to best the school bully. What was I thinking?

We stopped in the street. I couldn't tell if my barb had struck home. You could never see that part of him. "Aarush," I said, but the apology never came out.

He shook his head. I wasn't sure if I'd hurt his feelings, and it bothered me.

"In the end, it doesn't matter," Aarush said quietly, his face earnest.

Words rushed up my throat, but I held them back. *What do you know of my embarrassment?* I wanted to scream. *That's easy for you to say. You weren't humiliated in front of the whole school.* No, he hadn't been today. He was made fun of every day.

I said simply, "I have to go. I'll be late for work."

CHAPTER 6

ROUND TWO

I WATCHED AARUSH HEAD down the street after we parted. I felt strangely lonely. I fought the urge to call him back and apologize. I really did have to get to work. Anthony Tuchroni had made it clear when he rehired me, if I was late I didn't have to bother showing up to the supermarket, ever.

The supermarket was not one of those big mega stores. It was a small boutique-like thing called the Purple Artichoke. The front of the store had rustic redwood picnic tables with fluttery purple umbrellas. People ate their meals out there with chopsticks all the time, even if it was Italian food. Go figure.

The place was set up like a farmer's market, only the prices were triple what you found in the local grocery store. They had fancy cruelty-free sourced tuna, although how you can pull a fish from the water, let it starve for air and call it cruelty-free, I'll never understand. Gourmet salami called *salumi*, and vegetables like lotus root and nopal that looked like they were showing up for a modeling shoot. There was no vanilla ice cream in this store. The freezer was stocked with balsamic-glazed fig gelato and pineapple dragon-fruit sorbet.

I tied the parcels, which was an elegant way to say that I bagged groceries, and the tips were generous. Most of the women ran in with nails that were still slightly damp from the manicure shop next door, which meant I was assured extra money to carry groceries to the car. Aluminum shopping carts were not allowed in the parking lots. Too many run-ins with the luxury cars, I guess. That worked for me. I was good for an extra ten to fifteen bucks a day; plus we got a hefty discount on the food I brought home, not that we had much use for quinoa-crusted turbot in beurre blanc sauce. The nachos, when we could get them, were pretty good, though.

Today I bagged loads of food, and carried out more than half of them. My right arm ached from the beating it took. My feet dragged on the concrete because the groceries weighed me down. With each extra bag, I stifled my groans managing to smile through the discomfort. This convinced the customers I loved my job ensuring extra tip money.

We were coming to the end of my shift. The last lady in the store looked like she had cleaned out the entire canned goods aisle. She chattered about a holiday food drive or something at the school. I loaded the cans into her reusable shopping bags, realizing it amounted to over ten bulging sacks.

"Can you hurry? I don't have time," she said as she blew onto her wet nails.

I looked for Anthony, who was stacking seltzer onto the shelf. *Help?* I mouthed the words. Anthony didn't even return my glance. I stretched my neck. He studiously avoided me. I called his name. This time we made eye contact.

The manager's face was red. Anthony Tuchroni was shouting without talking, a rare feat to watch. He was able to impart the message with a flamboyant display of waving arms and a beet-red face. All this action translated into *Really, Whill? Stop being a baby and take the lady's bags.*

I opened my mouth to reply. The cashier's response saved me from an acid retort from my boss. She stopped chewing her gum long enough to say, "You gotta do it. He can't spare nobody else."

I looked around. Indeed, everyone was racing to get stock displayed for the Easter holiday. The chocolate bunnies were only half-shelved. They had to go this weekend or face the ignominy of the half-price bin. Anthony must have noticed this oversight at the same time. He snapped his fingers impatiently causing a pile-up in aisle seven of stock guys in neon vests. "Get those things up!" he ordered and five of them began ripping open boxes to get the chocolate bunnies displayed.

I looked over my shoulder at the growing mountain of bags. It was not only too much, it was freaking heavy. I wasn't a weight lifter.

"Oh, look at the time. Look," our lady of the canned assortment said while she glanced at her watch, "there's a fifty in it if you can get it into the car in one shot. I am so late."

Fifty. Fifty whole dollars was more than half of what I earned for the day. It was a game-changer.

"You think they'll let me take a shopping cart?" I whispered to the cashier. I looked longingly at the row of aluminum wagons interlinked like a shiny new ride at a theme park. They were small, almost the sports car version of a shopping cart, but one or two of those would make my trek to her vehicle easier.

The cashier shook her head as she filled another two bags. "Nope. You wanna get me fired. No carts allowed in the parking lot. No buts, Grady," she said through her teeth. "It's a rule with the landlord, or go take it up with Anthony. Don't make such a big deal about a few bags of groceries."

A few bags of groceries? This was the equivalent of carrying enough aluminum to create an airforce jet. I sucked in a deep breath, praying my asthma wouldn't act up. I felt my shoulders slump. I had been humiliated at school in front of everybody when Elwood beat me at arm wrestling. Now I was on the verge of being embarrassed at work as well. It was turning out to be one of those days I wished the ground would open up and swallow me.

I was thinking it couldn't get much worse than this, and then...*it did.*

Elwood Bledsoe walked into the store.

He was accompanied by none other than his designated driver, Lindsay Carruthers. Lindsay was swinging her key chain noisily, announcing to one and all she had gotten her license.

She was a cheerleader, of course. Despite her prettiness, to me she had all the appeal of a Tasmanian Devil. I had no idea what Aarush saw in her. Love, I guess, is a chemical thing. While Lindsay was a few years older than us and in high school, I suppose Elwood's prowess on the football field compensated for his youth.

Elwood's eyes lit up with unholy glee when he saw me. He made a beeline directly for the checkout, eyeing the stack of bags.

"I'm not parked far," the canned goods customer informed me.

Elwood turned to whisper something to Lindsay, who laughed nastily. She pulled out her phone and began recording the moment, I assume for the amusement of the school population. My life was turning into a documentary. I guess she was pinch-hitting for Elwood's film crew.

I spied the shopping cart full of bags, and I sighed with resignation. "You could make two trips." The ever-helpful cashier cracked her gum and rolled her eyes.

"Or ten," Elwood added to the conversation. He did a few bicep curls with his wrestling arm.

"Come on, the school is waiting for all these cans." The shopper looked at Elwood. "Young man! Would you like—?"

"No," I said quietly. "I can do it."

"Not in one trip, Super Bag Boy." Elwood leaped over the counter in a single bound. "Mightier than a paper bag, with more dexterity than plastic, it's Super Bag Boy!"

I regretted our game of naming ourselves superheroes when we were younger. While I didn't mind with Aarush, I had forgotten the game originated with Elwood. He took it to a whole new level.

Elwood held out his arms in front of him, acting as though he were flying. "You know, Whill, you could use the plastic ones as a parachute if you forget how to land."

Lindsay for some unknown reason found this hilarious, as did the chocolate bunny stacking crew, who now stood laughing at Elwood's antics. I never quite understood the dynamics of this kind of humor.

When Anthony smiled fondly at him, I fought the urge to hurl.

"I can take care of that for you, ma'am," Elwood said sweetly.

How did he do that? Look menacing and friendly at the same time. I shuddered. *Ugh,* those sparkling teeth again. And don't get me started on his smile. The only thing stopping it from going all around his head was his ears.

"I can handle it, Elwood," I said through gritted teeth.

"Yeah, sure." He moved to stand close to me, his hand on his hip, his chin tilted upward as if defying me to fail.

I turned slightly away and slipped my inhaler from my pocket. I caught Elwood's narrowed gaze and saw him open his mouth to make fun of me. My jaw tightened with resentment and I slid the asthma inhaler back into my pocket without taking it. That was dumb, but I had some perverse notion that taking it would make me look feeble in his eyes.

I looped several overstuffed bags in one hand, more in the other, my eyes never leaving his. I stood, half expecting the heavy bags to make it impossible to walk. While I don't consider myself a ninety-pound weakling, my guess is carrying your weight in canned goods has a definite effect on teenage musculature. My legs trembled, and the skin on my hands turned white as if all the blood was being squeezed from them.

Moving toward the exit, I could feel Elwood's gaze boring into my back. I paused at the door and told myself the bags were filled with feathers. Myself answered back and said, *They must be made of iron, then.*

Maybe if I focus all my attention on something, I won't feel my shins splintering from the weight, I reasoned. My body must have had a plan because I felt my lungs expand, and I sucked in a steadying breath. It felt good. Surprised, I took another deep inhale, concentrating on the power of the air traveling into my lungs. It circulated throughout my whole body, as if it was nourishment. I was shocked there was no breath-less wheeze.

I didn't realize my eyes were closed until I heard the woman say, "This way, please. Can you hurry?"

I took another invigorating breath, my blood pumping in a strange rhythm, I had never noticed before.

I searched the nearly empty parking lot, my eyes settling on a small seagull in the distance. It was standing on the top of a light pole, the wind ruffling its feathers. It stood stoically, unmoving. Furrowing my forehead, I kept it in my sights, my mind on the bird rather than the sheer weight of the bags. The bird became a beacon to the finish line. It watched me, its beady eyes non-judgmental, unlike the group in the store behind me. I acknowledged it with a wink, then realized I must be looking a little nuts, winking with a bird. Still, I never took my eyes off of it.

It was hard to believe I was holding so many cans. They smacked against my calves as I walked and for some strange reason, not only did it not hurt, they didn't feel heavy. My arms bounced with each step. I could feel their tactile strength holding the bags securely.

The customer stuck her foot under the trunk, the door to the SUV opened. Taking another steadying breath, I lifted one arm and deposited one set of bags into the trunk. The other swung in easily.

I turned back to look in the store window to share my triumph. Okay, maybe it was really to gloat. No such luck. Elwood was gone.

The customer handed me fifty bucks, which, while it made me happy, wasn't the thing that had made my day.

Aarush was right. I realized something today. While I was

puzzled about my asthma, I was sure about something else. *Strength does not have to be determined by size.* The ultimate source of power is hidden not in muscles but in one's ability to believe they can do it.

I wondered if others knew this secret. Aarush's, or really Mahatma Gandhi's, words came rushing back to me: "Strength does not come from physical capacity. It comes from an indomitable will."

CHAPTER 7

LIFE IS FLUID

UNCLE LEO TEXTED that he had a meeting and would be staying late at work. While I would have enjoyed going home and having both the remote and the house to myself, I knew I owed Aarush an apology for my rude behavior earlier.

I walked to my friend's home, and came in the back door. I rarely knocked. I had been treated like a member of the family from the time I was a baby.

The house smelled luscious when I entered. Gita was busy preparing dinner.

"Grady, dear, so glad you made it. I am ready to serve soon."

I smiled at Gita. My gaze was always drawn to her *bindi*, the red dot on her forehead. Aarush told me once it was her third eye and gave her insight to see things others couldn't.

I looked through the steam of the granite-topped center island. Gita held up a pot lid, showing me the bubbling *bhaji*.

My mouth watered when I saw the vegetable curry dish. I never ate greens with Uncle Leo. I was too lazy to buy them, and he was too lazy to cook them. Anyway, the few times he did make them, they were horrible. I loved the taste of the potatoes, carrots, peas, and green beans stewed together in Gita's rich sauce of exotic spices.

She held out a plate of toasted homemade *pav*. Nobody else in the house was a particular fan of this dish. Gita usually made it on my birthday, since it was a favorite of mine. I paused to think about the date. *Well, it wasn't my birthday.*

"What's the occasion?" I asked, taking the plate of bread to the table.

Gita shrugged, her eyes bright.

Aarush's mother walked into the room. Mrs. Dr. Patel had the ability to make me lose whatever air I had in my lungs. I reached for my asthma spray.

"Grady, take a deep breath. You don't need that," she told me.

Mrs. Dr. Patel was small and delicate, with long blue-black hair. Her dark skin was smooth, her almond-shaped eyes a more feline version of Aarush's. She moved her hands as she spoke as if they helped her with her thoughts. It was lyrical. She was the most beautiful woman I had ever seen.

"Aarush is upstairs. Go get him. Dr. Patel is on his way home."

I looked over at Gita, who seemed to be smiling at a joke I must have missed.

"I wasn't going to come over today." I was a little surprised by the reception I was getting.

"Life is fluid, not written in stone," Gita said in her inscrutable way.

I frowned. I looked at her face, which seemed to float in the steam from the many pots. Gita was always saying things like that.

I opened my mouth to reply, but Mrs. Dr. Patel chose that moment to grace me with her smile. It lit up the room. "Go get Aarush. Dinner will be on the table in a minute."

Aarush lay on his stomach across his bed, his books surrounding him. His laptop was open on the floor, and as I walked in, he was hanging over the side of his bed typing information.

"I said I wasn't hungry." Aarush didn't look at me. He was absorbed in his studies.

"You will be when you see what Gita made."

He wasn't expecting me. His head shot up, his lips tilted upwards in what only I knew was a grin. "You came, of course, to apologize?"

"No, I came to tell you that you were right." I flopped down on the beige carpeted floor beside the bed.

"No surprises there. Having confidence in yourself is half the problem. Hand me that." He pointed to a scattered pile of papers on the rug. I reached for the closest sheet. "Not that one."

I stopped for a minute to address the comment of confidence, but Aarush was deeply engaged in arithmetic homework. Anyway, what could I possibly say... that it's hard to feel confidence when you know the outcome. That's the difference, I thought. I'm more of a realist. Not that Aarush is the dreamer type, but in the end, you can't manufacture confidence. Truth was, I didn't know how someone got it... it's not like you could buy it on the internet, or something.

I picked up the next paper. It was full of math equations

in his sloppy handwriting. He grunted as I handed it to him and proceeded to scribble in his notebook.

"I actually did come to apologize too," I added in a soft voice.

"You don't have to. I knew you were rattled. I keep telling you all that stuff is not worth getting upset over."

I turned to look at him. Aarush could talk and do math at the same time. I could barely walk and chew gum. Well, that's not quite true. I could do those two things, but I definitely couldn't do math and hold a conversation at the same time.

"Doesn't anything bother you?" I asked him.

"No," Aarush responded without looking up at me.

"Seriously, dude. I mean, they are always making fun of you."

Aarush stopped what he was doing to examine me with those inquisitive eyes of his. "Why would I care what anybody thinks of *me*?"

Sometimes I felt like he came from another planet. "It's important," I told him.

"Why?"

I sputtered for a moment, at a loss to answer him. "Forget it. It doesn't matter."

"Exactly." Aarush closed his book with a satisfying snap. He sniffed the air and looked at me. "It's not your birthday. I wonder what's gotten into Gita?"

"Well, I'm not one to question miracles." I pushed myself up. "I'm sorry about what happened. You were right about strength and where it comes from."

That slow smile spread across his face again. Man, I wish the other kids could have seen him like this. But then again, it seemed that out of the two of us, I was the only one who cared.

"Boys!" Gita yelled up the stairs. "Your dad is home, Aarush."

"Come on, let's eat. Race you down the steps." Aarush took off in a flash toward the kitchen.

The Doctors Patel were sitting at either end of the table. Gita placed a steaming bowl of stew in front of me and gave me two crispy pieces of pav, the bread soaked in butter. I tore into it, enjoying the rich flavors.

Mr. Dr. Patel had a neat way of moving the conversation to someone else's occupation, making it sound as if their job was the most interesting work in the world.

We discussed school and assorted moments of the day. It was nice, the exchange of conversation, the give and take of talking and the flow of ideas that followed. Sometimes I watch the Doctors' Patel as Aarush spoke, the way their eyes met when he recounted some experience that happened. I wished someone looked at me that way when I spoke. Uncle Leo and I barely grunted our way through a meal, and mostly it was about how something on our plates tasted. I found myself relating my daring feat across the parking lot carrying the entire canned section of the Purple Artichoke. I included the part about my inhaler.

"So how many cans did you carry, Grady?" Mr. Dr. Patel held his knife and fork arrested in the air, as if I had told him I climbed Mount Everest…barefoot.

"It's no big deal." I looked down at my empty plate, wishing I hadn't eaten so fast.

"Indeed no, it is. I think it is remarkable the way you were able to concentrate on the light pole."

"It was the bird. I fixated on the bird that was on the light pole," I corrected him.

"And he managed without taking his asthma spray. I've told you, Grady, if you remember to breathe deeply you'll be fine. I think you've outgrown your asthma," Mrs. Dr. Patel said.

I looked down at my plate. Last month during my yearly check-up, Mrs. Dr. Patel said the test indicated my asthma might be anxiety-driven, whatever that is. All I knew is that sometimes I had trouble breathing.

"Still, you were able to carry everything." Mr. Dr. Patel exchanged a smile with Aarush. "It's a matter of mind over matter."

Aarush acknowledged his dad's statement with a nod.

We finished the meal with coconut ice cream, the frozen dessert cooling my mouth from the hot curry flavors. I loved the Patels' food, the seasoning, the way Gita cooks. I sat back with a satisfied sigh.

"Are we finished eating, then?" Mr. Dr. Patel got up. "I'll be right back."

We all watched him return. He held a gray envelope in his hands. He approached the table. Aarush's mother gasped. Only Gita sat with a secret smile on her face.

Mr. Dr. Patel placed the envelope in front of Aarush. "It came to my office. Well…open it, son."

Aarush's hands were on his lap. I looked around. Everybody was watching him, their faces so filled with love, and something else…respect.

"Go on, Rooshie. Open it," his mother urged.

Aarush looked up at me. "What if…what if I don't make it in?"

For the first time he looked miserable. I had never seen Aarush look unhappy.

"Don't worry, Aarush. I'm confident you'll make it into Templeton. In fact, they'd be just plain stupid to think of opening without you." I meant it in all earnestness. At that moment, I wanted him to be accepted more than anything in the world.

I glanced up to see that Mrs. Dr. Patel's eyes were watching me the misty way I yearned for before. I coughed a bit, not understanding why I felt like I was choking up. I resisted the urge to wipe my eyes, forcing them not to tear up. They stung in a way I have never experienced. Heat rose to my cheeks and I know I lowered my head. Mrs. Dr. Patel reached over and touched my chin gently. "You're a good friend, Grady."

Much as I would like to say the warm and fuzzy feeling was all I had, there was another sensation as well. I wondered if it was possible to be torn in two. While I was thrilled for my friend, there was a deeper feeling I was fighting. It poked me with sharp little claws reminding me of its presence.

A cold sensation of dread lurked under a layer that I tried hard to suppress. Aarush reached a shaking hand for the envelope. My best friend could be leaving me. He will go on to a superior school I could only dream about and learn things that will make both me and life back at Middlebury seem boring. *I could lose him forever.*

I fought the green-eyed monster, crushing it into a little ball and burying it into my chest. I glanced up to see Gita watching me. Her dark gaze reached into my soul making me sweat. I turned away trying hard to mean the next words coming from my mouth. "Open it, Aarush. I hope you get what you want."

He reached out and carefully separated the glob of wax

that kept the envelope sealed. His fingers slid into the envelope, and I swear, you could hear a pin drop in the room.

The folded letter inched out. The space filled with a bright light as the silver paper reflected the tiny pinpoints of the chandelier above us. Aarush dropped the foil as if it were burning hot.

His mother rose, her hands covering her face in a mixture of horror and joy. Tears pricked my own eyes, and I convinced myself they were tears of joy for my friend. "I don't know if I am happy or sad," she said, but her face glowed with pride. "We will miss you so very much!"

"Oh, happy," Mr. Dr. Patel said after clearing his throat. "We are all happy!"

"You deserve it, Aarush. You're smart." I looked at him. "And strong."

Aarush's mom held out her arms to hug him. His father surrounded them both in an embrace.

Gita was watching me. She nodded. "Good things come to those who wait."

"Yes, well, I have to go home. It's late." I touched his arm. "See, I told you." I tried my best to smile. I hope nobody saw it wobble.

"I'll drive you," Mr. Dr. Patel offered.

"No, you stay and celebrate."

Aarush glanced up. "You will get accepted too."

I didn't answer him. I didn't want to ruin his day. You can't get accepted if you don't complete the admission papers. While I did send in an essay, I never followed through with the application. That ended the day I threw it in the Patel's trash chute.

I left their house just as it was getting dark. The sun was

setting. The sky looked like black velvet, the stars a sparkling curtain. I wondered what the sky would look like over Templeton Academy.

CHAPTER 8

MIRACLES DO HAPPEN

*T*HE WALK HOME was for reflection. The weather was beautiful outside. There was a slight nip in the air. I concentrated on the dark landscape around me, trying to ignore the stinging behind my eyes.

Aarush Patel had made Templeton Academy. Elwood Bledsoe had made the school as well. *Me*, I was staying behind in Middlebury and learning to develop my prowess at carrying canned goods to their owners' cars.

I swiped a hand across my face, wiping the tears before someone noticed a big ape racing home crying like a baby.

It's all your own fault, I reprimanded myself. I had had my chance and chose not to fight with Uncle Leo. I never finished the application process. I had given up.

Get over it. I told myself. *Who wants to go to some secret school in the middle of nowhere to learn from the most interesting people in the world? Me, that's who.*

The house was empty when I got home. No big deal. I brought in the mail and tossed it negligently on the kitchen table. The kitchen was both dark and cold. I walked from room to room and turned on every light. Uncle Leo was going to have a fit. He was always yelling about wasting money.

I headed for the bathroom to stare at my face. I had that *I've been crushed* look, having spent the last half hour sobbing, so I scrubbed hard. I pulled Uncle Leo's acne medicine and washed my face until it glowed like the moon outside. I don't want you to get the idea that I had acne. I used his product so my flushed skin was the result of an abrasive medicinal treatment rather than sheer disappointment.

I heard the door slam, followed by the sound of Uncle Leo's keys being tossed on the table.

"Squirt?"

I was tempted not to respond. I didn't want him to see my face. I was also getting tired of the nickname. I still had the raw look and shiny eyes of one who has either been crying or using copious amounts of caustic acne medicine.

He approached the bathroom and saw my face. His jaw dropped. "Grady, have you been using my stuff again?"

"I had a zit."

"You don't get breakouts. It's expensive, man. Use your own soap."

Uncle Leo still had acne breakouts even though he was at the tail end of his twenties. You had to feel sorry for a grown man who suffered from teenage issues. I guess everybody had their own private hell.

"Sorry. I'll replace the bottle."

"You used the whole bottle?" Uncle Leo touched a blossoming pimple on his chin, and pushed into the bathroom to check his stock. Joni was due to come tomorrow.

"Don't shave. At least you have a beard to cover it." I felt lower than a snake. Some days it didn't pay to get out of bed.

I raced to the living room, threw myself onto the couch, put on the television, and looked for a *Walking Dead* program to appease my uncle. I heard him moving around in the kitchen. Uncle Leo brought in a couple of sandwiches on a plate and put them between us.

"I ate at the Patels'."

Uncle Leo's face lit up with hope. "Did you bring any home?"

"No leftovers." I didn't tell him that I'd forgotten to even ask for some. I should have been locked in a cave to rot. I was a terrible person. I hung my head with shame.

"No problem, Squirt. I'm sorry I overreacted about the soap." He offered me one of the sandwiches. Uncle Leo's forgiveness brought on a fresh wave of shame.

"Huh." He had a pile of mail on his lap and was separating the bills from the junk.

I looked up. He was holding a familiar gray envelope. It had the Templeton crest on the corner, my heart did a jig in my chest. It was impossible. My breath hitched and for a second I couldn't breathe at all. I knew it was not asthma.

He looked at me. "It's addressed to you." He raised his eyebrows up in a credible imitation of me.

"Let me see." I reached over, trying to snatch it from his grasp. My uncle pulled it away so I couldn't reach it.

"I thought you didn't apply."

"I didn't." Sweat broke out on my forehead.

"Grandpa would not be happy if you got in."

"Grandpa is dead." I stared at the envelope as if my vision could burn a hole through the paper and see inside. "Give it to me, Uncle Leo."

"We've talked about this, Grady."

We had and none of it made sense. Uncle Leo had been mysterious as he was evasive in his responses. It was the only time in my life he pulled the *I don't have to explain* card.

"Yeah, and I still don't have an answer as to why it should matter to anyone living or dead if I go to Templeton. Why, Leo!" I demanded. I had never spoken to him like this before. My uncle looked away. I saw his throat moving as if he were holding back. His hand gripped the letter so tightly his fingers had whitened on the paper.

My heart was beating wildly. Maybe miracles were contagious. I couldn't explain why I had an envelope, but I did, and on the slim chance I could make it in, I needed a good reason why Grandpa or anyone else would object.

"You still need parental permission," Uncle Leo said evasively.

"You're not answering my question." I wasn't letting go of the argument anymore. I felt closer to the reality of Templeton than ever before. Aarush's confident words that I would be accepted filled me with euphoria. I was buoyant.

Uncle Leo looked at me and shook his head. He sighed deeply and said in a low voice, "I never signed on for this."

I closed my eyes feeling sorry for my young uncle. While I am generally an easy-going person, it still can't be a walk in the park taking on parental responsibilities when you are barely out of your teens yourself.

"Who says I got in?" I changed my tone. "I never applied.

My essay was rejected. Let me see it." I held out my hand pleased to see it wasn't shaking.

Nobody knows Uncle Leo as well as I do, and I could see he was struggling himself. He placed the envelope on the seat between us. "Before you open it, Grady, I want you to understand that Grandpa wouldn't have allowed you to go there."

I looked up with what I'd hoped was a penetrating glare. "How would you know that? The school didn't exist when he was alive."

"Trust me."

I didn't care.

I grabbed the envelope and ripped the seal, exposing the flash of foil. I tore it open. The shiny paper illuminated my face. I swear I could feel the burn of its reflection on my hot cheeks.

My eyes met Uncle Leo's. "They accepted me. They accepted me," I repeated with wonder. "I have to call Aarush."

"I can't in good conscience let you go, Grady. It goes against everything I promised our grandfather."

I made it. Nothing mattered. I was going. Uncle Leo would have to sign or... I'd liberate myself from him, somehow. I didn't even care why he thought my long-dead grandparent wouldn't want me to go. That was silly. It sounded like a dumb excuse, anyway. I sprang off the couch and ran to my room. I called Aarush. He wasn't surprised at all.

"Well," Aarush said rather smugly. "Of course, you made it into Templeton. Gita and I filled out your admission papers."

"You what!" I exclaimed. I wasn't sure if I was supposed to be angry, but Aarush's next comment made me feel good.

"How could you expect me to go to Templeton without you?"

In the end, I reasoned. It really didn't matter. I was in and that's all that counted.

I avoided Uncle Leo for the rest of the night. I didn't want to hear him tell me that Grandpa wouldn't want me to go. How could he possibly know and what were his excuses for even suggesting it? There was no concrete reason and I refused to live my life by speculation.

I picked up my parents' picture with no small amount of annoyance. If they had been alive, I wouldn't have had to deal with my uncle's refusal to enroll me in the school. I didn't understand it.

I stared at my dad's face. He was so young, not much older than Uncle Leo now. Just as the accident had robbed him of his youth, I guess, caring for me stole Uncle Leo's as well.

I bit my lip, wondering why Uncle Leo wouldn't want to get rid of me. He could do whatever he wanted: take off for weekends with Joni, sleep out, eat whatever he desired. Why would he care so much about keeping me home? It wasn't as if Grandpa would even know if I went.

We ended up not speaking for days. It developed into a kind of cold war—no words exchanged, but there was a definite chill in the house. If he wasn't going to be honest with me and give a real reason, I didn't feel any obligation to give in blindly. This was my future.

I avoided Uncle Leo for the next week, keeping to my room. I could hear him pause outside my door. Once, he tapped the wood surface. I didn't answer. I put my ear to the door, hardly breathing until I heard him pad his way down the corridor.

Sooner or later we'd have to address the issue. I was going to Templeton Academy whether he liked it or not.

Joni was pulling a lasagna from the oven when I arrived home the following Wednesday. I sniffed appreciatively. I heard the door slam behind me.

"Sit down," she said, placing the casserole on the table.

I shook my head. "Not hungry," I lied. I was starved. It seemed the legend of my can-carrying feat had traveled, and I was being sought out for all of the heavy lifting the store had to offer. Even my manager spoke to me differently.

"We have to talk," Uncle Leo said behind me.

I turned around. He looked terrible. His face was pale, his cheeks hollow. His eyes had big black circles around them as if he hadn't slept for a week.

I staggered against the chair, guilt weighing me down.

Joni was busy putting real plates on the table rather than paper. I heard the clink of metal silverware.

"It's a celebration," Uncle Leo said as if to answer my question. "It's not every day my nephew gets accepted to the finest school in the world."

"I'm sorry, Leo—" I started. I had decided to stop calling him Uncle Leo. it made me feel more on equal footing. If he noticed, he didn't say anything about it.

He held up his hand to stop me. "I wish I could tell you what it's all about, but I can't. I also can't see another life ruined."

"Grandpa never even heard of Templeton."

Leo smiled sadly. "There are things you don't understand, Squirt." He stopped and looked at me. "I mean, Grady. What I've learned…" He appeared to be wrestling with the right words. "Well, that is, life's a journey."

"That's profound," Joni said with no small amount of awe.

I was even impressed. "Who said that?" I asked.

"I did," Leo said as he sat down. "I did, and it's time your life isn't trapped in other people's trajectories."

"What?" I asked, wondering who was this man? When had he changed from walking dead to the wisdom of the ages?

"Leo," Joni said reverently, "that was beautiful."

We sat in silence. I didn't want to ruin the mood. Joni looked at Leo as if he were a god.

To be honest, I was feeling pretty good about him right then. By the way, the lasagna was delicious too.

Elwood, it seemed, wasn't the only student from our school to have been chosen. Middlebury Middle School had the unprecedented honor of having three students selected. My picture hung in the great hall with Aarush's and Elwood's. There were assemblies celebrating our achievements.

A national magazine interviewed me and I tried my best to respond to the questions with gravity. I answered all their queries except one. I didn't know why I was selected.

While I understood Aarush got in because he was smart and Elwood because he was…Elwood, I couldn't for the life of me figure out how or why I got in. But, as I said regarding Gita's stew, I wasn't going to question a miracle.

CHAPTER 9
THIS IS PARI

ONCE WE KNEW we were going to Templeton the months flew quickly. Mrs. Dr. Patel volunteered to take me for the school physical along with Aarush. Leo had so little spare time, he was grateful for her offer. I did put my foot down for the orientation, though. I wanted to make sure Leo knew exactly what to expect.

"Only think of the type of school it is," Aarush said in awe as we waited for blood work done by robots at a state-of-the-art facility a full day's ride from home.

I had many physicals in my short life, Mrs. Dr. Patel doing the honors. I mentioned earlier that she is my doctor. Some might find it disconcerting, but Mrs. Dr. Patel is not the clinical type and when I see her or feel her cool hand on my head, it's the closest I can imagine to having a mother.

The exams were done in a facility that boasted long walls

of scanners. We walked in a single column through a type of tunnel that not only measured us, but somehow set us up with dental records. Aarush barely spoke, he was so excited from all the space-age machinery.

While most everyone was in awe, Mrs. Dr. Patel seemed not to be impressed by the technology. She waited at the end of the tunnel. I heard her speaking to an anxious parent as we walked to the other sections where we waited for more tests. Nothing was invasive, which I have to admit was a good thing, but I did feel a little bit like an astronaut.

"We're not going to the moon," Aarush told me after I mentioned it.

"It's the latest in medical science," Mrs. Dr. Patel said as she put her arm around me. "I was lucky enough to be invited to a seminar sponsored by the Templeton Foundation last summer. I am so excited about these new innovations, Grady. Medicine is making leaps and bounds that will trickle down to private practitioners soon, and with Dr. Templeton's help, I intend to be one of the first."

She was soon lost in a cluster of parents eager to ask questions. If I didn't know better, I'd venture to say Mrs. Dr. Patel seemed more like an ambassador for Templeton, but I had no time to think more about it.

They took hair and saliva samples as well, and I grumbled to Aarush that I didn't understand why they needed our DNA.

"In case our bodies are in a freak accident and are unrecognizable," Aarush answered calmly.

I didn't see Mrs. Dr. Patel come up behind us, but her voice didn't give me the reassurance I was looking for.

"Aarush," Mrs. Dr. Patel admonished. "What a silly thing to say. Look at Grady, he's gone all pale."

Middle school ended with a bang-up graduation. Aarush, Elwood, and I stood with the honors students. I don't think they were particularly happy to have me there, I realized, observing their dirty looks. I was not an honors student like the rest of them.

Elwood had a nice speech squeezed between Aarush and another one of the smartest kids in the school. I couldn't figure out why Elwood was so popular, but they cheered mightily at his infantile oration. If you asked me what he said, I really couldn't tell you. He chanted a few slogans, his fist in the air, and made cow eyes at Lindsay Carruthers, who sat with his parents.

The Patels gave both Aarush and me a nice party, inviting Leo and Joni as well. They served my favorite dishes. There were a lot of doctors there, all Aarush's cousins, uncles and aunts. Every time I said, "Dr. Patel," eleven people answered. I gave up and went upstairs to play video games in Aarush's bedroom.

Aarush and I sat on the floor, our backs resting against his bed. We were engaged in an epic battle between Super Dude and the Syblis of Silenia. It was the newest version of the game, still in the testing state. Mr. Dr. Patel had a friend who'd asked him to have Aarush try it out.

I wasn't sure I liked the new enemies, a pack of female harpies who tore at Super Dude's skin and attempted to peck out his eyes. They were unpredictable, and I missed the reliability of Master Disaster. It was easier to play when you understood your enemies. Aarush, of course, was Super Dude, and I had the pleasure of moving the three serpentlike females around the Sea of Dispara. He was pursuing me as I retreated, trying to catch me with his magical lasso.

The door opened. I knew it without looking up because the sitar music playing downstairs intruded.

"Shut the door!" Aarush ordered, his attention glued to the screen.

I heard an impatient sigh and glanced up. The air left my lungs as if it were vacuumed out. Standing in the doorway, her silhouette dusted by soft light, was the most beautiful girl I had ever seen.

She was tall. I guessed her to be my age, with thin, delicate hands and a heart-shaped face. Dark eyes glittered from a face framed by long, wavy black hair. She was dressed in a sari, the shiny gauze waterfall of light blue tumbling from her shoulder.

"Aarush," she said, her gaze direct. "You said you would introduce us." She glided into the room, and I sat slack-jawed, my thumbs frozen as she whispered passed me in a rush of silk.

Aarush, absorbed in decimating me, ignored her. I glanced from Aarush's blank face to her curious expression. She looked at me then, and I could hear angels singing, I think. I elbowed Aarush.

"What, Grady? You are making a poor performance today." He was busy clicking away and wrapping my characters one by one in his lasso.

"Aarush!" I said through gritted teeth.

As if coming out of a trance, he shivered then turned to Pari. "Oh, hi, Pari. This is Grady Whill."

Pari. Her name was as beautiful as she was. "Pari?" I stammered, wishing I didn't sound so lame.

"Yes. My cousin from Mumbai."

"Um...I didn't see you at dinner," I said.

"Yes," she replied sitting daintily on the edge of the bed

slightly behind me. "We've just arrived. Customs took a long time."

I wanted to look at her but thought it would appear too strange to sit on the floor drooling, so I fiddled with my game remote.

"Grady! Pay attention!" Aarush was annoyed.

"Aarush," she said, her hand touching her cousin's shoulder. "Be nice. Please introduce us. I would like to get to know your friend better."

Aarush was absorbed in cremating my icon, and responded woodenly, "Pari, Grady, Grady, Pari. Grady, pick up your speed, or you will run out of lives."

I colored up for Aarush. He was being rude. "Aarush," I said quietly. I lowered my controls.

She smiled indulgently at Aarush, then looked at me and said, "I thought it was you, Grady."

Aarush barked what passed for a laugh. "Yes, like I have *so* many friends, Pari. You know it has to be Grady."

Wait—What? She knows about me?

"So nice to finally meet, Grady. My aunt has told me a lot about you." She was watching me with a smile on her lips.

"*Really?* Like what?" I asked with all the manners of a gorilla.

Pari waved a hand in the air. "You are a good friend to my cousin and that makes you a good friend to me."

I watched her thinking about what she said. She was gazing at Aarush fondly. Our eyes met and I felt a frisson of electricity, as if Aarush was the conduit linking our friendship. I wanted to know more about her.

"Um …" I cleared my throat. "Are…are you staying long?"

"For a while," she answered cryptically.

I put down the remote and stood, wiping my sweating

hands on my jeans. Aarush tossed his remote and jumped to his feet. "It's just as well. You were no competition. Be careful, though, when you play against Pari. She is the best gamer I've ever competed with. She's a brilliant strategist."

"Like with chess?" I asked.

Pari nodded. "Yes, and some other things."

I picked up a control to hand it to her. "Would you like to have a game?"

Pari took the remote from my hand, her head tilted. "I'd rather talk and get to know you."

"Aarush!" Gita's voice came over the intercom. "Come down for cake."

Pari looked disappointed. "Another time," she said.

I, on the other hand, hoped I didn't look crushed.

"Oh, don't look like that, Grady. You'll have plenty of time to play *Super Dude* with Pari. She's going to Templeton with us."

Aarush and his cousin Pari left me in shocked silence as they raced downstairs for cake.

The first few weeks of summer passed in a blur of anticipation.

Orientation was a six-hour event on the local college campus. I thought I'd have time to meet some of the students, but we barely had a minute to acknowledge each other, much less socialize. It was run by Mr. Thompson, our principal, which was a surprise. It seems he became a Templeton representative based on the fact that he was the only school to have three students recruited. Plus, I guess he could add his stellar performance on Elwood's reality show to his resume. He explained as we gathered in the auditorium, that we comprised only the tri-state area and amounted to about twenty students. I recognized a few kids from the television program and remembered one or two from articles I'd read on the internet.

The twins Lydia and Forrest Cullen were there. They kept to themselves, but when we passed them on the great lawn of the school I heard them speaking what sounded to me like another language.

"Not any that I recognize," Pari said after I pointed it out.

"Cryptophasia." Aarush nodded.

"Also known as twin talk, a private language only they understand," Pari explained.

I'd never heard of it. More nerve-wracking than that, I hadn't heard of a lot of things that were thrown around or overheard in bits of conversations. Students mostly sat with their parents, but the snatches of discussion I caught felt way over my head. That old monster of worry nipped at my heels making me think that I may not belong with this group.

Our day was filled with videos explaining what life would be like. No distractions, no acknowledgment of the outside world, total isolation for eight months. We could call home once a month, but our parents or guardians could contact the school as much as they wanted to check on us. No cell phones or video games were allowed.

When I caught up with Pari and Aarush at one of lunch I mentioned the harsh rules. We sat in the school's cafeteria at a small round table. Students buzzed around us, rushing to get their meals done. Some were absorbed in books, others appeared to know each other. Either way, nobody approached us.

"It's clear they want blank slates," Pari observed.

I looked at her much like the blank slate she was talking

about, until the light bulb went off in my head. "They want to be the only influence."

"It's intriguing," Pari said.

I don't know if that would be the word I would have used. I felt my chest tighten and I wheezed a little bit. It came on when I got nervous, much like Mrs. Dr. Patel had said. I took a quick puff from my inhaler.

Aarush put down his sandwich and looked at me. "Grady, you are just as smart as everyone else."

I wanted to ask him where he got that information.

Pari smiled. "He's right, Grady."

Before I could ask how she knew what I was thinking, she responded. "It's all over your face. You'll do fine."

I looked around the room at all the students deep into their studies or discussions. I wasn't as sure as they were about it.

Leo signed the permission papers soon after orientation. We didn't bring up possible objections and it was a bit like walking on eggs around the house. I didn't want to have any more confrontations about it, and frankly, I didn't care about his reason. None of it made sense. If he was upset about the draconian rules, he didn't mention them and neither did I.

I was afraid they wouldn't do well under close scrutiny anyway, and didn't choose to open that particular can of worms. If I felt any apprehension about the school, any doubt evaporated under the excitement of being included with such a special group. As time to leave grew closer, I felt compelled to go, as if I was being drawn there.

Thankfully, there wasn't much to prepare. I was to take nothing but the clothes on my back. Everything from school uniforms to books and electronics were to be furnished by

Templeton. It seems we didn't have to worry about scholarships or grant money, either to my immense relief.

"I'll write," I told Leo at dinner. While calls weren't encouraged, emails were allowed, both Leo and I knew it was baloney. I wasn't much of a note-writer and neither was he.

It was our final meal until I returned when the semester ended, and dinner had a heavy quality to it. The school term would end by May, and didn't feel like an especially long time from now.

Leo was oddly silent. He watched me thoughtfully, while picking at his taco. My nerves jangled with fear he'd bring up the old fight, or misgivings about the school, and I didn't want to leave on a bad note.

Joni cleared the table. "Go play your last video game. They don't have any games at school. *Sheesh.*" She looked me straight in the eye. "Why do you want to go there for high school? I mean, it's on a rock in the middle of nowhere."

I opened my mouth to say something, then snapped it shut. I didn't have an answer. I don't know why I wanted to go. I just did. I also didn't want this argument to escalate.

It was as important to me as...*I don't know.* I couldn't even think of something that valuable. I knew from the time I'd heard of Templeton Academy I was supposed to go there. It was as though it was my—

"Birthright," Leo interrupted.

He took the words right out of my mouth. I looked up at him, my jaw hanging open as if it had been unhinged. That word. *Birthright.* Not normally in my vocabulary, but it fit what I was feeling. The word was strung like a wire between us, creating a connection. I felt it tug at my chest, linking us to some unknown force. I rubbed the spot where it joined us, wondering how a word had the power to do that.

He searched my face, his Adam's apple bobbing up and down. He didn't speak for a while. The world narrowed to just my uncle and me. I never felt such a closeness with him before, as if we were the only people in the room.

I didn't trust my own voice and I instinctively knew his voice would crack if he spoke. The room was thick with silence. I felt the remote drop from my nerveless fingers. *Don't ruin it, Leo.* I begged him from my brain. Whatever he was going to share was hard for him, and I understood there was no going back from it.

He leaned forward, his hands resting on his skinny knees. I realized he had something cupped in his palm. He opened his fingers slowly revealing what looked to be a school ring. "Your father would have wanted you to have this."

He offered it to me. I didn't move. I stared at the gold ring, the fiery red gemstone in the center sparking a memory. I couldn't speak if I wanted to. I knew that ring.

Leo took my hand and placed the ring in the center. "I wasn't going to give it to you until you got older."

"I...um...I don't know what to say." I took a shuddering breath. "Was this my dad's?" I didn't need to ask. It felt heavy in my hand, the cool weight of the metal feeling foreign. I put the ring on my finger and it rolled loosely around.

"He's going to lose it. Here." Joni reached around her neck and pulled a leather cord over her head. She untied it, took off her charms, and held out her hand for the ring. She placed the newly tied cord with the ring around my neck. The ring landed with a thud on my chest. I put it under my t-shirt.

It was weird. The ring fell into the hollow of my chest as if it belonged there.

"Don't lose it, Squ- Grady."

I was so touched by the ring, I forgot to ask what Leo meant by saying attending Templeton Academy was my birthright.

The next morning, the Patels arrived early to start our journey. Pari and Aarush were already in the back seat. The car was taking us to the airport. Aarush's parents were dropping us off. "Everybody has their wristbands?" Mrs. Dr. Patel asked. She had twisted in her seat to look at us.

We all raised our arms. We each sported identical rubbery wristbands that had shown up last week with the instructions to wear them upon departure. No one would be allowed on the plane without one. I had seen my share of these types of wristbands that people wore to measure their steps or body functions. These were different. There was nothing on them, no markings or other forms of identification. They were thick, but without any indicators, and once on, we couldn't get them off. This made us all give a weird type of chuckle, that wasn't even a laugh. Well, at least, Pari and I, Aarush didn't laugh much. He shrugged and said, "If it's from Templeton, what could be bad?" I kept moving it up and down my wrist, and while I couldn't help the small voice in the back of my head wondering why we had to wear them.

"Hmmm... yes," Mrs. Dr. Patel said, her face troubled as she looked at us.

I heard Mr. Dr. Patel respond in a low voice, "It will be okay."

She lifted one shoulder. "I don't know, Apurva. Not even

a photo, they are taking nothing from home? What if he misses us?"

I was surprised by her reaction. Aarush's mom had been excited about us all attending until that day at orientation. She had gotten quieter about it after that.

"Aarush, you mother is worried if you don't have a picture you'll forget us," Mr. Dr. Patel said.

Aarush looked puzzled for a minute and said, "That's impossible, Mom."

"Still," she began.

"You were fine about it last spring," Aarush's father said. "Don't make them nervous."

"What if—"

Mr. Dr. Patel shook his head. "We talked about this. I trust the Templetons."

Pari patted Mrs. Dr. Patel's shoulder. "Don't worry, Auntie. Grady and I will make sure none of us get homesick. We have each other."

Going to Templeton was an unprecedented experience for anyone. It felt strange to be leaving without baggage, not even a backpack or lunch bag for any of us. The rules were very clear. Templeton was brand new. We were the first class to attend, and in four years we would be the first graduating class. We would be the only grade in the school until next year when fresh recruits were chosen. Students were not to be distracted by anything.

The plane was packed with students flying down to Miami. There were some chaperones on board. We all knew they were not students. Their clothes as well as their age gave them away.

The chaperones had no interaction with us, almost as though they were there to observe. They were positioned in the four corners of the plane, and once we were seated, they sat down and appeared to get busy with tablets and gold styluses.

The airplane was filled with the excited babble of students. Elwood sat a few rows in front of us. He refused to look at me. I saw him introduce himself to a group who had transferred from international arrivals. They were connecting with our plane after flying in from Europe.

These boys looked older. They clustered around Elwood's seat. I could hear them speaking with thick accents. I strained my ears. One boy turned. He was barrel-chested with a shock of dark hair. His brow hung low over his narrow eyes. I saw a scar stretching from his cheekbone to the corner of his upper lip. It pulled at his mouth, making his face look like he was frozen in some weird grin. I smiled back. I swear I could hear him growl.

Aarush chose the moment to observe, "He reminds me somewhat of Marcie, I think."

I laughed for a second. The boy gave us a smoldering look that sent shivers down my spine. He couldn't have known what we were talking about, but I got the distinct impression he knew Aarush was comparing him to the neighborhood pit bull.

We exchanged a sizzling look, and I knew at that moment I had made an enemy. I spent the rest of the trip avoiding eye contact with him.

We took off for a two-and-a-half-hour plane ride that appeared to be over in a snap. I tried to watch half of a movie, but somehow the lips seemed out of sink with the actors, and I lost interest. By the time they served us snacks, I could feel the pressure change indicating we were approaching our destination.

I glanced out, my head pressed against the plexiglass of the window to observe the cloudless elegant skyline. Miami rose like a jewel out of an aqua ocean. The plane was energized as a rush of excitement swept over the kids; Aarush started to fidget. He stacked and restacked the magazines from the plane's seat pockets. He had read them several times over, quoting information that nobody was interested in exploring. While I could understand it driving some people nuts, it was Aarush and one of his quirks. People who liked him, accepted it as part of the package.

I heard Elwood make several acid comments. It's times like this that strangers judge Aarush. He gets overwhelmed, his hands start moving too much and he'll fixate on something that doesn't bother most people. Sure enough, his hands were tangled in the headset as if they were handcuffed. I caught Lydia Cullen staring at him, her eyes wide and unblinking. Her expression unnerved me no little bit. If Pari saw it she didn't say anything.

The steward made his way down the aisle with a plastic bag in front of him to collect our borrowed headsets. Aarush was enveloped in the wires, somehow both my lines as well as his were tied together, and he was in a state of panic to straighten them out. His anxiety must have affected me because I felt my chest compress. The familiar wheeze of asthma came making me pat my pocket for my inhaler. I took a quick puff, but got little relief. Whispers followed by a few chuckles erupted from the seats across from ours as Aarush's moves became jerkier.

Before I could reach over to help him, Pari calmly placed her hands on Aarush's fiddling fingers, and with quiet efficiency uncombed the wires to place them in the bag. Her voice was low and soothing. The whole episode made me wonder what her special talents were that qualified her for Templeton.

Later at the airport in Miami, we were hustled into a waiting area. Buses arrived to take us to a ferry. It was an easy transfer as no one had baggage. There were dozens of vehicles that formed a caravan, and I craned my neck to catch a sight of the city. I was dismayed to see Elwood on my bus. *Was there no escaping this guy?*

One of the chaperones stood. All heads turned to stare at her but the volume of noise on the bus was too loud to hear. I would have thought we all had a healthy curiosity about these strangers, yet that didn't stop the group of teens from ceasing their conversations. She waited, the intensity of her scrutiny giving me the creeps as she looked up and down the rows. Then she did the strangest thing. Miss Parker raised her hands, then placed a single finger against her lips. As if by magic, the entire bus went silent as if our vocal cords had been cut off. *How did she do that?* I wondered. I twisted in my seat, every one of the students was facing forward and watching her. Even Elwood complied and stopped talking to the dark-haired goon from Europe.

The woman held onto the top of the seat, the swaying vehicle making her lithe body move with each turn. "Can I have your attention?" she said, the timbre of her voice low. I felt like I had to concentrate to hear her voice. "My name is Miss Parker." I couldn't tell how old she was. She could have been anywhere from twenty-five to forty. Her skin was like porcelain; not a wrinkle marred her completion.

She wasn't nasty or anything, yet every time her gaze rested on me, darts of uneasiness made me squirm. She had brown hair and pale skin. Now that she was standing, I could see she was in some sort of uniform made of a dark material. I didn't want to stare, but I couldn't see a seam, zipper, or button anywhere. It was a form-fitting charcoal gray jersey.

I guess it was better than the guy walking down the aisle in the bus to my left. He must have weighed two-forty and was wearing teal-colored spandex. He looked like a relic from an eighties muscle gym.

Miss Parker surveyed us, moving from each student to the next, as if she were memorizing our faces. "I need you to hand over all your cell phones." There were gasps and groans followed by some more verbal protests. I mean, we all knew this time was coming. I guess none of us believed it would truly happen. She held up a surprisingly firm-looking hand. "You knew the rules. There's no cell service on the island anyway. Valencia Templeton, Dr. Templeton's daughter, has mandated that electronics will not be allowed."

"I've never been separated from my phone," a girl across the aisle wailed. "I don't think my parents are going to like this."

"Tabitha Cartwright?" Miss Parker held out her hand for the cell.

"How did you know my name?" Tabitha clutched her phone tightly to her chest. "Can't I please keep it?"

"To answer your first question, this was fully explained at orientation."

Tears filled the girl's eyes.

Miss Parker went on, "Think of this as your first test. Can you leave the mainland truly behind?" Without waiting for a response, she grinned, but the smile held no warmth. "I know you all very well."

I heard Lydia and Forrest Cullen chattering away in their secret language in the seat behind us. Lydia seemed worried, her voice had a soothing quality, that while I didn't understand what she was telling her brother, eased my tension as well. I looked at Aarush who was calmly observing Miss Parker, then exchanged a glance with Pari. We both acknowledged our discomfort without words. Pari with pursed lips, me with an epic eye roll. At least we spoke the same language. I gulped with indecision. My hand tightened on the bar of the seat before me. It was getting real. I didn't want to leave, but this felt, I don't know, a bit like we were going to some reform camp or something. I must have communicated my unease, because Pari gave an almost imperceptible shake of her head and a small smile. I nodded back and sat more comfortably in my seat. *Whatever,* I thought exhaling a pent-up breath. The only ones I needed to talk to were right here on the bus. I guess I really didn't need my phone.

Another girl stood and banged her hand on the seat before her. "I can't believe this!"

"Then you may leave when we get to the next destination and will not be permitted to finish the journey to the school." She looked at the group as if she was speaking to each of us individually. "Our curriculum demands total concentration. Your parents not only agreed but loved the idea of distractions being removed from your life. I will remind you that you will be able to speak to them monthly, and they of course, will be in constant contact with the school to check on your progress."

"Sounds more like a prison," a boy from the second row called out saying what we were all thinking.

"Fine," she said, her voice flint-like. She spoke into a black band around her wrist, her eyes never leaving ours. "Mr. Grisham will be leaving us at our next stop." She scanned the bus as if daring us. "Anyone else?"

Miss Parker walked forward and slid the phone from the girl Tabita's unresisting hands. She strolled down the narrow aisle, stopping to ask for all electronic devices, knowing each student's name as well as where they lived.

"I can keep my watch?" Aarush asked hopefully. He always wore it.

She paused by our row and rested her hand on the seat back. I could feel her watching me, but I had nothing to hide. I handed her my cell phone.

Aarush had never broken a rule in his life, so I don't know why she was observing us.

"I can keep my watch?" Aarush repeated

She shrugged. "Watches, earrings,"—she looked right at me—"and rings are allowed."

Those intense eyes raked me from the top of my head to the bottom of my feet. She stopped on the center of my chest. My father's ring rested in the hollow of my breastbone under my shirt. The metal warmed, as if it had been exposed to a flame. I gasped, feeling the ring heat up under her steady perusal. I placed my palm on my shirt over the ring, pressing it against my skin, my breath caught in my throat. The ring continued to heat up until I could feel it scorch my flesh.

Burned, I jerked the leather cord away from my skin. Miss Parker smirked, then moved on to the kids in front of us.

She stopped before Elwood, seemingly unconvinced when he held up his empty hands.

She raised an eyebrow and stood firm. She bent over to whisper something in the kid from Europe's ear. He paled and handed her a bunch of stuff he pulled from his pockets. Elwood reluctantly followed suit.

"I wonder what she told them," Aarush whispered.

Miss Parker spun, her face settling on Aarush, and said, "I said I would order a full-body cavity search at the port."

How had she heard us? I wondered. I could barely hear us.

There was some forced laughter. Elwood and his new friend, I decided to call his Eurobuddy, scowled back. I smiled, thinking of Elwood being subjected to a forced pat-down.

"She's a hot number," Aarush shared, making me laugh out loud.

"What do you know about *hot numbers?*" I asked him, my chuckle edging a bit on hysteria.

Miss Parker turned to stare at both of us. I certainly didn't want her attention. "Be quiet," I warned Aarush.

For the first time in all the years I'd known him, Aarush blushed. He looked down at his fidgeting fingers. Biting my lip, I considered the teacher wondering why her expression appeared so hard when it settled on me.

I poked Aarush then and pointed to a huge sign announcing we were approaching the Port of Miami. Imagine our surprise when the bus made a left, turning away from the entrance, to pull up next to a giant wall of greenery. There were a few calls of dismay and a wisecrack about using GPS when we noticed the barrier being swung open by guards wearing the same uniform as Miss Parker but in a different color. The bus made the turn onto a long driveway that was flanked by rows of tall palm trees.

"How interesting. It's a private dock," Aarush observed.

"How do you know that?" I asked him.

He pointed to the ocean where it met the beach. Turquoise water lapped the white sand.

A huge craft looking for all the world like an ocean liner bobbed in the harbor. There was a gangplank and men in dark blue uniforms lining the dock. I fought the sudden urge to say, *Yo ho ho*. It didn't matter. Someone else said it, and the kids on the bus broke up with laughter.

Our vehicles pulled up, disgorging five hundred babbling students. We were divided into groups of twenty-five so that the dock now resembled a military parade ground. The sun beat down, and Miami's humidity made my shirt stick to my clammy skin. Pari shuffled from one foot to the other in the hot sand. I heard that girl, Tabitha from the bus griping about the heat. I was sorry I had left my water bottle on my seat in the bus. In my haste to get moving, I had forgotten it. Sweat trickled from my scalp down the back of my shirt. I saw Aarush wipe his forehead with his arm.

I stood in line with Aarush and a few others. Elwood strolled past us to park himself in the front of the queue. I felt a hard shove, and Eurobuddy, pushed past me as if there was no room in the street and the only way to get there was by walking over me. I resisted, holding my ground, but his beefy size barreled over me as if I didn't exist

I had no time to think about stepping on his foot in retaliation before I felt a gentle tap on my shoulder. Twisting around, I found Lydia Cullen watching me. "Don't do it," she warned. She lifted her brows, sliding the direction of her gaze sideways toward Miss Parker. I could see the teacher observing me as if I were the only person there. I bristled wondering if she was watching Eurobuddy and Elwood as close as she appeared to be following me.

Lydia gave me an impatient shove. I opened my mouth to say something, but the look on her face arrested me. It wasn't mean. I got the distinct impression she was being nice. I'm not quite sure how I got to that conclusion, but I knew it and the anger escaped out of me like a deflated balloon.

Our group was moving toward the gangplank. My head arched backward. It was a long way up. I was not fond of heights. As if sensing my discomfort, Aarush moved closer in front of me, Lydia, behind me, her shoulder bumping mine.

We followed the students before us, Elwood and his new friend leading the way. As if we were on a great moving conveyor, we climbed aboard.

The minute my feet touched the metal of the gangway, I felt my uneasiness recede to be replaced by excitement. I forged my way up the steep gangway, determined not to look down or even backward. I was onto my new life.

CHAPTER 10

HOT DOGS ARE ON THE MENU

*T*HE SHIP'S HORN gave a deep blast, and the engines rumbled underneath our feet.

"We will be docking in two hours and forty-five minutes. I suggest you visit the snack bars on decks four, five, and six. There will be a barbeque, and hot dogs are on the menu."

A cheer went up as we all laughed. It sounded more like a party boat. I didn't see Miss Parker, and I can tell you that didn't bother me at all. I was the tallest of our group that had morphed into a crowd of five. Lydia and her brother attached themselves to us and after a brief introduction, it felt like they belonged to us.

Lydia and her brother were short and heavy-set, identical in almost every way except for their hair. Lydia's being a bushy halo around her face, Forrest shaved close to his head.

"Deck five," I said, leading our new group to the middle

deck. The wind buffeted us on the higher altitude, and we watched the land recede taking us into the deeper blue waters. The cabin was refreshing after the intense heat outside, and cooled by air conditioning. I lost sight of Elwood after we entered the food concession on Deck Five. He was probably outside comparing his biceps brachii with Eurobuddy.

Pari, Aarush, and our newfound friends found the line for food, and we chatted happily about finally being on the last leg of the trip.

"She creeps me out a bit," Pari whispered, her head close to mine. Both Aarush and I knew who Pari was talking about without question. It was as if we were on the same wavelength. I liked the feeling. We made our way through the crowds, the five of us, and for the first time, I felt like I had my own clique.

"Miss Parker? I thought she was beautiful," Aarush answered.

"You think every woman is beautiful. She is ..." I couldn't think of a word.

"Odd," Lydia said, with a frown. "She's odd."

"There's a lot of odd here," I said with a meaningful look at some of the other students. Indeed they were a varied group. I don't want to give the impression I'm some sort of snob, but these kids were...*different*, and I don't mean like they were diverse.

There was a giant digital clock indicating the time. It was going on one in the afternoon when my stomach rumbled. I was famished.

I glanced around, realizing with a start that they were looking at us with the same expression. *Did they see Aarush and me as strange too?*

"All the teachers are special. If that makes them odd, then

so be it," Forrest volunteered. "I think we are going to experience many new things here." He spoke in a low volume and I had to lean forward to hear him. Lydia repeated what he said so often it sounded like an echo chamber.

I touched the ring resting against my chest remembering the heat when Miss Parker was around.

Maybe it was in my imagination. It had to be. Rings didn't turn warm on demand.

I recognized students from the television show, the kids who got in with their essays. Lydia began a commentary on their identities. It seemed that she knew everyone.

There was Devon Neely, the blind boy. He had his hand on the shoulder of a short kid I didn't recognize. She mentioned about ten others, but they seemed to blend together. I couldn't remember anything extraordinary about any of them and she didn't say what special abilities enabled them to come to the school.

There were so many others, milling in small groups, making friends. I could see cliques developing already, the jocks in one group, a pretty group of girls in another. *Sigh.* Some things never change.

We found a spot, squeezed into it, and watched students form into clusters and I wondered if Lydia and Forrest were sad they hooked onto us so early. We shared whatever we nabbed from the buffet. Aarush didn't eat meat, so I gave him all the fries, and he happily placed the hotdogs in front of me. Aarush was a slow eater. He observed our surroundings, using a french fry to gesture when he questioned who they are and why they might be at Templeton.

I downed two dogs before he made a dent in the bucket of fries. Forrest looked longingly at the dessert bar; Lydia prevented him from eating a fourth *churro,* with a whispered comment.

"Aarush," Pari admonished. "That's rude." She gave his fry a pointed look.

"Talking about them or pointing to them?" he asked.

"Both." She giggled.

Pari must have been a draw, several students, mostly girls came over to introduce themselves to her. We made the social cut, Pari was the nicest person I'd met making it a point to introduce us to each one of them. Both Aarush and I stayed silent, listening to their stories. Lydia was more animated than Forrest, but not as popular as Pari. She didn't seem to mind, and I sensed she was not competitive like some of the other girls.

Pari also had a way to make people feel at ease about themselves. I was beginning to realize Lydia had that same quality. Forrest, I noticed, rarely interacted with anyone. Built like his sister, he was a short, heavyset boy, with probing eyes. His voice always made me jump. It was unexpectedly like a deep bass drum.

We discovered the kids came from all over the world. No one mentioned what gave them the edge to get into the school, and to be honest, I'm not sure if any of us really knew. I didn't see anything more than a group of students that looked no different from Middlebury. Of the three of us, I knew the one with the most promise was Aarush, easily the smartest person I knew. Every so often I glanced at the giant clock on the wall of the ferry. We'd been traveling for most of the day, having left at the crack of dawn. The excitement, the rush of adrenaline dissipated, I yawned loudly.

Now that I'd eaten, I found I was exhausted. No one else

was complaining, and I thought it would make me sound weak and babyish to mention I was tired.

Elwood and his newfound friend, it seemed, had discovered our peaceful area of the boat. Of the three decks allotted, I thought the gods were playing an evil trick when I saw him push his way through the crowd. He and his new friends cleared out a small group of kids from a table, knocking their food onto the floor. There were a few cries of dismay, but Elwood puffed out his chest intimidating the smaller students. They scattered like a dandelion blown away in a breeze. Elwood laughed, then knocked their sodas onto the floor splashing anyone close enough to them.

I saw a blonde girl leaning casually against the wall watching him. She moved toward them, her chin raised defiantly.

She called out "Hey!" which I thought sounded cool the way she said it.

Elwood looked up innocently, pointing to his chest. "Me?"

"Yeah, you." She stalked over to him, then stood, her hands on her hips, her face a tight snarl. I saw Elwood lean close to say something. She didn't shrink back, she actually leaned toward him. Eurobuddy was right behind her. I didn't like it.

Soon they were standing so close, you barely see daylight between them. I could hear a heated exchange. Kids crowded around them encircling Elwood and the girl, the sound amplified by the confined space. I could tell by the look on Elwood's face this was going to be a problem. *Where was an aide when you needed them most?* Memories of the arm wrestling debacle flooded my brain. It didn't matter. It was two against one, and I knew what I had to do. She had no idea with whom she was tangling.

I reluctantly stopped eating my third hot dog, dropping it onto our messy table in case the blonde girl needed help.

"Where are you going?" Pari asked.

I turned my gaze to the girl and Elwood.

"I'll come too?" she said. I shook my head, my eyes resting on Aarush. Pari nodded with understanding.

I left the safety of my haven to move closer, but Elwood's Eurobuddy must have seen me move, because he turned to step into my path blocking me. I looked over the guy's huge shoulder and saw Elwood's arms moving around menacingly. The girl didn't seem impressed. I turned to Pari, and asked if she knew her name.

"Not sure." She thought for a minute. "Wait, I remember her. She was on the show. She's a champion wrestler, I think. Benly or Binly, some name like that."

Hopefully, her specialty was arm wrestling. It was heating up with a lot of cursing. Eurobuddy was diverted by a juicy phrase allowing me to squeeze past him, Forrest moving into my place as soon as I vacated it.

I stood opposite the girl, trying to get her attention. She was glaring at Elwood, her shoulders erect, her hands fisted. She seemed to come out of her rage, looked up and saw me. Her back to the wall of students encircling them, she walked sideways until we stood beside each other.

"I didn't think you noticed me," I told her.

She didn't answer. Elwood was yelling, "Hey, you! Blondie, I'm talking to you!" She glanced up, her legs splayed as if she were a pirate captain on the deck of her ship. "Me?" I heard her snicker.

"Do you need help?" I asked out of the side of my mouth.

I saw her lids lower as she gave me the side-eye. "I'm good, but I'm glad you're here," she said with a confidence I envied.

All talking ceased and the students cleared a larger space with the blonde girl and Elwood in the center. They circled each other like predators.

Elwood responded with a nasty bout of laughter that sounded like a machine gun.

I couldn't see her face now, she moved directly in front of me. She was hunched over, her hands opening and shutting, her knees bent.

There was a commotion when Eurobuddy broke through the knot of students pushing himself between the two would-be combatants. Something must have transpired, he was whispering to Elwood whose brutish head was bowed as he listened. I saw it come up to look at something behind me. The hairs rose on my neck, twisting around, I saw Miss Parker there, her arms folded. The loudspeaker let out an ear-splitting whistle then followed with the announcement we would be docking.

Between the loudspeaker squawking and Miss Parker's presence, the rumble atmosphere was ruined. Elwood pointed to the blonde girl and said, "You got lucky." He and Eurobuddy ducked out of the cabin. Miss Parker followed them out, her gait unhurried.

I wanted to find out this girl's identity, but the area hummed, the crowd becoming a mob. The air in the cabin became charged as if by electricity. The students shuffled *en masse* to the exit doors, the level of noise deafening the ship. Since our table was in the other direction, I had no trouble returning to it.

"She's unbelievably brave," Pari said as I approached. "So

were you," she added, a bit shyly, I thought. Still, I felt my face go all hot.

"Oh, Grady is a student of size is no indication of strength. In fact-" Aarush began.

I interrupted him before he could share anymore, "We are about to dock. Let's stay together."

Aarush threw his cold fries into the garbage.

I tossed my last hot dog into a trash can and grabbed the back of his shirt, stopping him from taking off. "Hold on." I held out my hand, motioning Pari, Lydia, and Forrest to follow before we got swept up in the current of people moving to the exit.

Outside, birds screamed overhead, circling. The island looked like it was floating on the aqua waters of the Caribbean. The front of it was relatively flat with a blindingly white sandy beach. One side of the land mass had a craggy mountain with several jagged peaks soaring into the clouds. It was covered with lush trees.

"Look at that!" Aarush said, pointing to the summit. "I can't see any buildings." He stood on his toes. "Grady, tell me what you see."

I stretched upward to spot a tower of dark polished rock rising out of the island like a giant's tooth. "Over there." I pointed in the westerly direction opposite the giant peaks. I opened my mouth to describe the vista but felt the words lodge in my throat. How do you relate the unrelatable? My mouth opened with disbelief. "It's...it's like a castle," I said dumbly. My words, or, really, lack of them, didn't give our new home justice. It was otherworldly, like something I'd expect to find on Mars.

Built into the rock like a carved monument was a fortress with long, narrow windows, the glass sparkling in the waning sun, winking at us. There was an organic quality to its shape. The hard edges were blunted as if nature's elements had weathered the walls.

We glided closer, falling under its ominous shadow. A large round tower loomed over the ship, blotting the sun. The boat deck had gone silent as we craned our necks, taking in our foreboding new home. The sharp tang of the ocean meshed with the earthy scent of land.

The waves crashed against the base of the island. It was desolate, not a walkway in sight. The windblown shrubbery was clinging to the craggy outcroppings of rocks that blossomed like mushrooms around the dense walls.

"This place is *sick*!" someone muttered.

"Holy crap, maybe I should have become a wizard," another joked.

"*Hogwarts* is in the opposite direction," the blonde girl responded. She stood behind Pari, her hands on her hips. Pari smiled at her. I watched the girl grin back. She looked at me and with a single nod acknowledged my role in her fight. It was probably the coolest thing that had ever happened to me.

"More like *Jurassic Park*! Where are the dinosaurs?" Forrest shouted.

There was a scattering of conversations followed by the sound of relieved laughter. The ferry cruised slowly, our boat as hushed as the island before us. The sun beat down on the ocean blinding us. The give and take of the waves hitting the shore filled our ears. I felt wobbly, but if it was from the movement of the ship or the fluttering in my stomach, I wasn't sure. Maybe it was the ingestion of one too many hotdogs, I thought.

We rounded a sharp point where a sleek lighthouse stood guard at the entrance. A long jetty was built from the recesses of the building. A pristine beach lay before us, with a impenetrable jungle hiding the monstrosity of the building. My tongue touched my lips and I tasted the salt of the spray. I felt the rush of excitement replace my jittery nerves with wonder.

We disembarked in hushed awe absorbed in taking in our new surroundings. I caught sight of Elwood and his friend pushing their way through the crowd to get to the gangplank. There was a receiving line on the dock on an elevated platform. A tall man dressed completely in black stood at the forefront. A woman in a scarlet tunic waited at his side. Miss Parker was next in line, and I wondered how she had managed to get through the mob and down to the dock, looking as cool as you could expect. There was definitely something strange about that lady. Teal-colored spandex guy was there as well and a bunch of other people I had never seen before. A ring of personnel in dark uniforms worked with the crew to dock the ferry.

We descended the long plank, our hands on the rope banister. The elevation unnerved me, but the comfort of being hemmed in by Aarush and Pari helped quite a bit. I was surprised it appeared as orderly as it did. Pari was followed by Lydia and Forrest. The blonde girl helped Devon Neely navigate the gangplank. I could see Elwood and his new friend down at the front pushing through the crowds to disembark first.

We were ushered onto the beach, which surrounded the platform holding the gray-haired man, who watched our procession with a benign smile on his face. He stood before a monumental flagpole with a pennant flying with the school logo emblazoned in red and blue. I could make out gold mythical creatures on the flag, but didn't recognize them. It must have taken an hour for us to assemble, and despite the fact that we were all young, I have to say we gave the impression of a well-behaved group. I wondered if Miss Parker told them about the confrontation on the ferry. The older man raised his hands, looking like Charlton Heston as Moses in *The Ten Commandments*. Everyone was staring at him.

"Welcome, welcome to the opening day of Templeton Academy." He wasn't shouting, yet his voice filled the beach area. He had no microphone or sound system that I could see. "I am delighted to greet you, the first students to attend our glorious school. You are the pioneers, the trailblazers who will set the precedent for all who will follow you."

He paused, then looked at the crowd. It felt as if his piercing gaze touched each and every one of us.

"You were handpicked from millions because we recognized something special in you. I know what you are capable of...Lydia Cullen." His eyes narrowed and he scanned the crowd, coming to rest on our little group. He pointed to Lydia, who flushed to the roots of her hair. "I am going to confirm what you think you know is real. It's all up here." With one hand he pointed to his head and then directed his attention to...*me*? "Grady Whill." A space cleared around me, I wanted to sink back in the crowd. "You will learn to harness your inner strength and perhaps lose the self-doubt that paralyzes you." Before I could even digest what he said, Templeton spun to the other side and pointed to Eurobuddy. "Lucas Reinhart, your overconfidence needs redirection. We are glad to welcome you and students like you from all over the world." Apparently that kid Lucas had too much of what I was missing. I wondered how many others had an abundance of what I needed and if I was starting school at a disadvantage. I started to sweat.

Lucas Reinholt. I now had an identity for a potential tormentor, but I was too wrapped up in the notion of self-doubt, wondering if the school was planning to harness me like a horse to a carriage.

Templeton went on, "In case you haven't guessed, I am Dr. Clifford Templeton." He continued naming other kids, setting us off murmuring between ourselves. I was trying not to obsess about the fact that he singled me and blasted my potential flaws all over the place. I mean, wasn't everyone full of self-doubt? *Nah,* there was a ton of other stuff, but I was the only self-doubter. I glanced at Pari's set shoulders, Aarush's gobsmacked face, the blonde girl's determined chin, and bit my lip. It seemed not everybody appeared as upset as me.

In the end, Templeton said a lot but gave no real information, except for me and my confidence level. It didn't matter. Between the trip, our exotic surroundings, and the weird welcoming committee, we were all awestruck. It was hard to follow all his words; I was busy analyzing what could have given me away, then I saw Miss Parker's eyes directly on me. I blinked, but she didn't and I knew in some way that was important in our relationship.

When I refocused, I heard Templeton say, "In the end, when you realize that what you think is your imagination is not, you'll have achieved our mutual goals. We are thrilled you've decided to join us for the journey of a lifetime. You are going to see and do things that you have only thought about in your dreams! Isn't that right, Valencia? I'd like to introduce my daughter, Valencia Templeton."

I could hear Elwood making monkey noises in the crowd. *Monkey noises...really?* I figured his days at Temple would be numbered.

Valencia nodded as if she were a queen. She was as tall as her father, with flaming red hair. I could feel the heat of her scrutiny when it traveled over us. I saw her gaze settle on...*Elwood.* It had a strange effect on him. He stopped wisecracking, going strangely silent and stood taller. Valencia Templeton was as still as a statue, her eyes were closed. We waited, the tension building for her to say something, but she remained as silent as a tomb. Finally, she moved forward and I saw she had a slight limp. She used a tall walking stick for balance. Holding out her hands, with the long staff in one hand, she looked like a priestess from some fantasy movie I watched with Leo. She inhaled what had to be the deepest breath I had ever seen someone take. Opening her eyes, she appeared as if she was coming out of a deep sleep. That's when I noticed she had some strange-looking peepers. They were such a deep shade of gold that they appeared to glow. She slammed her staff onto the floor and cried out, "They are ready, Father!"

The crowd gasped collectively rearing backward. I felt like I was in some bizarre theatrical show in a theme park and anticipated fireworks next. I was not prepared for what happened next.

Dr. Templeton waved his arms, looking for all the world like a windmill. *A nutjob*, I guessed, not a little disappointed.

I observed Aarush with a side-eye. He was staring straight ahead, hooked on the spectacle.

Pari met my gaze with that same silent communication we shared on the bus. It made me feel special and I raised my eyebrows in my special way. She grinned back. I felt a sense of relief, a kinship. She pursed her lips in a grimace of distaste directed toward the display put on for our benefit. At least, I hope it was for that and not me. I winked and was rewarded with a smile that made me feel better.

I bent forward trying to catch the attention of the blonde girl, wishing I had asked her name. I was curious to know her take on it. She seemed absorbed in the program, her brow furrowed in a way that looked troubled. I think she was biting her lip.

The atmosphere changed, the air filled with ozone, as if there had been a thunderstorm. I saw sparks, followed by the crackle and buzz of our charged surroundings. A low ceiling of darkening clouds moved over our heads creating an oppressive atmosphere.

Collectively, our heads snapped up. The wind started whipping at first, making the Templeton flag flying over our heads crack like a whip. Birds circled...I mean really circled in an organized fashion, swooping down in a sweeping arc to graze our heads. They screeched loudly. I was thinking that rather than Templeton, we had made some wrong turn onto the island of Dr. Moreau.

The waves rose, pounding the beach; the stinging spray misted around us. The crowd grumbled. I heard a few alarmed screams. Some of the kids were ducking, others crying out as nature shifted around us.

"And just like that," Templeton shouted, snapping his fingers. "We will start the semester."

The sun broke through the clouds, and a rainbow formed over us like a ribbon. There were cries of surprise and a few *ahhs*.

"Turn," Dr. Templeton commanded. We pivoted as one,

and the entire vista opened to a green field where scattered sheep placidly ate away. It was as if the jungle had evaporated. Rolling hills stretched before us. The island seemed endless, the tall mountains framing the monolith that was to be our new school.

"Did he just do that?" I asked Aarush.

Aarush didn't hear me, still captivated by the surroundings. I looked at Pari, a question in my face.

She shrugged. I would venture to say she did not seem affected by it and while I admired her, I was impressed. "Maybe," she went on. "Could be mass hypnosis."

"Whoa," I said. This place rocked. While I admit I was more than a little freaked out by all the waves and bird stuff, I was dying to know how Dr. Templeton had made it all go away. From the sound of the crowd, I was not the only one wondering it.

"I would say he's doing it with screens, but I can't see any," Pari said, searching for clues.

If he was, Aarush was still under whatever spell they concocted. He ignored us.

"Yes," the blonde girl agreed, speaking over his head. "And by the time we leave, we'll be able to do those kinds of things, too."

I opened my mouth to ask her her name and she supplied it before I had a chance to speak.

"My name is Bailey Sloane."

"Hello, Bailey," Pari said, her voice warm. Now our official ambassador, Pari proceeded to introduce us all to her. "What do you think of the show?" Pari asked with an edge to her voice.

Bailey shook her head. "I doubt many will achieve the

abilities I saw here today. Half of them will be going home by the winter holidays."

Everyone seemed to agree with this notion. I was consumed with the thought that I would be one of the first to be sent packing. I decided to turn my attention to our surroundings.

All around us, the dark uniformed crew herded us down a hidden paved road that appeared as if by magic. We walked down the winding path, surrounded by dense greenery. My eyes took in the lush gardens with the wide variety of flowers. It looked like a painting from a museum. I could hear birds cawing, and the fragrance of the blooms filled my nostrils. Pari sniffed, nodding appreciatively.

"Frangipani," she said.

"Franga-what?" I asked.

"It's a flower," Bailey explained. "I don't know. It might be. Smells more citrus-y to me."

Franga-whatever, citrus-y, the old gargoyle I now identified as self-doubt landed on my shoulder making each step heavier and heavier as we walked into the building. *What was I doing here?*

Strange birds I had never seen before flew overhead. I heard Forrest identify two varieties, my stomach sank to my knees. Aarush argued the species couldn't be found this far north. Oh boy, I had a bad feeling about this. Maybe Leo knew something I didn't.

Feeling more in my element, I could have sworn I recognized monkeys chattering...or maybe it was Elwood and his simian buddy. Either way, I clamped my mouth shut, not willing to share in case I was wrong. I didn't want to look as stupid as I was feeling right now.

It was an upward climb. Rising out of the land, the rock

fortress appeared. It was surrounded by a giant moat with a rushing stream of water. I looked down, feeling like my eyes were jumping out of my head. It was filled with squirming alligators.

I elbowed Aarush. "Do you think that's allowed?" I whispered, so only he could hear.

He glanced at the snapping snouts and shrugged. "Well, we are in a jungle."

The portcullis was up, and the drawbridge stretched across the roiling water below us. We walked across the wooden bridge, our feet echoing hollowly like an army marching into the dark interior.

CHAPTER 11

FAILURE IS GOOD

*T*HE INTERIOR OF the building was filled with natural light and hewn from coral. The walls were flecked with prehistoric fish trapped forever in the stone. I had to grab Aarush when he slowed to pick at some creature embedded in the rock wall.

The crowd propelled us along, and I didn't want to become separated. I saw Pari was speaking with Bailey like they were long-lost friends.

The air was cool as if we were underground. We walked the curving corridors that featured rough-cut entrances to hallways. The chatter of voices sounded almost like a chant and had an underground, vault-like quality, except that the ceiling had clear panels of plastic letting in the sunlight. The corridors opened up into a giant hall, not unlike a train station. Sound was magnified in the barrel-shaped room. The ceiling soared high above us like a cathedral. Sunlight filtered in through the tinted plexiglass roof filling the room with muted light. Several entrances were spaced along the circular walls in assorted colors of the rainbow. Students poured in from all different directions. I could hear the sound of running water, like an underground stream nearby.

An obelisk that must have been fifty feet tall was stuck right in the middle of the terrazzo floor. It towered over us with the magnificence of a monument. A hush fell over the crowd, we pushed toward the center of the room becoming a concentrated mob. Between the stone walls and the splash of a nearby waterfall, we sounded like a pack of humming bees. The closer I got, the louder it seemed. We milled around the stone obelisk like the apes in the movie *2001: A Space Odyssey*, and as my shuffling feet drew me nearer, I could see a couple of sentences of carved writing running across the top of the black stone.

"You'll have plenty of time to read it later," a voice behind me said. It was Bailey. She looked at me, sizing me up. She bit her lip in annoyance. It made her seem tougher, almost unapproachable. She had a challenging tilt to her chin as if she was ready to defend her territory.

I stared back at her. She was taller than me, her body as wide as a college linebacker. I made eye contact and said, "Nice job back on the ferry."

"Grady, right?"

I nodded and replied, "Grady Whill."

She shuffled a bit and then said in a low voice, "I didn't need your help."

I had a feeling that any way I answered would define our

relationship for the next four years. "I saw. Still, I wanted you to know I was there if you needed it."

Her gray eyes thawed and knew I made the right move. She smiled and held out a fist for a friendly fist bump which I was only too happy to return. There was something in her face behind the mask of toughness that told me she would be a friend. It could have been the way she spoke to Pari. Don't ask me. Maybe my superpowers were already developing, and I would be able to read people. Maybe my self-doubt was evaporating already. I thought about it for a moment. *Nope. Still there.*

We stayed in our friendly locked stare for another minute. She bobbed her head, then motioned toward the yawning doorway behind me. "Go on. You're holding everybody up."

I opened my mouth to say something, but Pari interrupted me. "Yes, do move faster, Grady," she urged. We pushed past the knot of students clustered at the base of the obelisk. Some kids chose to stay and read the carvings on it.

I looked backward trying to catch a glimpse of the writing on the stone surface. I squinted but couldn't make out a single word in the gloom. There appeared to be four sentences. The rest of the highly glossed monolith was bare, as though they had stopped in the middle of carving the words in and weren't finished.

The jabber of hundreds of voices echoed in the room. I turned to say something to Aarush, but my words were swallowed in the vastness of the space. He wasn't listening anyway. His eyes were darting up and down the obelisk like a computer scanner. Pari grabbed his shirt and pulled him into the entrance.

Truth be told, I was feeling a little trapped myself. The

group continued to move like a herd of sheep. We walked through the cathedral-like hall and entered a dining facility. There was a collective gasp as we entered the room, followed by excited rumblings.

Our wristbands lit up. The room pulsed with color from them...well, only two colors, red and blue. I noticed mine was red. I have to admit I was happy to see so were Aarush's and Pari's. Bailey held up her arm, and I saw the red reflected on her pale skin. She smiled crookedly at me.

The room had a double entrance with a flashing light overhead. One was red and the other blue. Remembering the flag, I assumed they were the school colors. At the door, a uniformed teacher directed the red wristbands to one side, the blue to the other.

Sunlight streamed from more skylights. Alternating red and blue pennants hung from the ceiling. The red ones had a golden two-legged catlike creature on them; the blue had a sparkling fire-breathing winged creature similar to a dragon. I looked down at my wrist. I guessed I was with the cat people.

The room was bright and cheerful. It looked like we had entered the innards of a giant vending machine. The walls were covered with small windows, each pane of glass filled with food. "The cafeteria," Pari uttered in awe. "Look at the choices!" I guess she was finally impressed with something.

Food. My stomach rumbled noisily. It seemed as if we had eaten hours ago on the boat, and to my fourteen-year-old body, not enough. My mouth watered when I saw all the different types of choices lit up behind their glass window.

An old memory of a restaurant my grandfather used to eat at in Manhattan called the *Automat* popped into my head. He told stories about the hundreds of choices of food available behind a little door. I smiled, thinking he would tell me this was the same type of setup.

We were led to long tables, each able to seat fifty kids. All the students who had traveled on our plane were gathered together. Overhead the red flag waved, identifying us. I noticed with dismay Elwood's red-colored wristband.

The jock sat at the head of the table, surrounded by the European group he gravitated to on the journey. Lucas Reinholt was glued to his right side. They were beginning to resemble conjoined twins.

Lucas was watching me from the other side of the room. He leaned over to say something to Elwood who glanced my way and snickered.

I decided to turn my attention elsewhere.

"Did you read that tombstone in Grand Central Station?" I asked Aarush.

He looked at me quizzically. "We didn't pass through Grand Central—"

"He meant the big hallway outside this room," Pari informed her cousin.

Bailey was seated on the other side of her. She was fingering her wristband while she examined the crowd. I was glad I saw a nicer side of her, otherwise, I'd swear this girl was the female version of Elwood.

"I managed to read some of it," Pari said, though I think she was distracted by the variety of food.

"Where are you from, Bailey?"

"Montana."

"I never met anyone named Bailey," I told her.

"Good thing you didn't make fun of my name," Bailey

spoke with an intonation that carried so much in delivery. I wish I could sound like that, I sighed.

"Why would Grady do something like that?" Pari asked.

Bailey twisted in her seat to look at Pari. "You really mean that?"

"Yes. Of course," Pari responded.

Pari was one of those people who seemed not to come from the same planet. She had this kind of calmness that brought a sense of peace. I had seen it when she helped Aarush lose patience on the plane when his headset wires overwhelmed him. She was kind, but more than that, like she had the ability to make you feel comfortable in your own skin. I guess Bailey, like myself, wasn't used to it.

Bailey was quiet for a moment looking like she was wrestling with some inner demon. She stared at me a while, and the conversations at the table receded to sound like noise. I kept thinking that I understood Bailey's distrust, rather than Pari's kindness.

I got the feeling she wasn't used to sharing personal information about herself. "It's my grandmother's maiden name," she blurted. It sounded like a challenge that nobody took up.

"It's nice," I said lamely. "Different, in a good way."

Her face had changed for a minute, it looked softer, I thought.

She squinted hard, as if she was trying hard to tighten her expression back up, like I had offended her in some way. Her mask of toughness firmly back in place, it felt as if she had tramped through my brain, almost as though she knew what I had been thinking.

My cheeks must have reddened. I shifted in my seat, sliding my gaze away. Bailey made me uncomfortable. I glanced around the table wishing Pari was next to me. I looked at Bailey with a hint of challenge and tried to clear my thoughts. There were things in there I didn't want anyone to know. My attention went straight to Pari again, and I cursed myself as undisciplined.

I made it a point to avoid looking at Pari. I let my thoughts scatter, picturing leaves flying away on the pavement. Bailey hit my shoulder with her large paw and gave a shout of laughter. She smirked and turned away.

Pari was considering a container of mango yogurt in a window to the right of us. She went on, oblivious to the tension between myself and our newfound friend. She started speaking, "There's some pretty mundane content on the obelisk. I need more time to process it, but the gist of it is basically—"

"Thoughts become things," Aarush finished, then shrugged. Everybody ignored him.

"What?" I asked, forgetting about Bailey for the moment.

"It's from the Templeton Codex," Pari explained.

"There's rumored to be about twenty or so statements in the Codex. That was only one quatrain. They are supposed to summarize the contents of the Codex." Aarush folded his hands neatly in front of him.

"Quatrains?" I asked, panic in my voice. I didn't know anything about *quatrains*. I wasn't even too sure about the Codex, the book of information that might or might not have been discovered buried deep underground by our illustrious founder. At this point there was so much mystery surrounding the Templetons, nobody was sure of anything. "All I could make out was something about failure. How do you know it's from the Templeton Codex?" I asked.

"I thought the Codex might be a myth...you know, a publicity stunt. After all, there's been little to nothing about it in the papers," Pari confided as if she were sharing a secret. I saw Bailey lean in to hear the conversation.

"Where there's smoke, there's usually fire. I don't know why anyone wouldn't believe it exists," Aarush answered her.

I had this strange feeling as if I had been dropped into a conversation, like when you turn on a movie in the middle and don't know about what happened in the beginning. I wanted to whisper to Aarush to fill me in on what I missed. Instead, I said, "Just because someone carves a bunch of stuff on a piece of granite ..." I shrugged, acting indifferent. I was going for a tough look, but I knew by Bailey's expression I somehow didn't succeed.

"It's basalt," Aarush corrected me. "Volcanic rock."

"Whatever. How do you know it was from the Templeton Codex?" I repeated trying to keep the desperation from my voice.

We had all heard rumors about the discovery of the Codex, but there simply wasn't a lot on *Wikipedia* about it.

"It said it on the top." Aarush rolled his eyes.

How had I missed that? "Anybody can stick a bunch of crap on a signpost and call it—"

My response was cut off by a tapping sound from the elevated platform where all the teachers were sitting. One of our new professors was testing the microphone on the podium. I glanced at the dais and counted over twenty teachers there. Valencia Templeton sat on one side of her father, Miss Parker on the other. Dr. Templeton's gray-haired head was inclined toward his daughter, with whom he appeared to be having a heated discussion. He was listening intently, but it was clear to me who the winner was of whatever they were discussing. The more impassioned Valencia got, the more peaceful Dr. Templeton seemed.

Valencia Templeton pushed her chair away from her table in a way that would have sent me to my room without supper. She limped to the podium, her expression angry and stark. Her hair had been pulled away from her face into a tight ponytail. She had matching silver streaks threaded through her red locks on either side of her temples.

Leaning heavily on the lectern, she cleared her throat, silencing the room. She turned once to acknowledge her father, who acknowledged her regally. She was dressed in the same outfit as Miss Parker and the rest of the faculty. She had changed from her tunic into a leotard, this one was blood-colored. I saw a large red stone on the top of the staff that she held firmly in her hand. It was the same color as my father's ring. Her gem pulsed with an inner fire, and the jewel on my chest warmed. I placed a hand over the ring as if I could stop it from heating up.

I was distracted by laughter. I saw Elwood and that boy Lucas horsing around at the other end of the table.

"Good afternoon, students." Her deep voice echoed. "Welcome to Templeton. In case you don't remember, my name is Valencia Templeton, and I am director of Templeton Academy. Can I tell you how pleased we are to finally meet you all?" She smiled, but it was a strange grin, forced, as if she weren't used to doing it often.

Her father clapped with joy, looking for all the world like he was watching something vastly entertaining.

She scanned the room, as if she were memorizing each of the five hundred faces opposite her. Valencia's eyes were amber and oddly luminescent. They circled the chamber slowly, carefully. Once they caught a recipient in her gaze, they glowed with a frostiness rather than the warmth you'd expect from someone with those color eyes.

Their intensity rested on me. Her face was calculating, as if she were measuring the mettle of each of us. I hate to admit that I broke away first, embarrassed by the fact that I was squirming in my seat. Even Elwood stopped moving around when she took the stage. She stared at him so long it made me feel uncomfortable. His grin evaporated, his face changing right before my eyes. His expression seemed as if carved from stone, it was so still. He sank into his seat slowly. I had never seen him so quiet, or... *captivated*.

"Classes, you will be excited to learn, will start tomorrow precisely at eight in the morning. You will receive your schedules after dinner. They will be posted in your dorm room monitors." She gestured to the wall with a forceful hand. It lit up with a screen that showed a sample schedule. "Most of the walls in the entire school are capable of turning into a monitor. I'm sure you've all noticed the obelisks in the main entrance. Indeed, it is the beginning of the Templeton Codex. Quatrain One has been carved for your consideration. As you continue with your education, more of the Codex will be revealed to you. Start with the first quatrain, discover its secrets, and use it to climb the ladder to the next one. The clues to its success are right at your fingertips." She folded her hands as if she were praying, then opened them wide to include us all. The room buzzed with excitement, the students murmuring grew louder, building a momentum I didn't share. I looked around at their rapt expressions. *Why didn't I feel that way?* I deflated into my seat wondering if I was missing something.

All I muster for Valencia Templeton was antipathy, even a bit of revulsion. This didn't bode well for my career here, and I wondered if I'd be one of the first to go home.

I glanced at Aarush who watched in total absorption. I wanted to lean over and ask what he saw in Valencia Templeton. Instead, both Pari and Bailey looked my way at the same time. I saw amusement on Pari's face, a wry smile on Bailey. My breath expelled with relief. Maybe I wasn't so alone in my thoughts.

Valencia's voice rang out in the cafeteria, loud and bell-like. Her expression was bright, lit with an inner fire. "The Codex, our creed—you must learn it, students. It will unlock the secrets of the universe." She walked from one side of the dias to the other as if she were a commander inciting her troops to go into battle. Two hectic spots of color splashed against her cheeks and now her hand fluttered as she spoke, her voice breathless. She pounded her walking stick against the stone floor with each statement as if it helped her emphasize her words. "Once you learn the first quatrain, we will give you the second, followed by the third, until you have mastered the entire Codex. There is so much to teach you! Some of you will be invited—"

"Valencia!" Dr. Templeton's voice was sharp. He half rose from his seat.

Valencia halted instantly, her eyes flashed with hatred for a second, then her face lost all animation, but I recognized resentment in the set of her shoulders.

"Did you see that?" I whispered.

"*Shush,*" Aarush said.

Pari leaned over, commenting, "I wouldn't want to get on her bad side."

Valencia took a steadying breath and said, "Father—"

Dr. Templeton gave a small shake of his head, his hand fisted on the table. Her lips thinned into a straight line, as if he'd muted her. The room was silent except for the uncomfortable rustling of the students in their seats.

"Very well. I will open the room for questions now." Valencia turned to us, her voice flat.

Bailey raised her hand, and at Miss Templeton's nod, she stood and asked, "Is there any chance to see the real Codex?"

Valencia glanced back at her father, who stared straight ahead not acknowledging her. She responded with a hint of mockery in her voice. "Sorry, Bailey Sloane. Much as I'd like to share the contents, seeing it now is forbidden."

"It's like a giant tease," Pari whispered. "Why tell us, if we can't see it?"

This comment egged Bailey who took a step forward and demanded, "I don't understand why we can't see the entire—"

"Next question." Valencia moved away without answering.

"How do they know our names?" I asked, my palm covering my mouth so they wouldn't see me speaking. "Did you meet her?"

Bailey sat down in a huff and replied, "Maybe they read minds."

We weren't paying attention to the conversation between Valencia and another student, but Dr. Templeton's gruff voice said one word. "Precisely."

We all jerked in our seats, not sure if he was talking to us or the inquiry of the other student.

Valencia cleared her throat. "My father feels that his curriculum is the only way to teach the Codex." She spoke slowly as if she were choosing her words carefully." This is his method, his system. The Codex has never been released. You will only learn the next part after you master the one before."

Dr. Templeton nodded with approval.

Valencia went on. "Dr. Templeton believes this in the only way to protect the Codex and… you."

There was a surge of rustling as the students absorbed this tidbit of information. Hands jumped into the air waving for attention to be picked.

Dr. Templeton ordered, "Continue, Valencia."

His daughter went on ignoring the sea of hands. "It remains under lock and key in a highly protected airtight facility underground. No one is allowed to see it. *No one.* However, during your time here, you'll become very familiar with it, and some of you will eventually be invited to read the actual document, perhaps even put your own interpretation on its meaning." She glanced back at her father at that, her stance defiant. "It's important for *us* all to study, to become scholars, so that we all may learn what is hidden—"

Dr. Templeton tapped his own staff on the floor stopping her from continuing. Valencia shuddered, her shoulders slumped, and turned inward. She sighed audibly and said, "I'll take more questions now."

Pari raised her hand. Valencia motioned for her to stand. Pari rose, then asked, "Who wrote the Codex?"

The teachers on the dais all smiled smugly as if they knew a secret.

"Well, I bet *they* know." I heard Bailey say in a low voice.

I turned my head ready to ask Bailey if she also read minds, when Valencia's response distracted me.

"Ah, Pari Patel. But that is for you to find out."

Valencia appeared to be looking right at us. She pointed

a finger for Pari to retake her seat. Pari sank into her chair, an unsatisfied expression I was beginning to recognize on her face.

Valencia's voice was strident, apparently, her self-confidence was back. "You will have four years to discover the entire mystery of the Codex. Some of you will not be capable of finishing your studies and will be sent home." She snapped her fingers and a ticket appeared in her hand. A collective gasp rolled through the room. I heard Pari murmur, "Parlor tricks." I didn't know about her, but I was impressed.

Valencia went on. "If you find one of these on your desk at any time in the coming months, it means we have decided you are not Templeton material and will be shuttled off the island the following day. This is nonnegotiable."

I could hear each student shift in their seat. I looked at Elwood; even he had paled a bit with this news.

"Enough of that. Today is a day of celebration. No one is going home...yet. You will notice the small dispensers on each side of the room. They are filled with your favorite foods. You need only to find what you desire to eat and punch in your name, and your plate will be retrieved."

She pointed to four tables on the right side of the room. "These tables will henceforth be known as Kashinka; the other side will be known as Weribus."

Well, I thought, *that explains the pictures of the livestock.*

"If you are at a Kashinka table, you will be on the Kashinka schedule of classes, the Kashinka dorms, and Kashinka teams. Likewise for the Weribus. Miss Parker is in charge of the Kashinkas." She pointed to Miss Parker, who nodded curtly. "Mr. Lee will handle the Weribus." An African-American man waved from his spot on the other side of the room.

I saw Miss Parker, her gaze boring a hole into my chest. It made me squirm again.

"Mr. Lee looks like a friendlier guy than our Miss Parker," Aarush commented.

"Yeah, I wish we were on the dragon team," I added glumly, my preoccupation with the Templeton Codex forgotten.

"Who is that?" Pari asked, gesturing toward Elwood.

"He is that boy I told you about," Aarush informed her.

"The bully?"

"I don't know if I would call him that," Aarush said.

"I would," I mumbled under my breath. "He's not a nice kid."

I saw Bailey turn to stare at Elwood. He rubbed the back of his neck with annoyance. Twisting, he sneered at me.

Dr. Templeton tapped his staff on the floor, the sound ricocheting off the walls. All talking ceased. He gestured to his daughter to speak.

"You will finish your meal, and your teachers will guide you to your dorm rooms. There you will find a trunk with all your clothing and supplies. I suggest you familiarize yourself with the contents. I would advise you to make an early night." She smiled that tight-lipped grin that made her face look like a skull. "After all, you've had a long day." Her voice was clipped. "Make sure you memorize the rules and bylaws of the school in your personal laptops. It's been loaded, and you cannot start your studies until you read the entire post and answer the questions. The first quatrain of the Codex will be in the hallway in the morning for you to examine. You'll have plenty of time to study it over the coming months. Oh, and your wristbands ..." We looked down at our rubber bracelets.

"Do not tamper with them. They stay on you for the entire time you are at school."

"Why?" Elwood called out, his voice belligerent.

Valencia watched him carefully. "Why do you think, Elwood Bledsoe?"

He shrugged. Lucas said something to him, and he shouted, "It's to track us."

Valencia laughed. A low rumble went through the room. She continued her speech. "After your meal you will go directly to your dorms. Now, enjoy your dinner. *Bon appetit!*" I wondered if nobody else realized she hadn't answered Elwood's question.

She left the podium, but rather than rejoining the dais, she stalked out of the room, her staff hitting the floor with a angry thump.

The room buzzed with excitement. We all made a mad dash for the wall. Every few feet there was an electronic pad. All I had to do was punch in the number next to the desired food. A robotic arm opened the portal, delivering it on a tray. Aarush found Indian food. All my favorites were there, mac and cheese, chicken pot pie. You name it, they had everything, all types, for every diet. I was overwhelmed and decided to keep it simple. "This stuff is amazing," I said between bites of bologna sandwich.

Aarush shook his head. "With all the choices that I know you love, Grady why would you pick something so-?"

"Plain?" I asked. I pressed the bread so that the mayonnaise bubbled out of the sides. It was as if my grandmother had made it for me herself.

"Sometimes Aarush, the simplest things are the most satisfactory," Pari said with a conspiratorial smile in my direction.

I nodded in agreement. I couldn't have said it better myself.

Bailey held up a glass of oatmilk. "To simpler things in life," she said. We all clinked our glasses in agreement, but I knew deep down inside my bologna sandwich was probably the most uncomplicated example I would encounter in Templeton.

I finished my feast with tiramisu. It was the fanciest dessert I'd ever had. At least the grub was good.

Everybody chatted happily. Aarush looked up and stared over my shoulder. I felt the skin on my back heat up.

I turned to find Miss Parker behind me, her face impassive. "Make sure you throw your trash in the can." She spoke quietly, but our entire table heard her.

We cleared our mess, left the dining hall following Miss Parker to the center of the fortress. Despite what the director ordered, I peered up. It seemed Aarush was correct. The Templeton Codex was carved into the granite...I mean, *basalt*. I also found the sentence about failure. This time I squinted trying to read the words in the dim light.

I didn't have to, Aarush recited them to me in his low voice. "*Do not fear failure. Failure makes us stronger. Failure makes us smarter. Failure is good.*"

Failure is good? This place is crazy, I thought.

Kids were talking quietly, their voices hushed. The crowd was definitely more subdued coming out of the cafeteria.

It was hard to believe this morning I was home in my own bed, and now I was about to start a new life with this granite tower as the starting point. It seemed odd to begin a supposedly great future contemplating failure.

I heard the splashing of water. We entered a giant hall with a jagged rock soaring to the tall ceiling. Jets of water shot up, arcing and then dropping into a deep pool surrounding them. It was oblong shaped and separated the hall into two distinct parts. The mass of students divided in half. I looked up to find a red flag hanging over one of the entrances. The opposite side had an identical flag in the color blue.

We entered another part of the building that again was divided into two corridors. Now boys were separated from girls. Another teacher appeared and took the females to the other side. I waved to Pari, Lydia Cullen, and Bailey.

Miss Parker led us past a lounge to a corridor. She opened doors, silently pointing to which of us was to enter. Three to a room. Our group got smaller. I hoped she wouldn't point to Aarush until she got to my room.

Miss Parker swung open the door. She nodded to Aarush, who paused, looked back at me, and entered the chamber. Next she took a long look at me and flicked her finger for me to follow. I was so thrilled that Aarush and I would be together, I didn't realize who was our roommate until I heard his hated voice.

"I get the bed by the window, Grocery Can Man."

Not that it mattered. There was a six-inch card with his name in big block letters assigning him that bed.

Elwood Bledsoe.

If you would have told me this morning I'd be sharing a room with Elwood, I would have said you were crazy. I mean, what are the odds that three kids from the same school bunking together?

Elwood Bledsoe was our third roommate. This was not going to be good. Not good at all.

There were three neat beds, each made up with crisp linens.

A metal trunk was located at the foot with a matching bed-side table and a lamp. A large picture window was covered by a dark shade. Since we brought nothing with us, I had to assume they'd be empty. I had no idea if we would get our uniforms and supplies delivered, or if we had to go somewhere and retrieve them. The sheer thought of them outfitting us all, the assorted sizes was awesome to think about.

Aarush took the bed assigned to him by the far wall. He was on his knees, opening the nickel-plated chest at the end of the bed.

I walked over to the window. The shade was between the glass with no cords to raise or lower it. I tried to see what was outside. I couldn't discern anything.

"How did they know our sizes?" Aarush asked, taking out a dark-colored two-piece uniform. He held the shirt against his chest, marveling at the perfect fit. "I don't remember anyone sending in measurements."

"Must have been during the physical." I gave up trying to see outside and walked over to open the lid of my trunk, ignoring Elwood. The jock was tossing something in the air and catching it. He did it so fast, I couldn't see what it was. I turned to look at him, and he twisted half off the bed.

"What are you looking at, jerk?" His face was red, his expression menacing.

"Noth…nothing. It's just that we aren't allowed—"

"Shut up!" He raised his arm to throw whatever was in his thick fist at me. I recoiled, and he paused, enjoying my reaction. He lay back, smirking, then continued to throw the object more rapidly.

Miss Parker knocked at the outside of our room and poked her head in the doorway. She looked at the three of us, her gaze staying longer on me. Elwood had his hand hidden beneath him.

"Give me your asthma inhaler." She walked toward me, holding out her hand.

"I always carry it."

"You won't need it here." She snapped her fingers impatiently.

"I can't."

"Grady Whill, hand it over," she demanded.

For a minute or two we stared at each other in a silent stalemate. I felt the ring vibrate against my chest. It distracted me enough that I broke off our battle. She held out her hand close to my face, then shook it impatiently.

I reluctantly pulled the asthma inhaler from my pocket. She snatched it from my hand.

"Here." She pressed a small item into my palm.

I held it up. It was flatter, lighter. My name was printed directly on the metallic device.

"You hold it like a harmonica and squeeze." She depressed the metal with her thumb and forefinger. A light mist escaped. It had a faint floral odor. I raised my eyebrow. If I didn't know her better, I'd swear I saw the ghost of a smile flit across her lips. "Don't forget to inhale," she said in that cold, clipped way of hers, making me realize I imagined any warmth from her.

I held it up and looked at its streamlined form. It certainly looked easier to carry. I put the cold metal to my lips, but since I wasn't having a problem breathing chose not to press it.

Aarush came up behind me. He reached into my trunk and pulled out a tablet. He sank to the floor, holding it reverently. "It's an M460," he said softly, pushing up his glasses on his nose. "My father said they weren't coming out until next year." He tapped the glass surface and watched it leap to life.

"Aarush Patel," it said in bold red letters, "this unit does not belong to you."

"Whoa," I said and bent down to take it from his hands. I swiped my finger lightly across the surface.

"Welcome, Grady Whill."

Aarush sat back with an appreciative smile. "It's somehow been linked to your touch or face image," he said with wonder. "Interesting since they haven't recorded it anywhere." He sat back on his heels thoughtfully. "I mean, that I know of." He shrugged.

I barely heard him. My fingers were gliding across the surface of the tablet, opening links and reading. It blossomed like a flower. "Aarush ..." I turned to talk to him and realized he wasn't next to me anymore. He was doubled over, absorbing data as his fingers flew over the surface of his own tablet rapidly. The screen illuminated his rapt face.

"I still don't get this failure business from the Codex," I said absently, almost to myself.

Aarush's soft words floated over almost like a whisper. "Failure can be used as a tool to succeed."

That kid, sometimes he said the strangest things.

I opened my mouth to reply but closed it when I glanced from Aarush's captivated face to Elwood's bored expression and the monotonous sound of his hand catching whatever he was tossing. Suddenly, watching zombies with Leo didn't seem like such a bad idea, and I found myself missing home a tiny bit.

CHAPTER 12

THE FIRST DAY OF CLASSES

I DIDN'T THINK I was going to sleep that night.

We shared a bathroom with the next dorm. There were three stalls and a long trough that served as a sink. Everything was new from the pajamas I decided I hated, to the slippers with our names written into the terry cloth. Toothbrushes, toothpaste, combs, soap, everything with the distinct Templeton brand emblazoned across it.

We each had a locker filled with supplies we were going to need, identified with our name printed on every product as if it had been manufactured for each of us. All the clothes fit my body as if they were made for me. Well, they must have been.

We didn't leave the room to explore our surroundings. It took most of the night to sort out the things from the chest at the end of the bed. My nightstand surface became cluttered with assorted notebooks, folders, and a few textbooks.

Aarush investigated his trunk. He discovered that by pressing a lever, it turned into a desk with a swivel chair attached. Soon, he and I were organizing our supplies. The incessant *thump, thump, thump* of Elwood throwing the ball on the wall jangled my nerves.

The lights went out precisely at nine. It was pitch black. There was nothing left to do but hit the sack. Aarush's steady snores filled the room, punctuated by the beat of Elwood's endless ball game.

The day swirled through my head like a kaleidoscope. I couldn't sleep. I felt pent up with emotion. I fiddled with the band on my wrist. It annoyed me. I couldn't get it over my wrist. Soon my skin grew irritated from the movement.

My thoughts drifted to the Codex. "*Do not fear failure. Failure makes us stronger. Failure makes us smarter. Failure is good.*"

None of it made sense.

Morning brought island sunlight pouring into the room. The shade had disappeared from the window as if by magic. I examined the glass and saw it was positioned between the two panes and controlled automatically.

We all dressed and met in the main area of our quarters. It looked like an airport lounge with a giant LED board taking up one entire wall. It had the name of every student followed by a list of classes. I touched my tablet screen and filled out my schedule, noting each class and its corresponding room.

"*Hmmmm*...Subconscious Studies. We don't have much time." Aarush looked at his watch. "Breakfast has to be in the cafeteria."

"Hurry." Pari walked past us, looking much nicer than we did in the form-fitting uniform.

I pulled at the material around my neck. The ring was pressed against my chest. I could feel it digging into my skin. I placed my palm over it, sure nobody could see I was wearing it. I patted my pocket and felt it was empty.

"You go on ahead," I said to Aarush. "I forgot my asthma inhaler." I darted back to my room.

Elwood was leaning over my trunk when I entered the room.

"Hey!" I walked over and slammed it shut. "What are you doing?"

Elwood looked up, his face hardening. "Keep your shirt on, Grady. There was a time when you shared everything with me."

I put my sneakered foot on top of the trunk. "That was a long time ago."

Elwood laughed. "What are you afraid I'll find?"

"We weren't allowed to bring anything. What could you possibly find?" I resisted the urge to touch my father's ring.

I'm not going to lie. When Elwood stared at me, it made my heart beat faster. The metal warmed uncomfortably. First Miss Parker and now Elwood. This was getting stranger by the minute considering I hadn't even owned the ring before leaving for Templeton Academy.

"We used to have some laughs. Dump the freak and I'll make sure your time here is…comfortable," Elwood said.

I stopped rummaging for my inhaler and looked at him. "What do you mean by *comfortable?*"

"What do you think, Asthma Man?" Elwood said, standing up to his imposing height. He towered over me, and I was tall for my grade. I think his shoulders obliterated my view.

"Is that a threat?" I asked.

"Take it the way you want. I didn't choose you…or him for that matter. You …"—he pointed to my chest—"I can tolerate. Him …"—he shook his head—"it's only a matter of time."

"I don't know what you are talking about."

Elwood moved to the door. "Fine with me. Things are going to get tough here. He won't last."

"Keep making monkey noises and we'll see how long you last," I mumbled.

"What? Did you say something?" he demanded. When I didn't answer he stated, "I ruled our school and I'll be *numero uno* in this place." He paced the room, his voice bordered hostile. "Didn't you see how I was singled out by Valencia Templeton?" He moved next to me so his face was inches from mine and pointed his finger at my chest. "Didn't you!"

"She spoke to a lot of students."

"*Ha!*" he said as he left. "A lot you know." I heard Elwood's voice from the hallway followed by a cocky chuckle. That kid had too much confidence. But I had to admit, he did leave me wondering if I missed anything in his exchange with Valencia Templeton yesterday.

I grabbed my new asthma inhaler, shoved it in my pocket, and left the room.

The rec room had emptied by the time I ran out. The halls were filled with students milling about. I retraced my steps from last night to the cafeteria.

Aarush was watching the door as I entered. He had an empty seat next to him. Pari was across from us, a bowl of oatmeal in front of her, Bailey at the corner of the table.

"I got you bacon and eggs," Aarush told me as I slid into the bench seat.

The noise level was deafening. Miss Parker and a few other teachers walked the perimeter of the room, observing us. I glanced up and caught her piercing glare. The smell of the buttery eggs made my stomach rumble, and I realized I was famished. I concentrated on food instead of Miss Parker's bizarre fascination with me.

I tucked into my breakfast. Aarush was leafing through a book on his tablet.

"Interesting theories." Pari looked up from the same book she was perusing on her own device.

"I know. I can't see how they are actually going to teach this type of thing," Aarush said thoughtfully.

"What do you mean?" I asked, mopping up my plate with a wad of bread.

I looked up. Both Aarush and Pari were absorbed in their books. At the other end of the table, Elwood was talking to Lucas. Though he was speaking to him, I could see Elwood look up, his eyes locking with mine, every so often.

"See here." Aarush pulled the tablet closer to me. "Each chapter is about opening up your mind and expanding it to increase your energy."

"Energy? I thought we were here to find our strengths, you know. Power." I ducked my head and whispered, "Our super powers."

"Energy is power." The ever-helpful Aarush contributed.

I opened my mouth to ask what he was talking about when Bailey interrupted.

"How?" she asked. "How do we build our—" She looked right at me and said in a sarcastic way, "Power."

"Meditation exercises," Pari blurted, her voice excited. "I know all these. I've done them my whole life in yoga."

I felt myself deflate. I wanted to come here more than anything else in my life and the first class was yoga. *Really?* "Is that all?"

"Is that all, Grady?" Aarush repeated, then pushed his glasses up the bridge of his nose. "This is just the beginning." He riffled the pages on the flat screen, stopping to point at a chapter. "The Art of Self-Healing." He went a few more pages. "The next one is about communication. Then it moves into strength. By the last chapter you can levitate."

"Levitate?" I asked incredulously. "Let me see." I pulled the screen closer and stared at the pictures. Miss Parker was the model. There were four photos of her, each one with an explanation underneath.

In the first photo, she seemed to be getting comfortable, sitting with her feet folded before her. In the second, her face was bland, devoid of expression. Clearly, she was meditating. The next picture had her body elevated above the floor, her expression serene. She appeared to be floating a few inches in the air. The last picture showed her lying in midair horizontally, her arms outstretched as if she were Super Dude about to take off, her feet separated from the floor by at least twelve inches.

I looked up, searching for Miss Parker. She was in the corner observing me. I felt my cheeks flush.

"This can't be true," I said. "It's a trick. People don't fly."

Aarush took back the tablet. His finger was on the text as he read. "I know it sounds improbable," he said absently. "It makes a strange kind of sense."

"What makes a strange kind of sense?" I asked.

"What they are going to teach us." Aarush lowered his voice. "That's why we are so far from the mainland. They are going to teach us the Forbidden Arts."

"Are you nuts?" My voice cut through the room and everyone looked at us. I lowered it and continued. "That's an invention from the website. There's no such thing as the Forbidden Arts!" Everybody in Middlebury Middle School knew about the Forbidden Arts but nobody took it seriously.

"*Shhh*," Pari warned me. "They say that information is based on truth."

"It's a creation, like Super Dude," I said, loading the Forbidden Arts website onto my tablet. It opened with a warning that the material on the site was deadly and parental discretion was advised. Then some dude with a supernatural-type voice laughed and the words faded to a black screen that demand a stupid amount of money to continue. Of course, I never had the funds to pursue it, but anybody could tell it was all fake. "You want to tell me this is *real*?"

The creepy guy laughed again and Pari said, "Shut that crap off, Grady. What I'm saying is that Templeton claims the Forbidden Arts are buried deep in the Codex. Lots of unscrupulous people capitalize on an idea to make money."

"Well, the Templetons are definitely not into this for the money," Baily said. "They haven't charged anybody a dime. Maybe that's the secret of the curriculum that Templeton doesn't want to share."

"Yeah, did you notice the tension between Dr. Templeton

and his daughter?" When nobody responded, Pari went on. "Maybe she wants to teach it and he won't let her."

We all digested this information.

A gong sounded causing us all to jump in our seats. Miss Parker clapped her hands once. "You will head to your classes now. Use the maps in your tablets. There are signs that will light up along the walls. Don't be late."

Students gathered their belongings. Another gong sounded, this one a different note. Then the oddest thing happened. Miss Parker was there and then she wasn't. She had vanished into thin air. The room buzzed with hundreds of shocked voices.

"Did you see that?" I asked, my voice squeaking.

Aarush nodded, his eyebrows raised with an *I told you so* air.

"It's got to be a trick. Smoke and mirrors. I agree it is a gifted school," I conceded as Pari, Aarush, Bailey, and I waded through the crowd. "I still am not sure about these classes."

I hadn't seen either Forrest or Lydia Cullen this morning.

We looked at the LED displays directing us to Subconscious Studies.

Other classes listed were Physical Education, which took place in an arena rather than a gym, Math, Ethics, World History, English lit, and Chemistry. Now, that was more like it, though I can't say I was looking forward to those subjects. We had them scheduled for later in the day.

We rounded the corner to see Miss Parker waiting outside her room, her arms folded across her chest. A bright sign flashed over her door announcing we had arrived at our first class.

The sound of another deafening gong filled the hallway. We all stopped dead in our tracks, terror on all our faces.

"That is your warning bell, students. You have one minute before I will mark you all as truant."

We dodged toward the classroom, becoming a panicked tangle of students. Miss Parker made us stop, line up and enter two at a time.

CHAPTER 13

SUBCONSCIOUS STUDIES

MISS PARKER WAITED until we all filed in and found a seat in the large room. There were fifty of us in the class.

I saw the twins in the rear. Forrest waved, and Lydia smiled, her face pale, her eyes wide.

There were no windows in the room. The walls were padded with soft material. Everything was muted, and when I whispered to Aarush, I noticed the sound of my words seemed to be swallowed by our surroundings. This was like no other classroom that I had ever been in.

Instead of a blackboard, a glass panel took up the entire front wall. Miss Parker entered, observing us. Raising one hand, she flashed it toward the glass wall, and her name appeared in bright orange.

Students responded by gasping in wonder.

"As you can see …" her voice rang out from every corner

of the classroom, breaking the hushed atmosphere like glass. We all turned to look at her, but her mouth didn't move. The voice continued. "My name is Miss Parker, and this is Subconscious Studies, a required class that you will take for all four years you attend the school." She walked down the first aisle, then slowly up the second. I think we all had our mouths hanging open.

This time she spoke directly to us. "Can anybody guess what just happened?"

"Hidden speakers," Bailey called out.

"Ventriloquism?" Elwood asked with a smirk. "But I don't see a dummy." He squinted. "Oh, yeah, right there." He pointed to Aarush.

There were a few uncomfortable giggles. Lucas brayed like a donkey.

"That's enough, Mr. Bledsoe. Quiet, Mr. Reinholt. No, not ventriloquism. No, not at all. Anybody else?"

She walked slowly. There was something faintly menacing about her. Her shoes tapped on the floor in the room, the only other sound the rustling of the students as we all followed her slim figure.

Aarush raised his hand tentatively. Miss Parker turned to look at him, her eyes sharp and inquisitive. I didn't know about anyone else, but she made me feel like a specimen in a science experiment. Even as the thought took shape in my head, I felt her attention turn to me. My heart thumped so loud I was sure she could hear it. I prayed she wouldn't call on me. The heat of my father's ring warmed against my chest. Miss Parker's lips turned up in a slight smile. She pointed a finger at Aarush, giving him permission to speak.

He cleared his throat noisily. "You used the power of your

subconscious mind to activate the board to write your name," Aarush stated.

Miss Parker leaned against a lectern at the front of the class. "You believe such a thing is possible, Mr. Patel?" she asked.

"I don't see why not." Aarush was warming to the subject. "A thought is developed. It is then examined by the conscious mind, which triggers an electrochemical activity within the brain. Neural pathways are created as the information works its way through the brain. As the data travels, additional cells in the brain are imprinted with the details. The conscious mind then attaches an emotion to the thought based on the understanding of the information, and a belief is created. It's then stored in the subconscious mind as reality." He paused, then added thoughtfully, "Your reality became our reality."

Miss Parker looked at us, her hands flat on the desk before her.

"Who's the dummy, Elwood?" I couldn't help myself.

The students tittered. Miss Parker snapped her fingers and we went silent.

She tilted her head quizzically, addressing Aarush. "Are you saying I imagined it onto the blackboard?" Nobody made a sound. "That fifty students in this room shared my perception and what happened was all in *my* mind?" Her hand touched the glass wall. "Is my name here, then, in our imagination, or does it really exist?"

"Well, I see it, so it must exist," Elwood called out.

Miss Parker snapped her fingers, and her name disappeared. "Now it's gone. Was it really here at all?" She looked at me. "Mr. Whill?"

Oh God, oh God, don't call on me. Not me, was the only reality in my brain.

Pari raised her hand. Miss Parker ignored her. I remained frozen like a deer in headlights. Without turning, or taking her eyes off me, Miss Parker said, "Miss Patel?"

"The subconscious mind will locate and provide information that has been stored from earlier memories. It manufactures a vibrating energy based on information that it experienced already."

"Go on," Miss Parker said encouragingly.

"Those thoughts are sent outward and matched with energy of the same frequency, and the result is the manifestation of what you see and experience in your physical world." Pari smiled in triumph.

My jaw dropped to my chest. I didn't understand a word she said. I was way out of my depth here. *Mainland, USA, here I come.*

"Excellent, Miss Patel. Now would you translate it into an explanation everyone can understand? As you plainly can see Mr. Whill has no idea what you are talking about?"

"I do so," I burst out.

"You do?" Miss Parker's head swung in my direction. She looked amused, but not in a *hahaha* way. "Explain it, then."

I heard Elwood snort. I twisted in my seat to see Pari looking at me, her face full of warmth. I opened my mouth to answer but snapped it shut as a collection of ideas gathered in a misty cloud in my brain.

Aarush's words in the lunchroom came rushing back to me. *What did he say, exactly?* I took a deep breath, stalling as my mind seemed to come into focus. The answer tripped easily out of my mouth. "Thoughts become reality," I said simply. I wasn't sure if Miss Parker smiled or grimaced.

"You're using technology," Lucas addressed the teacher, interrupting us. "Or magic tricks," he added disdainfully.

Miss Parker's face turned purple with rage. She faced the glass wall. Her arms were outstretched, her hands undulating. The clear surface darkened, first becoming foggy. The crash of water hitting the wall surrounded us. Impossibly, it felt like we were submerged.

There appeared to be a raging sea behind the glass. Waves hit glass panels, the angry, foaming water roiling.

"Walk up to the board, Mr. Reinholt," she ordered him.

Lucas swaggered up to the glass screen.

"Touch it." Her voice was like ice.

He turned and smiled at his friends, then placed his hand on the surface of the panel. The wall reverberated when a large object hit it squarely where Reinholt had placed his hand. Something solid and sickly bluish-gray smacked against the glass. The mass took up the entire panel. Reinholt arced away, his face frozen when the pale object turned, its single eye the size of an ostrich egg peering into the classroom. It blinked, and we all must have jumped as it swiveled its unblinking gaze around the classroom.

A girl screamed. A portion of the glass shattered; seawater poured into the room through a large hole. A slimy tentacle reached out to grab Reinholt. It wrapped around his neck and held him against the glass. Reinholt gasped, his voice choking.

Students were screaming. I glanced at Elwood, who sat frozen in his seat.

Lucas's face turned red, then lost all color.

I didn't think, I reacted and ran to the choking boy. I grabbed the slippery tentacle. It was cold and powerful. With both hands, I wrestled it from its punishing hold around

Lucas's neck. My fingers slid under the muscular flesh of the octopus, imprisoning my hands. I couldn't move. Another tentacle appeared and wrapped itself around my thigh.

I felt Aarush bump into me. "Grab that tentacle!" I yelled to my friend as it moved toward my other leg. It was dragging us toward the glass wall.

"Technically it's an arm. Octopi don't have tentacles," Aarush said breathlessly.

"I don't care! Stab it with your stylus!"

Aarush struggled to release Reinholt when suddenly the tentacles were gone. The wall was a glass board again, and my hands were around Lucas's neck. He was pressed up against the wall, his body rigid.

I heard laughter from the doorway. I blinked stupidly and dropped my hands. The floor was dry. I turned to look at Miss Parker, who was scowling at an intruder.

Valencia Templeton stood by the entrance, her hand on the doorknob.

"Interesting way to introduce them to subconscious studies, Erin." Her gaze traveled around the room. I saw them pause on Elwood and then move over to me. It made me shiver.

"You shouldn't have interfered, Valencia. I had a lesson worked out." Miss Parker walked briskly to the front of the room. I thought I had a monopoly on disliking another person—Elwood. My animosity was nothing compared to the tension between these two.

"Some lesson," Elwood sniffed.

"You don't approve, Mr. Bledsoe?"

"It's stupid. Trickery, illusion, or whatever," he said, his voice insolent. "Either way, it's not real. They're not even wet."

"The creature didn't scare you?" Miss Parker asked with deadly calm.

I felt my pulse pick up a rapid beat. I looked around the room, everyone's face looked pale, and I knew my palms were wet.

"Are you absolutely sure, Mr. Bledsoe? Anybody else?" she asked.

The only thing I was sure about was that Miss Parker was scaring the crap out of me right now.

"I'm not impressed. I didn't even get up. I knew it would stop on its own. What were you going to do, kill Lucas? I don't think so." Elwood waved his hand as if he didn't care. Lucas laughed a bit, making my heroics feel unnecessary. Elwood capped it by saying, "Not all of us fell for your magic trick."

Boy, did I feel stupid right then. Elwood was right. I had walked right into that—run, more likely, risking myself and Aarush, for…nothing. And I ended up looking like an idiot on top of it all.

"Maybe the lesson wasn't about the victim," she began, then stopped, her lips tightening. I saw her glance at Valencia Templeton.

"Go ahead, Erin. Explain it to him," Valencia Templeton chuckled coldly.

"Get out," Miss Parker said, her voice glacial. "Now. You, Mr. Bledsoe—leave my classroom."

"Why?" Elwood demanded. "Because I challenged you, Miss Parker? Is that what this school is all about?"

"No," Valencia said from the doorway. "I have some lessons that may prove more challenging. Come with me," Valencia told Elwood.

Elwood got up and walked toward the door. Valencia held it open for him and followed him out.

The chamber was quiet after they left. I could see a white rim around Miss Parker's flared nostrils. She took a steadying breath, and I found myself doing the same. Something in the room shifted; it seemed less hostile.

"What just happened here, was it real or imagined? I expect a five-hundred-word essay tomorrow," Miss Parker announced.

The gong sounded. "Class dismissed."

It was as if she had dropped a mic.

CHAPTER 14

ROPE TRICKS

"**W**HAT JUST HAPPENED in there?" I asked Aarush as we jogged toward the arena for physical education. Pari and Bailey walked ahead of us, having met another girl, a Native American named Kelsea Talltrees. I could see their heads bobbing together as they spoke. They turned a corner and disappeared into the girls' changing rooms. Aarush and I went in the other direction.

"Just when I think you don't hear a word I say, Grady, you surprise me," Aarush said.

I slowed my pace and looked down at him. Aarush was at least a full head shorter than me. "I always hear what you're saying," I retorted.

Aarush smiled enough so that his teeth showed. He shook his head. "No, Grady, sometimes you don't hear anything at all."

I wanted to ask him what he meant by that. I felt faintly annoyed, insulted even, but we were running late. The gong I recognized as a warning bell sounded, drowning out all the chatter in the hallway.

While the building was brand-spanking new, a school gym changing room can be a breeding ground for smelly pests. Templeton Academy was no exception. As I said before, the room and lockers were spotless. That wasn't the vermin I was describing.

It also, for some reason, was not quite finished. Stacks of aluminum air-conditioning tubing were pushed against the wall, as if they hadn't completed all the work.

We took our time getting there. There were rows and rows of lockers. Our names were printed above them in alphabetical order, they were pretty easy to find. Aarush started to move to the following corridor, did a double-take, and walked backward toward me. The room had emptied of most of the students except for one or two. Elwood Bledsoe was waiting for me, Lucas Reinholt beside him. He stood by my aisle, his hands clenched, waiting like a vulture. Wherever he had gone with Valencia Templeton was unfortunately not permanent.

"Where did you go?" Aarush asked.

"What's it to you, Robot Boy?" Elwood moved from the locker he was leaning on.

"Just curious."

Aarush! It's a trap! Don't talk to him. I wanted to yell, but he walked right into that one.

"You know what curiosity did to the cat?" Elwood towered over Aarush like a mountain. His muscles looked like granite...or basalt...whatever—he looked menacing.

"Cut it out, Elwood. Stop trying so hard." I came between them, thinking I would diffuse the situation.

"Why did you choke Lucas?" Elwood sneered at me.

"I didn't."

"Are you insinuating it was my imagination, Grady?" Elwood's eyes looked like polished marbles.

"You okay, Elwood? You don't look real good," I asked him.

"Shut up, Grady," Elwood said through gritted teeth.

"Do you really want to do this, Elwood? I don't think it will be tolerated here." I tried to sound casual.

Elwood's face relaxed into a confident smile. "I'm juiced in. Teacher's pet."

"What?" Aarush responded. "Miss Parker threw you out of her class."

Elwood laughed. "Best thing that ever happened to me. Miss Templeton seems to recognize real talent when she sees it. Miss Parker can kiss my—"

"Hey," I interrupted. *Now, who's the stupid one?* I wondered. I didn't even like Miss Parker, but here I was, playing defender of her honor. "Don't say it."

"Or what?" He held up his hand. His red bracelet was gone. In its place was a black one that throbbed and glowed with purple energy. The color seemed more vibrant and way cooler than ours. "I'm protected now. Maybe you're going to be the one to get thrown out."

Lucas marched over and pulled off his shirt. "Yeah." He replaced it with a form-fitting gym shirt. He still wore our red bracelet, so apparently, he wasn't in Elwood's league yet.

"You're no longer a Kashinka?" Aarush asked.

"You mean on the pussycat team?" Elwood sneered.

"Technically speaking, I wouldn't call it a pussycat—" Aarush started.

"Shut up, freak." Elwood slowly turned toward Aarush.

Elwood had changed, his temper seemed more volatile than before. He was known to push boundaries as a bully in the past, this was different. Elwood enjoyed the audience's reaction to his teasing, as if he could display his superiority, then he would draw back just short of violence. Now, he was menacing, his face devoid of humanity, the timber of his voice sounded as if it were coming from deep in a cave. Elwood's brows lowered, his shoulders squared like a mountain range, he raised a boulder-like fist aiming it toward Aarush.

"No!" I yelled.

He twisted toward me, his face a snarl. Lucas intervened and pushed me. What else could I do? I pushed back. Needless to say, both Aarush and I ended up with an ignoble introduction to the joys of physical education.

Lucas Reinholt stood like a steel exit blocking my escape. Elwood took over, shoving me hard into a locker, my head slamming against the metal doors. I wasn't sure if it was my brain or the lockers rattling. I moaned from the pain. I heard Aarush gasp with shock then do something both out of character and astonishing. He leaped onto Elwood's back. Elwood roared with amusement. He seemed to have perfected an evil laugh in the short time he'd been at school. Aarush looked like a baby koala bear hanging on its mother's back. Lucas plucked him off, and together, he and Elwood tossed Aarush into the tallest tube of metal used for the air-conditioning. I heard him banging against the confines of the interior.

I rose, the world spinning. "Aarush, are you okay?" I called out.

Lucas and Elwood grabbed me under the arms in an iron grip and walked me toward the wall of lockers. They stuffed me in what I presumed was the largest and slammed the door so I couldn't get out.

While it was a big enough locker to accommodate my skinny body, it was claustrophobic. I rattled the locking mechanism frustrated when it wouldn't budge. It was jammed. Sweat broke out on my forehead, and I could feel my lungs contract. The metal box holding me filled with my wheezing. My arms were trapped against my heaving sides. I couldn't reach into my pocket for my asthma spray, so I pounded the door with my knuckles. I could feel the skin split above my fingers.

I could hear Aarush yelling for help. Rescue came by way of that kid I had first seen in our dorm. I had a vague memory of Dr. Templeton saying his name, but I couldn't remember it. I had noticed he wore a red wristband, which meant he was a Kashinka, like us. He yanked the door open, pulled me out of the locker, and said quietly, "You're alright. Take a deep breath."

I pulled out my new asthma inhaler, pressed it to my lips like a harmonica, and was surprised at the quick and efficient way the medicine flowed into my airways.

"Aarush!" I yelled, restored to myself again.

The kid gestured for me to follow him to the other side of the room. Aarush called for help from deep inside the tube.

"Give me a hand," our rescuer grunted. He was short, reaching only to my shoulder. He didn't have enough strength to tip the metal vent.

"We could sure use Miss Parker to imagine you out of there," I muttered.

Aarush attempted to climb out again. I could hear him slide down the sides.

"There's nothing for me to use to climb out of here," he called.

We shoved at the big thing, but it was like moving a sack of rocks.

"Should we get a teacher?" I suggested.

"The kid looked at me with disbelief. "Yeah, and how are you going to explain your friend got in there?" He paused. "You gonna rat on the big kid. This is the first day, bro. You'll be done in the eyes of all the other kids, the bully's gonna get'cha, and then-"

"Okay, forget it. I agree," I interrupted him. He was right, after all. Another gong sounded. "Let me think. Wait a minute."

"Think fast, class starts in about two minutes," the new kid said.

I looked around the room. There was a narrow utility closet in the corner. I opened the door to find a bunch of push brooms with sturdy wooden handles. I grabbed two of them and raced back.

"Here." I handed the other kid a broom. "Let's rock the tubing and stick the broom handles underneath.

Using our shoulders we both pushed. The tubing teetered then fell back with a noisy thud.

"Let's try it again. Brace yourself, Aarush."

I put the broom flat on the floor near my foot. "When I say push, kick the broom with your foot."

He nodded. We both shoved at the tubing, I know my arms were shaking from the effort. The metal rocked and I kicked the broom handle underneath the bottom.

Our rescuer followed my lead, sliding his under as well, leveraging it against the floor.

"Get ready, Aarush," I warned.

Aarush braced himself as we shoved the tube. I put my shoulder against it as it tipped forward. It teetered for a moment, then flipped forward, falling with a jarring crash, spilling Aarush onto the floor.

Aarush scrambled up. "Thanks. Stupid place to leave unfinished vents."

I looked around. "I'm beginning to think nothing happens for no reason here."

The other kid looked at me. "What do you mean by that?"

Before I could answer Aarush held out his hand. "I'm Aarush Patel. This is Grady Whill. Thanks again for helping."

"Shaquille." He shook Aarush's hand. "Shaquille Jefferson."

Another gong sounded.

Shaquille made a noise with his tongue. "That means we're late."

I nodded. "We better get moving."

Aarush spoke as we changed into the clothing that had mysteriously been placed in the lockers with our names.

"That was good thinking, Grady. When you couldn't extricate me with brute strength, you found a viable solution."

Shaquille's face lit up. "He used the first Codex. I wonder if there's extra credit for us in all this."

I must have looked puzzled because Aarush continued, although he was speaking slowly, as if he knew I didn't understand. "Failure is good."

I didn't see the connection, so I replied, "Ha! Real good. Let's go before we fail gym."

I was not happy. Nothing had changed, only the scenery.

It didn't matter, I thought. Elwood had been protected by the principal in our last school. It appeared he felt safe enough here to flex his muscles. I would just steer clear of him and remind Aarush to avoid him like we avoided Marcie. The pit bull—you remember?

The three of us jogged into the gym together.

Mr. Lee, the lead teacher of the Weibus or blue team, was our gym instructor. He wore an outfit similar to Miss Parker's, but in green. His hair was closely shaved to his dark head. He pointed to the floor where the other students were seated, their legs crossed.

I apologized for our lateness and he waved me off.

"First day," he explained. "I won't be so lenient next time." He seemed more flexible than Miss Parker. I heard Elwood making word noises and then go quiet. I noted with satisfaction he looked vastly uncomfortable. His hulking frame was hunched as if he had no give in his tendons. Lucas Reinholt was listing sideways and practically sitting on top of him.

We shared the gym class with girls. Another teacher, her brown hair pulled into a ponytail, walked up and down the rows of female students, her hands on her hips. She introduced herself as Jane Garcia.

"Welcome to gym class," Mr. Lee's voice boomed in the room. "I want you to leave all your perception of the real world behind and be prepared to lose yourself in a new reality."

"Yes," Miss Garcia continued. "You are going to learn that everything you thought was true ..." She paused and looked around the room at each student. "...is not. In the next four years, we are going to show you how to use physics to your advantage."

"I thought this was gym class," Elwood said, with a grunt. He was clearly uncomfortable sitting like this. His comment, as well as the defiant way he said it caused the students around him to giggle.

"If I remember your application, you got in here with your ability in athletics." Miss Garcia raised an eyebrow. She watched Elwood struggle with his position. "You think you're a good athlete, Mr. Bledsoe?" Miss Garcia asked.

"I don't think I am. I know I am." Elwood straightened his back, then flexed his arm muscles to prove his point.

"And here I thought you got in due to your superior intelligence," Mr. Lee said.

Elwood's jaw hardened, not sure if he was being mocked. "I got in with that too." He fiddled with his new bracelet.

I saw Mr. Lee's attention was drawn to Elwood's new wristband. He focused on it and was silent for a bit. The class tittered, oblivious to this new development. I have to admit, I was enjoying Elwood's slide from the rarified air of supremacy into the trenches with us ordinary people.

I sucked in my breath. I had to be alert.

"Look." Elwood stood defiantly. He pointed a finger at his chest. "I was the regional wrestling champ for the entire East Coast two years straight, not to mention the greatest quarterback our junior high had ever seen."

"Is that so?" Mr. Lee said softly. He looked at Elwood for a bit, as if he were measuring his capabilities. "Let's take a look at what you are capable of doing." Mr. Lee snapped his fingers, and two ropes dropped down from the ceiling to dangle a few feet above our heads. "A race, then. I want to see what you are made of."

Mr. Lee looked around at the assortment of students, stopping when he noticed Lydia Cullen. He gestured for her to approach the rope. Forrest sat on the other side of the room. I could see him smile at her with encouragement.

Lydia looked uncertainly at Miss Garcia, who nodded in agreement. The teacher placed her tablet on the floor and held out her arm. "Come on."

Lydia shook her head, but Miss Garcia motioned for her to go up to the front. With a heavy sigh, she rose and approached the rope.

Lydia did not look like someone used to physical activity. She was heavier than most of the other students, and moved her body ponderously. Her sneakers squeaked on the floor as she tripped in her reluctant journey. Elwood was at one of the ropes, making gorilla sounds as she walked up. He mugged a few funny faces to Lucas. A few of the kids laughed, but a stern look from Mr. Lee quelled any further comments.

I wasn't sure where the teacher was going with this. I have to admit, I was happy he didn't pick me. I am a dismal rope climber. I did feel bad for Lydia. She was about to be humiliated in front of the entire class. I knew the feeling well.

Mr. Lee stood between the two swaying ropes. "Two very different people. Can anyone tell me who they think will win this contest?"

Elwood took this time to show off his ripped deltoid muscles while Lydia stared owlishly from behind her round glasses.

A few hands went up. Mr. Lee nodded to a boy in the first row, who pointed to Elwood.

"Why?" the teacher asked quietly.

This time Lucas laughed out loud. "You have to be blind not to know why."

"Quiet, Reinholt," Mr. Lee said shortly. He turned to the other boy. "Go on."

The boy shrugged. "She's probably never had to do a rope climb."

Elwood opened his mouth, his lips twisting. I knew he was on the verge of saying something nasty. Miss Garcia walked closer to him. Elwood was a big guy, but this woman towered over him. I hadn't realized how tall she was. He looked like a troll next to her.

Miss Garcia exchanged a look with Mr. Lee that must have made Elwood squirm. I know it had that effect on me.

"We shall see." Mr. Lee walked back to stand before them. He made a wide circle as he raised his hands in the air. While Lydia looked at him intently, Elwood's shoulders shook with suppressed laughter. Mr. Lee brought his two index fingers to the bridge of his nose. He was breathing deeply. He stared intently at Lydia. I watched, amazed as Lydia slowed her breaths to match the teacher's. I couldn't see Lydia's face, but her body was still, other than the deep lungfuls of air she was taking in.

I found my own chest rising and falling in time to theirs. I turned to see that all the students appeared to be breathing in unison. We all sort of fell into the same pattern…well, except for Elwood.

Mr. Lee placed one hand on each side of their temples. Elwood recoiled; Lydia visibly relaxed into him.

"When you climb the rope, think of a person or animal that can do it with ease," he told them.

"A monkey," Lydia whispered.

I was shocked to realize that I had pictured a monkey in my mind.

I looked at Aarush. His eyelids were at half-mast, and he was moving his lips silently. I glanced at Elwood, whose face reflected his sullen attitude, his stance rigid.

Mr. Lee removed his hands and spoke almost in a whisper. "Yes, be mindful. A monkey, a squirrel, a cougar. Pay attention, class. They all climb. Pick an animal you can identify with and imagine what it sees, hears, and smells. See the world through their perspective. You don't want to be heavy. That will hold you back. You don't want your legs to feel like dead weight or your arms to be weak."

Miss Garcia walked up and down the aisles, repeating the words, "A monkey, a squirrel, a cougar." She kept repeating them, her voice as soft and light as air. Mr. Lee droned on too.

I felt myself drift. Sound receded. My body melted away. "Picture it. Smell the surroundings, Feel the cool air of the forest, or the heat of the jungle. It doesn't matter, just pick something and live it, breath it, feel it." They kept talking until I couldn't really hear them, their voices became background noise.

I was in a forest, knee-deep in dead leaves, running through the debris on four legs. I could feel the wet earth, my fingers clawing in the soil as I rushed along the ground.

I spotted a tree. The uneven bark loomed before me. It was cracked in a striated pattern, parts of it coming away from the trunk. I looked up to the leafy canopy. Water dripped. The blue sky peeked through the umbrella-shaped leaves. Gripping the rough bark, I felt it cut into the pads of my fingers. I hung on and raced up the side. Looking down, I watched the forest floor grow distant. The sky was right above me.

I came back into myself slowly to see Lydia gripping the rope inches from the room's high ceiling while Elwood hung midway, his arms shaking with the effort. Sweat poured down the sides of his head. He appeared panicked.

I glanced at the entire class. Our mouths were all open in astonishment.

"You can come down now, Miss Cullen. We don't have time to wait for Mr. Bledsoe's leisurely climb to the top." Mr. Lee turned to consider us, and Lydia made her way carefully down as if she were born doing this. "Rule one," said Mr. Lee. "Looks can be deceiving. I want a four-page paper about that for Friday."

We all groaned. He turned slowly. "Add to that assignment but due tomorrow, your personal experience today. What did you see, hear, and smell, and what do you *think* happened? Class dismissed."

I hung back as we left the room, adrift in the adrenaline rush of Elwood's humiliation. Elwood stalked from the room in a huff, a nasty expression on his face.

Aarush stood next to me, babbling about failure and how it had helped me figure out a way to get him from the air-conditioning tubing. I half-heard him.

My ears picked up a disgruntled Mr. Lee as he complained to Miss Garcia. "Jeez, a black band already? It's the first day, for Pete's sake. She was supposed to wait until the evaluations."

"She must have seen something to earmark him," Miss Garcia replied.

"Then she needs glasses. That kid is a problem."

"You didn't have to embarrass him," Miss Garcia said.

"Cocky son of a…He is everything that the Codex abhors."

"You know what Valencia is like when she gets the bit between her teeth." Miss Garcia bent to pick up the tablet she had placed on the floor.

"Templeton's a fool to let her—"

"*Shhhh*," Miss Garcia cautioned. "Little pitchers have big ears." They were looking directly at me.

I felt my ears redden to the tips.

The rest of the day passed in a blur. Science class was similar to what I had experienced at home. I was loaded down with English, history, and other homework, but the two classes that seemed to stand out more than any other were Subconscious Studies and physical education.

After we ate dinner, Aarush and I unfolded the desks and got to work. It was going to be a long night. Elwood, I am happy to say, didn't return to the room leaving Aarush and myself alone for the evening, which wasn't a bad thing. After the confrontation in the gym, I wasn't too thrilled to see him and I wasn't sure how our first meeting after that would go.

Aarush had come to my defense today, surprising me. He was quieter than usual. A thought occurred to me. "Aarush, you miss home?" I know I didn't particularly, but Aarush had acted out of character earlier and may have needed to talk to his parents.

Aarush was on his bed, the tablet illuminating his face.

"Of course, I miss my parents and Gita, but I don't miss home. This is exciting stuff we are doing."

I couldn't find much excitement in the regular studies, but I will admit what happened in Miss Parker's class and gym was intriguing. "Do you think that kid, Shaquille, is right? Should we talk to anybody about what happened?"

Aarush was quiet for a bit and said "No. We handled it. Let's see if it becomes a regular thing. I don't want to look like a… a…"

"Snitch." I understood exactly what he meant. "Elwood is a bully, but today, he seemed different."

Aarush nodded. "He was probably showing off. It should wear thin as the workload increases, he won't have time for it."

We fell asleep soon after that. I have no idea where Elwood was or even if he was doing his assignments at all.

CHAPTER 15

SCHOOL DAZE

*T*HE NEXT FEW weeks we settled into a routine, rising at dawn to try to catch up on the vast amounts of homework they gave us. School was hard, the hours were long, and nothing was what we expected. We did go outdoors more and more each day. That was the only place where Elwood and his buddy found ways to torture us. They were never covert. Someone was definitely advising Elwood to reel it in, but he still managed to get his digs in.

Our school was divided into two groups. I have to say, other than in the hallways, we didn't see much of the blue group. It was as if we had the whole place to ourselves. You remember, we were the Kachinas, some weird two-footed cat. The blue group had a better-looking image to emulate. The Weribus was a winged dragon-like creature. Maybe they kept us apart so there would be no competition between us.

I kept wishing we'd see some Weri's, as we called them. Lucas and Elwood would have had a field day with them, and that might have given some of us—you know, the cat people—a break. No such luck.

I remember the first day we went outdoors. We emerged from the building to find the tropical sun hard on the eyes after days of being in the tomblike interior. The sea sparkled dark blue in the distance and, as it moved closer to shore, faded to an aqua, where it lapped against the white beach.

Fencing in our island on the southern side was a craggy, uneven hill appropriately named, I learned from Bailey, Scarface Mountain.

"How do you know what it's called?" I challenged her after she told me.

"I asked, dufus," she did say it in a friendly way; I couldn't be mad. Bailey was a few months older than me, but in some strange way, she felt like an older sister. She was firmly in our inner circle. I expected that girls and boys would stick to separate groups. At Templeton, we formed a ring and spent most of our spare time together. Shaquille, Bailey, Pari, Lydia, Forrest, Aarush, and I were all extremely different, but we each contributed something, whether it was in homework or conversation. There was a comfort level when we got together. Bailey was not as sheltered as Aarush and Pari, which made me feel a kinship with her. She didn't speak about home, but I instinctively knew she was used to fending for herself. Her responses in class, the way she assessed situations made me realize she had an understanding that other kids lacked.

We walked outside on the path and I observed my group of friends. I was beginning to realize that each one of us excelled in something, contributing to make us a more solid pack.

Aarush was logical, his scope of knowledge far beyond what I had previously known. Pari was his perfect foil, while equally brilliant, she brought a humanity that Aarush appeared to be missing. Bailey's power ran deep, reflected in the strength of her body as well as character. Always ready to defend, I learned her loyalty was unshakable. Shaquille was quiet and fast, sometimes you almost forgot he was there, yet he turned up whenever there was trouble, ready to help. Forrest and Lydia read situations better than anybody in the clique. They had a clear understanding of what motivated other students or even teachers. Of my own attributes, I hadn't figured them out yet, and I wondered many times what I was doing at Templeton.

"Scarface," I walked next to Bailey to see if she would fill in more information. "Who told you that?"

Bailey studied the ragged stone outcroppings. The rocky incline was covered by towering palms and scrubby brush covering the parts that weren't bare. It looked unfriendly, foreboding, and impenetrable.

"It looks like an ugly sore," I commented.

Bailey shrugged. "It's part of the island, a sum of its parts. Like everything else, we all have good and bad parts."

That's what I'm talking about, Bailey made me think. Everybody in our group did. When I was younger and friends with Elwood, everything we did had a mindlessness about it. A lightbulb went off one day and I realized that was the real reason I stopped wanting to be with him. Well, that and the meanness he developed.

We skirted past the base of the mountain on a dirt trail once we left the confines of the developed part of the school grounds. We jogged around the perimeter of the island and I marveled at the vast differences, the wide expanse of turquoise sea caressing the fine white sand and the lump of a mountain, uneven and jagged, with its harsh lines and forbidding presence made me realize it reflected life in general.

Bailey looked at me, her head tilted. She nodded and once again I shivered feeling she tramped through my thoughts. "I get you," she said cryptically, and took off leaving me baffled. *How could she get me, when I didn't even get me?*

Soon, gym class was moved outside, so we ran a partially paved track that wove through the jungle past that cliff. I felt like the sea represented openness and truth, the hulking shadow of the mountain, the hidden secrets I longed to discover from the Codex and the mysterious teacher staff.

The only class Elwood remained in was gym. An uneasy stalemate developed between Mr. Lee and him. The gym teacher did not goad him again. In fact, it appeared he went out of his way to ignore Elwood. It was as if he had to have him there and couldn't do anything about it.

I will admit phys ed was not my favorite activity. In fact, I dreaded the daily routine. When I practiced with my friends, they adjusted their running speed to mine. I was not a fast runner on a good day.

Today the air was thick and muggy, not to mention swarming with mosquitos. *West Nile virus, anybody?* I asked Mr. Lee about it one day. He looked back at me as if I were speaking another language.

As the entire southern side was a series of hills, the first time I followed the course, I had to use my asthma spray at least twice.

The class took off as if they had been born running. With the exception of Lucas Reinholt and Elwood, who couldn't resist knocking me to my knees and then jogging away, snickering.

I stood panting, my hands on my thighs, breathless and gulping air. I hung back, wheezing, watching Pari, Bailey, Shaquille, and even Lydia and Forrest Cullen tear up the track as they reluctantly left me in the dust. I didn't remember seeing Shaquille go past me, but he must have. I knew he wasn't behind me.

Shaquille was strange. It was as if he were in the room, then not, and then materializing again. I don't want to give you the impression I thought he had the ability to be invisible. What I'm saying is he could disappear in a group, and then when you searched for him, it turned out he was standing right next to you.

Aarush deliberately tripped over a tree root, causing him to fall on the path. I saw him observing my feeble attempts to run. As soon as I neared him, I reached over to help him up, thinking he'd really fallen. I realized it was a clumsy attempt to keep me company. Aarush rose easily, brushing dirt off his gym shorts. Mr. Lee exchanged a look with Aarush, then trotted to the front where Lucas and Elwood led the pack.

"Aarush, why are you doing that? You can run better than me." I was angry. Our dynamics shifted and it felt wrong. I was the one to always bail him out.

"Use your spray, Grady," he told me. I glanced at the group running far ahead of us, then back to Aarush. "Maybe you should imagine yourself as a cheetah," he added helpfully.

I wanted to smash my fist into one of the tall palm trees that surrounded us. *A cheetah, really? Cheetahs don't have asthma!* I wanted to shout. I gritted my teeth in anger.

"You think I can't keep up with everybody else?" I was

incensed, but it didn't show as I was doubled over hacking away.

Aarush shrugged. He looked at me through his thick glasses. His eyes appeared different. I couldn't put my finger on it. With dawning horror, I realized he was worried about me. All that did was make me angrier.

"Go on." I waved my hands. "I don't need company." I felt like a complete loser. "Go!" I snapped.

I saw Aarush struggle for a moment, then turn and run ahead, his pace snail-like. I leaned against a tree trunk, my face tight with embarrassment.

"Cloudy thoughts prevent the body from functioning," said a voice coming out of nowhere.

I must have jumped five feet in the air. Too bad we weren't practicing pole vaulting.

I spun to find Miss Garcia studying my face. She had her hands on her hips, her legs planted on the track.

"Watch," she said. I saw her screw up her face, her skin becoming red. Sweat broke out on her brow to coat her temples. Her breathing became labored. I recognized the wheeze of asthma. She reached into her tunic and pulled out an asthma inhaler similar to mine. She didn't take it, though. Her eyes lost their focus, and she began a rhythmic breathing pattern. I watched her face relax, her breathing slow. I felt my own breathing fall into sync with hers.

"You have asthma?" I asked.

"Yes." She nodded, placing the spray back in her pocket.

"You didn't take your rescue inhaler!"

"I am never without it, and I always take it when I need it. Panic will make it worse, you know."

I agreed about the anxiety, it always made it worse. Miss Garcia looked fine. "How did you do that?"

"You have to learn to know the difference between when you want to take it and when your body really needs it."

"I think I know the difference when I really need it," I said with a little heat.

We started walking along the pathway. She picked up speed. I kept up with her. Our arms swung by our sides. My body pulsed with anger and I couldn't think about anything but the way I knew Elwood would tease me when I reached the end. It consumed me.

I felt myself becoming short of breath. She looked down at me. "Clear your mind."

I lowered my eyebrows, my thoughts spinning. As much as I wanted to, I felt the air squeeze from my lungs. "I can't. I can't do this," I gasped.

Her steps slowed, and I heard her voice. "Take *I can't* out of your vocabulary."

"I can't focus!" I choked out.

"That's part of the problem. Failure is good," she said enigmatically.

All that did was make me want to throw up, and I was so busy trying to figure out what she meant by that, my breathing had eased.

"Grady, thoughts shape reality." Miss Garcia said it twice before I heard her. She continued, "Your understanding of what's real is a product of your inner voice. If you want to change your reality, change what you say to yourself."

"Is that a quatrain?" I rasped.

All I got was a secretive smile. I was heartily sick of those.

If you know something and want to share it, then just say it, I wanted to shout.

"Try," she urged. "Think of things that make you happy, things you excel at."

I sighed, giving in, maybe grumpily. Her encouraging attitude made me feel like a jerk, so I closed my eyes and gave it a whirl.

Images flashed in my mind. I concentrated on the ones that brought me pleasure, ejecting Elwood from my thoughts, Miss Parker, and anything else that made me miserable. As soon as I felt myself drifting, I created an image of me winning at *Super Dude*, carrying nine hundred cans of food to a car, and eating a huge dinner at Aarush's house, looking at my parents' picture. I thought of Pari.

My feet were pounding the pavement. I opened my eyes. I didn't even realize they were closed. We were jogging, my breathing even. I glanced at Miss Garcia sideways. She was smiling at me.

"Don't stop thinking about the things you enjoy, Grady. You will always need your asthma inhaler. You have asthma and will have to take it, but try first to not let your body trigger it." She turned to look beyond us. "See, you can do it."

I nodded.

"Sometimes, we are able to control our bodies by staying centered," she said.

"I wasn't centered," I said, surprised I wasn't even breathless. We kept up our trot.

"Asthma is brought on by all sorts of things and when we can't control it we have to take the medicine. But, if we know anger or worry sets it off, we have to reduce those stresses preventing it from bringing it on."

I guess she could tell I wasn't too sure about this, so she continued, "You can carry matches. By themselves, they won't cause damage, but when you strike one it can cause great devastation with a fire."

"So, I have asthma, and always will."

She nodded. "Go on."

"If I control my surroundings-"

"No, your reaction to your surroundings," she corrected.

My mouth dropped. I had never thought that I could be the one setting off my own issue with my breathing.

"Never forget to carry your medicine, and don't depend on your mind to get you out of it. Remember, if you know anxiety makes your breath short, then try to avoid putting yourself in that state."

I had nothing more to add to the conversation. We caught up to the rest of the class, now lounging on the powdery sand of the beach.

Miss Garcia turned, still running, and said softly, "Remember to use your spray when you need it, but try to clear your thoughts and relax so you'll avoid that situation."

We stopped and faced each other. I was barely out of breath.

"Is there more?"

She smiled. "Oh yes. This is just the beginning. You will learn—" She stopped abruptly, her face closing up. She acknowledged someone behind me.

The ring under my tunic pulsed with energy against my chest. I spun to see Miss Parker watching us. It made my skin crawl. I turned back to Miss Garcia, nodded, and waved goodbye.

I ran over to sit with Aarush. To anybody else, he would

have seemed expressionless. Not to me. I saw the hurt in the set of his shoulders, the downturn of his mouth.

I felt myself flush with guilt at the way I had spoken to him earlier. I started to apologize. Aarush changed the subject, as he always did. He never stayed upset for long.

Our excursions outside became easier for me. As the weeks passed, I ran faster than anybody else in the class, including Lucas Reinholt and Elwood.

No matter how much time we spent outdoors, I never saw a boat or airplane or, as I said before, the blue dragon kids who shared our habitat. Maybe they had all been sent home. It was as if we were alone on this planet. No distractions, for sure.

I wondered if I'd still be able to beat Aarush at *Super Dude*. I was even more surprised as time wore on when I realized I didn't care. I stopped longing for video games as the lessons went deeper.

I noticed that most of us seemed quieter; the volume of our combined noise had subsided. And while we still buzzed like a pack of bees, it was more of a controlled hush. I think we were less silly. There seemed to be a gravity settling into the students. Then I spied Elwood. I changed that statement to most of the students.

Time went quickly. I have to say I enjoyed these classes more than school at home. Weeks turned to months. I called Leo on the first of the month. We mostly talked about the weather. He teased me that he was using my game system and there was little to do about it. I didn't mind, my brain was kind of full, digesting what we were learning.

I had studied the obelisk in the main hallway more than once. It drew us like bears to honey. During those first three months we'd been at Templeton we'd congregate there, reading the first and only quatrain, wondering when they'd carve in another. "There's more, right?" I asked one day.

Bailey nodded in her serious way. She had cut her hair very short. In fact, I think mine was longer. Phys ed had affected her body as well. She appeared taller, her muscles more developed than anyone else's in our group. I observed she moved with ease, and while she didn't say much, she did interact socially a bit more with students.

We parked ourselves at the base of the obelisk like a group at a picnic. Some of the kids were studying; others, like me, were hanging out.

I heard Lydia gasp. Elwood had cornered Forrest by the entrance of the cafeteria. Lydia turned to Bailey. "My brother," she choked out.

Bailey was beside Forrest an instant later placing herself between the heavy boy and Elwood.

I followed, ready to help in time to see Elwood stomping away.

"What happened?"

"He left the minute Bailey arrived," Lydia informed us, dancing from one foot to another. "She's amazing. I wish I could do that."

Bailey snorted a bit. "Anybody can do that. It doesn't take any special skill. Lydia, I think what you can do is incredible."

"He's a coward," Pari said disdainfully.

"Bullies usually are," I added, puzzled that the confrontation hadn't escalated. Elwood only attacked when we were outside, when he thought his prey was isolated. "Still," I said to Bailey. "That's the second time you've stopped him. I would watch my back."

"I'm not afraid, " Bailey's voice boomed in the room. I'm sure Elwood could hear her. We all walked together to our place in the cafeteria.

I thought of us as an interesting group. For all that we were nerds, not all of us were brainiacs. "What's their specialty?" I asked Pari, referring to Lydia and Forrest.

"You haven't figured it out yet?"

I shook my head.

"Empaths," Pari said, her face puzzled. She stopped to look up at the monolith. "What is the next quatrain?" she yelled with frustration, stamping her foot.

I wanted to talk about them being empaths but was diverted instantly. "Yeah, where are the rest of the quatrains?" I asked Bailey, who shrugged her big raw-boned shoulders.

We sat at our usual table.

"I suppose they will put up another one when they think we are ready for it," Aarush offered without looking up. He was working with his tablet and some project he had volunteered to do for extra credit, not that he needed it.

"What do you think the next one is?" I asked the group.

Aarush's head snapped up. He tapped his glasses with his stylus. "*Hmmm*...interesting question. I have searched, and there is nothing other than the discovery of the ancient scrolls of the Codex. Only the Templetons have studied them."

"And they are not sharing any information," Lydia said. "It makes me wonder about the rest of the students. Why are they keeping the Weribus separate?"

"Why do you think?" I certainly had no idea.

"Control," Pari answered. "It's obvious. Whoever controls the Codex ultimately controls who can study it."

"Okay," I said, considering this idea. "I can buy that. But what's up with our divided student body?"

"Perhaps that too is for control," Aarush said thoughtfully.

I tilted my head, which was a sure sign I didn't know what the heck he was talking about.

"Think of us as some kind of science experiment," Aarush continued. "Perhaps they are giving us the same syllabus with one difference, and they want to see which outcome will be more successful."

"*Eww,* that makes me feel like I'm in a petri dish." Lydia shivered.

"Quite," Aarush agreed in a Spockyway.

I opened my mouth to respond, but a commotion interrupted me.

Valencia Templeton had entered the cafeteria. She was following her father. I studied her. Something was different. Her limp was gone. Dr. Templeton walked beside her, his hands clasped behind his back. She was moving her hands around as she spoke. Her face looked just a little twisted. I was glad she didn't notice us. They moved past us, pausing nearby. I leaned to the side, catching some of her conversation.

"Father, it's been enough time. If each of the teachers promotes their electives—"

"It's been almost three months, dear. You know how I feel about haste. How can you expect them to understand that external changes are fleeting?" He looked down at her leg, his gray eyebrow raised. "You really shouldn't have gone ahead without someone there, Valencia," he chided.

Valencia made an impatient noise. "It worked! Thoughts shape our behavior."

"That's true, dear," he said patiently. "But you'll remember that alterations on the outside not supported by matching changes on the inside are…at best…superficial."

Valencia's exasperated reply rang through the hall, silencing all chatter. "Please, can't we go somewhere to talk about this? I think we've waited long enough!"

"Your choices leave a lot to be desired. You rush things, Valencia. Remember what happened when we rushed."

He looked around the room. His gaze settled on *me* of all things. He frowned. I gulped. He turned to Valencia and said, "This is not the time or place. Besides, the boy is obstinate, hardly what we're looking for."

I wondered what boy they were talking about. I hoped it wasn't me.

Valencia stopped where she stood, took a fortifying breath, and responded, "Sometimes, Father, I can't believe I am your offspring." She balled her fists, her face becoming redder, then stomped away, leaving her father standing alone.

Templeton stood in the center of the room, looking around at the students' faces. "Carry on, children." He paused, then said, "Anyone? Why is failure good?"

Aarush raised his hand.

"Ah, yes, Mr. Patel. Apurva's boy. I'm not surprised. Go ahead."

"It is clear, sir, that if you fail, your brain develops new pathways to succeed and overcome the challenge. This builds our intellectual strength the same way we create muscle in the gym."

"Quite. Quite. Nicely done."

I looked down at Aarush in wonder. So simple yet so profound. *Why didn't I think of that?* My mouth dropped, not just from Aarush's statement. I realized Aarush didn't sound like Mr. Spock at all. He was sounding more and more like Dr. Templeton.

"So, back to our discussion. What will the next quatrain be?" Lydia asked the group. "Anybody want to take a wild guess?"

"It could be anything," a new voice volunteered. Devon Neely was sitting next to Lydia. He had a walking stick with a ball carved on the end that he used when he moved around. I knew he had been sightless since birth. I never expected him to last at the school. I lowered my head with no small amount of shame. I certainly felt differently about many of the kids since we'd started. Not for nothing, I learned not to judge a book by its cover.

However, many of our fellow students went home. Some of them were total surprises: smart kids, athletes, student prodigies who couldn't cut it. Then there were the ones who were allowed to stay. They surprised me even more. When I had been paired with Devon in class for an exercise, I often forgot he couldn't see.

"Perhaps it will be something about frame of reference," Devon volunteered.

Forrest turned around but stayed silent. He rarely spoke.

"I think I know," Lydia piped up. "My frame of reference is different from, let's say…Bailey's. Her thoughts and ideas are based on her experiences. Her responses are born from her personal past."

"Interesting concept," Aarush commented. "You will contribute an opinion to a conversation different from Bailey's based on both of your personal histories. So when we see the world through your eyes, we have to understand it as your perceptions."

Here we go again, I thought with mounting frustration. "This is all speculation!" I stood up. "Unless you know what the next quatrain is, you're all just guessing."

"I think you're right, Grady." I heard Shaquille's voice but didn't see where he was. I looked around, and he waved from one of the small windows, where he was retrieving a sandwich. *He must have flown there*, I thought.

When we left for class, I read the inscription of the quatrain on the obelisk again. I didn't have to look at it. I knew it by heart. We all did.

It seemed simple enough. Failure is good and all that, if a little stupid. Failure could never be good, in my opinion, even after hearing Aarush's explanation. What can I say? Old habits die hard. It just didn't sit well with me.

I thought about Miss Garcia and when she said that while we were running. I didn't get it. Failure meant expulsion, didn't it? I didn't realize I had said it out loud until Pari responded. *Or maybe I didn't actually say it out loud.* With this crowd you could never be too sure.

"People are leaving here not because they failed, but because their minds are closed," Pari explained.

"Oh, that makes sense," I muttered, wondering why she said that if the words had never left my mouth.

Aarush, Pari, Bailey, and the rest of the group argued about it again at dinner, oddly enough drawing sides. To my dismay, Aarush and Pari agreed that failure was the most important component of success.

"Jermain Rodgers was sent home yesterday because of the mistake he made in chemistry class," I said hotly, and very loudly.

"It's only a mistake when you don't learn from it," Aarush said between mouthfuls of vegetable curry.

"Yes." Pari nodded. "Don't confuse the learning curve with mistakes."

"Semantics. It all means the same thing." I shook my head. "A mistake got him thrown out, so it's a big, fat failure as far as I'm concerned. I don't know if I even believe there is a Codex."

Aarush and Pari gasped. Bailey looked up from her sandwich, and Forrest Cullen dropped his fork so that it clattered against his dish and landed on the floor. They stared at me, then resumed their conversation as if I hadn't said anything at all.

Everybody sided with Pari. Bailey had no opinion. It was all too convoluted for my understanding, yet we all went out to the hall, copied the words over and over as if they would suddenly make sense, and then discussed them in the cafeteria during meals. I didn't tell them about what Miss Garcia had said.

Weeks passed. We argued and found no solution. More kids were gone. Classes became easier with ten, then twenty fewer students. I wondered if those kids felt *failure* was a *good* thing.

I struggled with it. *Failure was good.* I repeated it like a mantra every day. I certainly didn't believe it. Nevertheless, it ran through my head as I jogged, it sat in my frontal lobe during Miss Parker's class, and it certainly came onto center stage during physical education.

One day I let my mind try the notion on like a pair of

shoes. I went back to the beginning when I had failed at running. With Miss Garcia's help, I found a way to make it work.

It had been months, and I hadn't needed to take my asthma spray. *Was failure the spark that fixed that problem?* Maybe Aarush was right.

I could think of little else. Not that there was time to do much more. We had bucket loads of homework.

Sometimes I had to admit a feeling of regret at coming to Templeton, especially when testing began. I toyed with doing something that would send me home, but then I remembered, *Home to what?* Not that I didn't like, or even love Leo, but really my group of friends felt like a family now.

I saw Elwood daily in physical education. He left every morning, and I'd catch a glimpse of him following the straight-backed figure of Miss Templeton. We learned that he was under her private tutelage. He didn't have to take any of the other classes. He sat in a room learning directly from her, and it was rumored straight from the Codex as well. He became distant. His skin changed to a grayish color. Maybe it was a harder workload. Who knows? He was as silent as a rock, plodding in the hallways, quietly trailing after her like a puppy.

Within a few weeks, Lucas Reinholt was added to Valencia's exclusive class. I will admit it rankled me. What made him so special that he received this kind of treatment? Was he being tutored because he was ahead of us, or was he being kept separate due to his inability to fit into our group? Was he the new mold or a broken one? Let's just say I was more than a bit confused.

Now he had failed with Miss Parker. Was his failure making him successful with Miss Templeton? Did his brain learn from the error of his ways to grow intellectually to a new level?

I looked at his hulking body, his blank face. *Nah.* He looked as stupid and mean as ever.

I sat morosely in the cafeteria while Pari chirped about her fabulous exam results. The others remained silent about their grades. I had no clue how they did. I was pretty sure Forrest was struggling more than me. I didn't need special powers to know that Aarush was acing all the exams.

I passed the giant monolith, the carved words mocking me. Well, if failure was good, then I was doing great according to my quarterly report card.

I wondered if they sent my grades home, and on a rare call with Leo, I waited to see if he mentioned anything.

CHAPTER 16

AMBER EYES

WE CARRIED OUR tablets, so there were no lockers in the hallways, eliminating places to stand and gossip or even observe other students. If you broke one, or it wasn't working correctly, they simply replaced it. Supplies, it seemed, were endless.

I knew Christmas came and went. There were no celebrations, parties, or dances at school. I reminded Pari who grumbled that she missed those types of things. She was tired of wearing the same uniform every day. Lydia and Kelsea Talltrees, agreed with her. Bailey didn't seem to care. Of the guys, we didn't discuss it much, like admitting it made you sound like you were not Templeton material.

The entire school was my age, which meant for the most part it was a level playing field. We were all in the same boat. In a perfect world, it should have meant a stress-free existence socially. The fact that we were the handpicked *crème de la crème* should have been enough that we wouldn't have the nonsense that plagued schools all over the world.

Nevertheless, people still behaved as if they were in middle school, instead of high school. They created inequalities, finding fault for the most minor offenses. Being tall and geeky, for example, was a major disadvantage. You'd think the subjects we were being exposed to in our classes would distract students from the adolescent need to torture another person, that such cruelty wouldn't exist, but sadly it did. Templeton was a microcosm of the world, and as such, we had good and bad people. Some were vicious enough that I wondered if their superiority in some way made them defective.

It was an interesting thought and was much on my mind as I walked through the hallowed halls to the restroom. Doors were closed, and I could hear the teachers within the classrooms giving muffled instructions. Light poured in from a skylight overhead. I took my time.

I heard a sharp hiss, followed by the staccato response of an angry male. I slowed my pace, not wanting the squeaking of the soles of my sneakers to intrude on what sounded like an epic argument. It appeared it wasn't only students who gave in to a temper's temptation, I mused, hoping to catch a glimpse of the teachers arguing.

The unmistakable sound of something large and solid being thrown made me stop and hug the wall. This was serious. I could hear loud breathing, then the response. "How could you be so foolish?" a female asked, her voice deadly.

"It wasn't there. What did you expect me to do? Sit and wait for it to be returned?"

Not a teacher but a student. Elwood. His voice had

deepened overnight. It sounded like it was coming up from a vast canyon.

"We looked everywhere, Miss Templeton." Another voice. Lucas's heavy accent didn't surprise me. I was going to have the rarefied treat of actually overhearing one of their private lessons.

I turned to walk away, fury making my sneakers squeak on the floor as I stomped down the hall.

"Quiet! Let me think," Valencia said out loud. A chair was moved again as if someone stood quickly. "Did you hear that?" There was some whispering and then, "Did you leave the door open, you idiot? I picked you because I thought you were smarter…" Her voice trailed off in a litany of complaints.

I wondered what she was teaching them, what keys to the kingdom were being shared. I stopped to stand silently in the middle of the hall.

The ring under my shirt heated up against my skin. I sucked in my breath and pulled it away from where it made contact with my chest. I could feel the intensity of being watched in the center of my back. I pivoted, then stopped in my tracks.

Valencia Templeton stood in the hallway, her odd amber-colored eyes pinning me. Her arms were folded over her chest, observing me as if I were an insect. I opened my mouth to say something, but the directness of her gaze froze the words in my throat. Her lips twisted as if she ate something sour.

I felt an icy sensation emanating from my gut, moving through my lungs. I inhaled, feeling my chest expand, the power rushing to all four of my limbs. I moved from foot to foot, fighting the urge to take off and run. It was as if I were being possessed. My fingers tingled. I made two fists, feeling the strength in my hands grow with each lungful of air. I knew none of this was coming from me. It was as if I had taken my asthma spray times...*a hundred.*

Miss Templeton was watching me, searching my face for a sign or something.

I was powerful, but powerless to know where this new force was coming from. I moved. My feet were light, as if the energy to move them was coming from somewhere else.

My ring turned icy rather than hot, the shock of it making me gasp. Whatever was happening, I knew instinctively I wasn't ready to handle it. I shook my head and turned to continue to the restroom.

The air left my lungs in a *whoosh.* I found it hard to breathe. Reaching into my pocket I withdrew my inhaler to take a puff.

She laughed then. Loud and clear, it filled the hallway.

I knew only one thing: that woman unnerved me.

I wanted to ask someone what had happened to me. *Had I imagined it?* Was that an example of my powers, and why would they appear in front of Valencia Templeton? I shivered, remembering the strength of the energy.

It felt like I was invincible, as if I could move mountains. I didn't tell anyone about it. Not even Aarush.

I was able to call home twice more from the special rooms they used for communications with the mainland. Phones were in small stations, like in an office building. It felt like I was vacationing on Alcatraz.

We were given fifteen minutes. Everyone was hunched over the desk, speaking softly. I could hear a few sobs. I rolled my eyes and looked toward the sound. It was Tobias Enwright. All that boy did was cry. It was a wonder he didn't find that ticket on his desk like so many others who had been sent home.

The ranks had thinned. There were fewer than three hundred of us left on *the rock*, as we called it. Every day another kid was gone, his or her bed empty after finding a boarding ticket for the ferry on their desk.

I had attempted to call Leo a few times that day. The first time, Leo missed the call altogether. He must have been at work. But by the second one, we connected.

"How's it going, Squirt?"

"It's fine." I tried to sound nonchalant. I had failed a big test. I was sure I'd be seeing Leo sooner rather than later.

"Grub still good?" Leo asked. He was always asking that. I guess food played a bigger role than I realized in my uncle's life.

"Yeah." It came out with a sigh.

"Sounds great....Grady...are you happy?"

I thought for a minute. I wasn't unhappy. The workload was gruesome, but for some reason, I didn't want to share that with Leo. I also didn't want to share my resentment at Elwood's advancements with Valencia Templeton. "It's definitely not what I expected."

"How so?" Joni asked. Apparently, I was on a party line.

"Hey, Joni."

"Hey, guy. Do you want us to come over there and spring you?"

I thought for a second. The idea sounded appealing but they didn't even know where I was. "You couldn't even if you wanted to. We're on this isl—" A loud buzzer drowned my voice. All sound was cut off.

"Hello?…Joni? Leo?" The line was dead.

Still unnerved about the phone call, I met up with Aarush in the library. I wanted to tell him about Lucas's inclusion in Elwood's special classes. I was curious to know his opinion. I knew he was studying in the library. Even I enjoyed going there. The library was one of the coolest parts of the school.

It was located toward the rear of the school and had soaring ceilings and an endless supply of books on shelves that went all the way to the top. If you needed to retrieve a book that was on one of the really tall shelves, you attached yourself to a booster that shot as much as five stories up and stopped automatically at the book you wanted. I had to admit that part was amazing.

Aarush had taken over an entire table with a collection of papers and books from the stacks. He was furiously typing on his tablet. Pari sat on his other side, absorbed in her work.

"Aarush!" I called softly. He didn't look up. "Aarush!" I said his name a second time. The third try was a whisper yell that traveled like a hurricane through the room. I got a stern look from the librarian, Mr. Clarkson, the fellow I remembered with the teal-colored spandex suit he must have had left over from the eighties. Pari jabbed him with her elbow.

Aarush looked up, his glasses crooked.

"What are you doing?" I slid into the seat next to him.

"The paper on fake news." He looked at me, his glasses

sliding down his nose. "You haven't even started reading. Look, Grady." He pointed to a book. "This fellow believes the world is actually flat. He said—"

"Nonsense," Pari said with a shake of her head, then went back to work.

I agreed with her and made a face. "This stuff is a waste of time. I thought we were going to learn how to be, you know, special here. It's the same boring junk we learned at home."

I didn't like to admit that learning to cope with my asthma did indeed make me feel special. It was just that it wasn't enough. Big deal, so now I could run or play tennis. What was so unique about that? Elwood's special classes irritated me more. What was Elwood learning that we weren't?

Aarush couldn't have looked more aghast if I had sucker-punched him. He shook his head. "Grady, we have to learn these things. How else do you think you'll succeed if you can't tell the difference between the truth and a lie?"

"Believe me, I know the difference. The world is round. I wish... I wish we'd do-"

Pari looked up, her expression amused. "What? Learn to fly? Become invisible? I believe you have to rethink what makes someone powerful, Grady."

I flushed. She wasn't mean, but she somehow made me feel silly, as if my expectations were those of a little kid. They weren't. Actually, I was so confused, I wasn't sure what my expectations were.

I considered sharing what had happened to my body when Valencia was watching me, but the words froze on my tongue. What if I imagined the entire episode? It sounded childish, even in my head.

Aarush studied me for a minute, then said, "A good leader

must surround himself with smart people with many opinions. He must listen to everybody to come up with his own ideas. Maybe the world is flat and we just don't know that yet. Remember when we talked about frame of reference? Our minds and opinions are developed from our personal experiences. They alone shape our responses and are as individual as a thumbprint."

"Yeah, everybody here is a special snowflake."

Pari giggled.

Aarush blew out a deep breath from his lips. He looked at me, his brow furrowed. "This sarcasm can't be good for you. You don't want to sound like Elwood."

I shrugged. "I don't care." I wanted to share that my phone call had been cut off when I mentioned we were on an island. Maybe it would be good to start sounding like Elwood. Perhaps that was the ticket to success.

I wanted to complain about the excessive workload. I wanted to…I don't know what I wanted.

Pari held up a hand. "Grady, we've been given a very special opportunity. Just look at this place. One hundred thirty-eight of us left. Don't lose a chance to grow by being impatient or closed-minded."

I shrugged. "You forget the dragon people, the Weri's. There may be more of them left than us. Maybe we are on the weak team." I was feeling persecuted.

"Grady, you're sounding persecuted."

What can I say? My mind was an open book to everyone, but me. "Yeah, Aarush, I get your point. But what is the point?"

Aarush lowered his stylus and looked at me intensely. "This is just the beginning, Grady. Only the best will survive."

"You're creeping me out, dude."

I think we all laughed a bit after that, and the tension eased.

"It will get easier," Pari said with a smile.

I wanted to believe her, but the lessons were hard. A lot of it still didn't make sense. *Thoughts become things*, I repeated to myself. Well, my thoughts hadn't become things, and failure wasn't so hot either.

"I gotta go." I stood and left the library. Aarush went back to his paper without a second glance. Pari watched me leave. I needed answers. Something didn't feel right.

One day I saw my pants didn't reach my ankles, the next day I found new uniforms in my chest at the end of my bed. It was like they were replenished by magic. We didn't question it, and as a result, none of us talked about it either.

I walked purposefully through the crowded hall one morning. I caught sight of myself in the reflection of the glass wall lining the corridor, and for a moment I didn't recognize myself. I had changed. It was happening at a rate that I barely noticed.

Come to think of it, Aarush was leaner and more muscular too. I was taller, my face longer, and the hard exercise had given my shoulders a broadness I'd never detected before. Months of steady workouts would do that to you. Don't get me started on Elwood. He looked like Mr. Universe.

I passed through the row of administration offices lining the corridor beyond the Codex monolith with its single quatrain. Dr. Clifford Templeton had an office there. Our founder had to have an answer. Leo always said, "If you want to know something, go to the top." I wasn't getting the answers anywhere else, and my interrupted phone conversation still rankled me. It didn't get higher than this.

A secretary looked up expectantly. She was ancient, her iron-gray hair in a neat bun on the top of her head. She too wore the jumpsuit all the staff wore; hers was a mustard yellow. She moved with a flexibility that belied her years.

"Mr. Whill?"

"Mrs. Morton, do you think I can speak to Dr. Templeton?"

"Oh, no, no." She shook her head. "He's a very busy man."

"I understand, but I have a question."

She took my arm and escorted me toward the door. "Yes, very well. You can send any questions through your tablet. Certainly, after all this time here, you've explored it and found the menu. All the instructions are there."

I pulled out of her grasp. "I understand, but I'd like to—"

"Grady Whill?" Another secretary walked into the room.

I looked up, holding my ground. "I'd rather talk to Dr. Templeton."

"Perhaps I can help you." She wasn't as old as Mrs. Morton and her jumpsuit was a deeper shade of yellow. I wondered briefly if that indicated she was more important.

I shook my head. "I'd really like to talk to the doctor. It's kind of... urgent."

"I'm sure it is," she said. She put down the papers she was holding and came closer, making me back against the wall. "I think I can help you with anything you need."

I swallowed. They both had me in a corner, blocking my view. "Dr. Templeton is probably the only one—"

"Bill Bradley said, 'Ambition is the path to success. Persistence is the vehicle you arrive in.'"

I heard Templeton's voice but couldn't see him. The two secretaries were like a giant mustard-colored wall.

"Oh…Doctor, I told him you were not talking visitors," the first one said.

"It's alright, Gwennie. Follow me, young man."

The women melted aside, and Doctor Templeton stepped in front of me. He was much taller than I remembered. His long legs seemed to make him storklike. He inclined his head, a slight smile tugging his lips. "I've been waiting for you, Grady."

"What…?" I opened my mouth but nothing more came out, I stumbled past them as the doctor ushered me into his office.

It was enormous. A desk was at the far end. Our feet were swallowed by the luxurious carpet. Books lined one wall. Another wall had a great glass panel with a ninety-degree view of a giant aquarium. A ten-foot-long grouper swam lazily past us, followed by blue and yellow neon-colored fish. The triangular underbelly of a manta ray sidled up to the glass, its fins caressing the surface, its sickle-shaped mouth opening with each measured breath. My chin must have been resting on my chest.

"Did you not realize we were underwater?" I heard Dr. Templeton ask from behind me.

I shook my head. Words stuck in my throat. I turned to look at him. "I mean, I assumed…We entered the building at ground level."

"Parts of the school are on ground level—your dorm, for instance. I built it on an infinitesimal gradient so that one doesn't even feel the downward decline." He smiled benignly. "The greatest minds in the world helped build this place."

He took a long reddish-colored stick from a jar. "Dried seaweed?" He held it out to me. "Try it. They're delicious.

Smart food, packed with magnesium and calcium. Good for the bones." He made a fist.

I took it from his hands and nibbled the end. "*Umm...* tastes like—"

"Bacon. Nothing better in this world than bacon. From the processing. I have it made right here on the *rock,* as you kids call it."

I chomped down. As far as I was concerned, anyone who liked the taste of bacon was okay in my book.

We finished our treats in silence. Templeton placed a bottle of water before me on a glass table. He moved to a large desk, gesturing at the seat in front of it for me. I walked over and gingerly sat on the edge of the leather seat.

He made himself comfortable in a luxurious captain's chair, looking for all the world like the commander of a starship. He steepled his hands in front of him. His keen gaze observed me. I watched him back. It seemed we were caught in a staring contest.

There was a peacefulness about him. He made me feel much different from when his daughter looked at me. They had the same odd-colored eyes, that strange amber, yet his were as kind as hers were cold. How could two identical people be as opposite as summer and winter?

"You are troubled, Grady?" It was more of a rhetorical question. I stared back at him mutely, not knowing where to begin. "You wished to speak to me?" he prodded.

Any thoughts of conversations froze in my throat.

"School is not what you expected, Grady? Has anything occurred that you need to tell me about?"

I gulped, suddenly afraid to answer, my fingers gripping the arms of the chair. Here was my chance to open up, spill out all my feelings and I sat like a statue. The office narrowed to the two of us. I felt my chest tighten. I didn't know how or where to start. *Do I complain about my studies? Let him know I was disappointed? Rage about Elwood? Question his precious Codex?* I felt like my brain was being split into two parts. It was all too much. I must have looked panicked because Doctor Templeton's next words were calming.

"I want to assure you that you are not alone." Templeton swiveled in his chair and considered the ocean floor. His voice had a hypnotic affect. For a minute, we sat in mutual silence. Then he said gravely, "Many of the students feel similarly. I can think of someone else who almost gave up once." His eyes clouded and he looked wistfully at the graceful sway of the ocean plants.

My ring vibrated against my skin with a life of its own, breaking the stillness of the room. It thudded dully, matching my beating heart. Dr. Templeton raised his hand like an orchestra conductor, and I could swear the ring quieted. I wondered if I imagined the feeling.

He stood and walked around the desk, then leaned on the corner. He placed a reassuring hand on my shoulder. A current passed between us. I felt weighted, my eyelids heavy. I might have even been drooling; I'm not sure.

"If you are questioning the phone line cutting off, they are programmed that way to keep us isolated," he told me. "You are at a critical juncture in your studies. Distractions will destroy all that we've done."

"I don't feel like I've got anything special to offer the school. It feels disconnected…the learning, I mean."

His buzzer blasted in the room like an air-raid siren. I must have jumped ten feet in the air. The doctor held up a single finger and picked up a sleek receiver. "Yes?" he answered softly.

I could hear the shrill voice through the phone. I think mainland China could have heard the screaming.

"Yes...*hmmm* ..." the doctor said, his lids lowered, shadowing his gaze. His finger traced an invisible pattern on the tabletop. He sat up, alert. "Stop right there, Valencia. I said we were not going to—" He halted and looked up as if he'd just realized I was there. "Not now, dear. Let's discuss this after dinner."

I heard a tense silence, followed by an exasperated sigh.

"Alright then, see you later." Dr. Templeton hung up the phone and looked up at me.

"Everything has a purpose, Grady. Everything in life happens for a reason. Each class is preparation for the next level of understanding. Think of what would happen if we just showed you how to use your innate skills to harness energy to achieve what you desire. Tell me, Grady...tell me of the consequences."

I cleared my throat noisily, then stuttered, "*Ummm*...If a...*umm*...person has skills, then he or she should be taught to use them. Will I be taught to use them?" I cleared my throat again. He nodded as if I should continue, so I finished the sentence in a rush. "I don't know why we have all those other classes. I mean, what use is chemistry going to be if I can channel thoughts into things?"

Dr. Templeton snorted. He stood up and walked around the desk to pace in front of the massive window where fish swam in shimmering schools.

"How can you turn your thoughts into things if you don't know their chemical composition, I ask you? Imagine, if you will, that by simply increasing the nitrogen in the air, you can suffocate yourself."

"I wouldn't…I mean, why would I increase the nitrogen?" I asked, shaking my head as if to prove it.

Dr. Templeton went on as if I hadn't spoken, his hands clasped behind his back. "Suppose you combine hydrogen and oxygen." He walked to the center of the room, then bent down to look at me. Our eyeballs were less than four inches from each other. I sat frozen, my knuckles white.

The room dissolved into blackness. I couldn't see my hand in front of my face much, less those weird-colored eyes. The air became icy. Frost appeared before my mouth when I gasped. I jumped from the leather chair and felt as though I were floating.

"Pay attention, Grady," I heard Templeton from far away.

I saw him floating next to me. He clapped his hands, and the room exploded with a deafening roar. I spun wildly, reaching out, but I couldn't get a hold of anything. I had no concept of where the room began or ended. For all I knew, I was in another dimension. The cold air flashed with tiny pinpricks of light. We were surrounded by stars.

"Did you know that when those two elements are combined in just the right way, it's possible to create nuclear fission? Have you any idea what nuclear fission can do?"

I concentrated, trying to think of the answer. *Um…no.*

I heard a laugh followed by his voice. "Precisely!"

When I opened my eyes I was on the floor outside my science classroom, Aarush leaning over me.

"You're acting strangely, Grady. Are you okay?"

"Aarush, what does the nuclear fission of hydrogen and oxygen make?" I blurted.

"Stars," Aarush replied. "It makes stars."

CHAPTER 17

SEE AND EMPATHY

WE MUST HAVE been getting used to the place when the teachers could do all these strange things and we treated them as part of the day. I pushed my questions about the phone call to the bottom of my list. I mean, the question paled when I thought about what he did to me, where he might have taken me.

I replayed my meeting with Dr. Templeton over and over again. *Did he take me to outer space?* I didn't think so. Yet he had been able to make me believe we were there. It was the same as Miss Parker and the first day when she made the glass in our classroom explode. Was there something wrong with me that I accepted both of these incidents as normal?

"Don't overthink it, Grady," Aarush told me that night. "It will all come together when you least expect it. I think...I think ..."

I rolled up onto my side and looked at Aarush. He was lying flat on his back in the bed. "What do you think?"

"I think it is all about what's inside of you. I think humanity is capable of doing anything if they can get rid of the things that distract us and concentrate on what we can do."

I grunted and lay flat. I was here and millions of kids were not. Templeton had picked me. Even if I couldn't see what they had done, there was a reason I was there.

I pressed the ring against my chest where, I swear, it throbbed with a life of its own. The pulsing served in the same capacity as the purring of a kitten. Rather than frighten me, I had come to realize it vibrated as my emotions changed. I was somehow connected to it. I slid it from under my shirt and considered the blood-red stone. It glowed with an inner fire. I rolled it around my hands and thought of Dr. Templeton. It warmed, growing hotter when I pictured Miss Parker and warmer still with Valencia. It was so hot it scorched my fingers when I thought about Elwood.

I examined the ring. It was another part of the Templeton puzzle, reacting to people there. At first, I had attached magical significance to it, thinking it was messages from the father I never really met. *Nope.* I decided, nothing supernatural there. It was reacting to me, somehow, the wearer and my feelings.

I learned to let go of my doubt, the constant search for justification to make it fit into my world, and…go with the flow. Maybe the school was teaching me something.

I was proud of my accomplishments in phys ed. I worked hard at the subjects I felt comfortable doing. Miss Garcia's tips on preventing asthma came in handy. She would take both me and Lydia Cullen to the side of the gym to practice focusing as class started. We stood in a small alcove between gigantic padded mats. In through the nose for the count of five, hold, and then out through one nostril slowly for another count of five.

I found I had more lung capacity and was able to participate without the need of my asthma spray. More importantly, I didn't get that panicky feeling right before an attack began. It was as if I knew I wasn't going to need it. I swear Miss Garcia sensed when my chest constricted. She would look straight at me and, with a slight nod, take deep, calming breaths. I mirrored her motions and found my chest easing. This enabled me to do things I had never done before in gym.

Lydia didn't have asthma. One day I asked her why she joined Miss Garcia and me.

"I have anxiety," she whispered. She had the same round face with chubby cheeks as her brother, Forrest. Instead of a cap of curls, she wore two frizzy pigtails on either side of her head. She usually sat next to Bailey, as if she hid in the larger girl's shadow. Her nose was covered with freckles. She was painfully shy. Frankly, I still wasn't sure what an empath was. I asked her what she thought had brought her to the school.

She looked around, her lips pursed. "Sometimes, I see things."

I rolled my eyes. "Everybody *sees* things, Lydia."

"Well, it's different for me. I see people…really see them. And then I can feel things about them."

I nodded, my eyebrows raised. "Like what?"

"Look," she said, her eyes darting around the room. They settled on Aarush. "Most people think he doesn't feel anything. He does."

No argument there. "Go on."

"And Shaquille." I had to search the gym to find him.

"He has the ability to disappear, become invisible. He doesn't know it yet."

"Invisible? That's crazy."

"Is it, Grady? You didn't notice him when you first arrived. If he hadn't helped you out in the locker rooms that first day, you still wouldn't have known he was in class. Admit it; he melts into every crowd. He can fade away but hasn't realized his own potential."

"How do you know that?"

Lydia's lips firmed; then she spoke again. "I told you, I...I am an empath."

"Does Templeton know?"

She nodded.

"Why am I here?" The words popped out of my mouth before I could stop them.

"You don't know your own strength, Grady. Your capacity for power is stored in the same place as your loyalty and heart."

Not the answer I was looking for. Having x-ray vision or the power to freeze somebody solid seemed much more appealing. Yet I hadn't seen anything that unique in the school so far. Being an empath was nothing special. I had seen tons of stories about them on the *TLC* channel. I wasn't sure what I was expecting, but it wasn't this.

"What about Elwood?" I blurted.

Lydia turned to look at him. She grimaced, making her look as if she were in pain. "He has capacity too...only it's not stored in the same place as yours." She looked straight at me. "While he has great passion about it, it comes from his...you know ..."—she touched her stomach—"his solar plexus. He is stubborn as a rock." She turned to look at Bailey, who was deep in conversation with Kelsea. "Bailey is not comfortable in her own skin."

"Most of us aren't comfortable in our own skin."

"Yes, that is true, but her especially. She is not sure why."

"Do you know why?"

She looked at Bailey and replied, "Oh yes, it's obvious."

I glanced at Bailey and didn't see anything that was obvious. She was wrestling with another boy and had him in an admirable headlock. To me she seemed confident and secure with who she was.

Miss Garcia came over for our breathing exercises, and while I followed her lead, my mind kept replaying the conversation with Lydia over and over again.

Elwood wouldn't look at me. He had tripped me twice. The first time I fell so hard, I hit my lip, and now I had a faint white scar. Pari had admired it yesterday and said it made me look dangerous. There was bad blood between Elwood and me, of that I was sure. I didn't need Lydia to *feel* that. Maybe I was an empath too. Whenever Elwood and I did anything, whether it was in physical education or the cafeteria, we ended up squaring off against each other. I asked him once why he hated me so much.

Elwood sneered and looked at Aarush, then responded, "You are so dense, it's not funny."

I shrugged. Yes we were friends once, and now we were not. I don't know what it mattered so much to him.

You could cut the tension between me and Elwood with a knife at times, and to make it worse, the teachers only seemed to be watching us. I swear that Miss Parker gave me the creeps. Every time I found her gaze on me, my father's ring lit up with a life of its own. I had to remind myself it was coming from me and not caused by another person.

I caught Valencia Templeton observing us, but I could sense a smirk under her impassive face anytime Elwood won and I was at a disadvantage. I should have asked Lydia what she felt about the headmaster's daughter. Frankly, I found Valencia colder than Miss Parker, an epic feat if you ask me.

I know Elwood disappeared from our dorm room for a few days. Never said where he went, but he was smug as ever when he returned. He seemed hardened, unapproachable. He stopped speaking to me altogether.

One day, soon after the holiday break would have been at a normal school, he and his stuff vanished from our space. Not that I'm complaining, mind you. He was nastier than ever.

CHAPTER 18

HEAD GAMES

WE ALL KNEW the winter holidays had come and gone. We had lost track of time with the burden of the workload. My brain felt tired. I missed days off, talking about holiday food or celebrations, even though ours were pretty downplayed. I never appreciated them more.

Since there was no recognition of any celebrations, or even Saturday or Sunday, for that matter, time felt different. When you don't spend your hours planning for those special occasions of the year, the days take on a quality of sameness. Time simply wore on.

There was no real seasonal change either in our neck of the woods. The weather was either hot or hotter. No television shows to remind us of what we needed to buy. No pop-up ads on our devices showing delectable chocolates for that certain someone on a holiday. Truth be told, there was a lot less pressure when you didn't have to think about those things. I don't know about you, but it was easier for me not to worry about being a loser because I didn't have plans for New Year's Eve or be with someone on Valentine's Day.

Time marched on. There were no packages from home allowed. Some of the kids grumbled. Didn't matter much to me. We were nearing the end of the term. We would be sent home for four months. I guess that was part of the deal: the opportunity to go to the school of the millennium, eight solid months of study, four months of vacation. Seemed like a fair exchange to me.

I knew we were nearing mid-April, because Lydia announced it one day. I guess being an empath gave her some extra perks, like she knew what was going on outside, as well as the inside of the school.

I didn't feel the days passing. I don't want you to get the idea that I loved school. I enjoyed my friends. It was certainly easier without Elwood's sour face in our room. He was gone from our dorm to who knew where, and that was fine with me.

Miss Parker's classes were long episodes of writing and thinking, and thinking and writing. It felt as though we were learning nothing.

There were times when I saw evidence of other students in the school, but we never saw them or shared classes. The blue pennants hung in the commissary, notes would be on blackboards, assignments I never recognized, but of the other students, I saw nothing. Sometimes this school gave me a massive case of the chills. It was as if we shared the campus with ghosts.

We tried prodding Miss Parker into explaining where the rest of the student body was, or even another display of the magic or whatever you want to call it that she did on the first day, but she was immune to our demands.

She lectured walking back and forth, discussing the history of the world and the different regimes that were in power. I realized we had a theme here. Day after day she discussed civilizations: the Greeks, the Romans, the Phoenicians, the Malian, the Mayan, the Huns, and the British Empire. The list was endless. She moved through history, from the Middle Ages, to the Age of Exploration, to the Renaissance.

I saw a pattern. Society was determined by the person in power. They set the moral code for the country. If they enjoyed learning and growth, then universities flourished. If they felt threatened and feared an uprising, freedom, and knowledge were crushed. What this had to do with subconscious studies, I had no idea.

Today for some reason we talked about World War Two. "Can anyone tell me why Winston Churchill withheld the information that they had broken the Nazis' codes and allowed the bombings to continue to destroy his air force and country?"

I was baffled. Churchill's people had broken the German communication codes. He knew every move the enemy was going to make, each city that Germany planned to bomb, yet he didn't evacuate. It made no sense to me. He didn't move ships and planes to safety. I mean, they had deciphered the code for the German messages and did nothing to save the civilians.

Aarush raised his hand. Miss Parker nodded at him.

"He sacrificed the British population because if he revealed they had that information, the Nazis would find another way to communicate it, which would put the eventual end of the war in jeopardy."

"That's despicable," Pari muttered.

"Is it? Mr. Whill? Do you agree?" I looked back at her, feeling like a cornered animal.

"It's horrible," I stated. "But if he had revealed the information, the war would have not ended, and many more would have died." I paused, then added. "I think."

"Go on," Miss Parker said, her voice low.

I thought for a long moment. "War is terrible. Prolonging it is, or was, horrible. I guess he decided that sacrificing the few for the bigger population was his only option."

"I want to stress that war is never a good choice. It is the result of a failure of diplomacy." Miss Parker pushed away from the wall she was leaning on. "One must always exhaust negotiations before resorting to conflict." Somehow I had a niggling idea this lesson was not about history. It was about us.

She walked up and down the aisles of our room, passing each of our desks. "Being a leader or being a powerful person is a responsibility. Sometimes they will be called upon to decide impossible things."

Now, don't get me wrong; I heartily disliked this woman. But I looked up and saw her face locked on mine. She stared at me as if she had invaded my skull. I fidgeted with my stylus, wanting to look away, but her gaze held me, prisoner.

"Say, for instance, you were called upon to save the world. ..." We all laughed uncomfortably.

She walked toward Pari and rested her hands on Pari's shoulders. "Let's say the opposition had Miss Patel...and offered her as trade. One million lives for ..." She looked sideways at her with a slight smile. "One million lives for Pari. What would you do?"

I can tell you, most of us did not like where this conversation was going. We all squirmed in our seats.

I raised my hand reluctantly, then lowered it. I saw her hands tighten on Pari's shoulders. Fury surged through my body. This was Pari. I pushed my hand in the air. I had to answer. "I know what the response is supposed to be." I shook my head, adding, "I don't know if I could do it."

Something passed between Miss Parker and myself. It was strange. I heard Lydia gasp in the seat behind me. I stared at Miss Parker feeling like we were the only people in the room.

"I appreciate your honesty, Grady. It takes a brave person to give a truthful answer."

I jerked my head around to look at her. Miss Parker had called me by my first name. She had never done that before. That was actually the nicest thing she had ever said to me.

When I locked on her face all I could see was overwhelming sadness. "Sometimes"—her voice was hoarse—"a person is put in a situation where they must...they must decide what is more beneficial...saving a few or saving the world."

Lydia raised her hand. "What does this have to do with developing our inner powers, Miss Parker?"

Miss Parker seemed to shake off whatever she was thinking about and turned all efficient and frosty. "Once you have developed these abilities, decisions will be harder. You may find yourself placed in situations where you will have to do what is right for the greater good."

"So?" Forrest muttered.

"It may not match what is right in your heart."

The ring resting on my chest came to life, warming me, or maybe I was reacting to the subject. For the first time, I wanted to stay and ask more questions.

The bell rang, and we scrambled from the classroom. Everyone was happy to have lunch, followed by some free time. I paused by the exit and looked back. Miss Parker was staring out of her glass wall. I could have sworn I saw her wipe away a tear.

We were sunning ourselves on the beach after lunch and after Miss Parker's two-hour class. I was hot; however, our uniforms had a built-in cooling agent that wicked the perspiration from our skin. I never felt the heat, but today it bothered me. I kept glancing at Pari, feeling worried for her. "What do you think that was all about?" I asked Pari.

"It's usually about how leaders or governments came to power. She went off on a strange tangent today," she responded. "By the way, Grady. I absolutely refuse to let you choose me over the masses," she said with a laugh. "You must never let the forces of evil destroy mankind because of me." She was smiling as if it were a joke.

I don't know about anyone else, but I had a shiver of dread. I couldn't find my voice to answer her, the thought of a world without Pari was unthinkable.

I shook off the gloomy thoughts and replied something like, "It doesn't matter because *that's* never going to happen."

I was absently playing with a sand crab. I kept creating piles of sand, turning them into mountains. The crab climbed them, and I would shovel the sand out from under him, preventing his escape. The creature would fall into the valley my fingers created, slowly attempting to get away again. I kept up the activity for a while. I felt sorry for the crab and was close to letting the poor guy go.

"Yes," Aarush agreed. He had a tablet on and was scribbling equations with his stylus. "I prefer the lessons about recognizing the different methods they used to achieve control."

I shrugged, making yet another hill for the little crustacean to climb. I didn't want to admit that I was still rocked by the lesson or the thought that Miss Parker might have been crying.

"It's important. How are you to deal with leadership if you don't understand how the government works?" Aarush said.

Pari sat cross-legged against a sturdy palm. "Oh, let him go, already, Grady."

I looked up sharply.

"The crab. Let him go."

"He likes our game." I made another obstacle course for my new friend.

"It's all a game," Aarush said from his spot on a slight incline. I looked up at him. Aarush continued, "You see, everything is about strategy. Like chess. Miss Parker is teaching us to get into the minds of other people so we can anticipate their moves. Like Churchill today."

"I'm not in the mind of my little crab here," I said. "But I can guess which way he is going to go. Watch." I shoveled a new mound, interfering with the direction he was walking. "See? I don't have to know…*owww*!" I yelled, grabbing my wrist and holding up my hand. The crab dangled from my thumb, his pincer locked on the flesh of my finger. I shook him off. He fell onto the sand with a plop and took off toward the shimmering water. I cut off his escape with my tablet, blocking him efficiently.

Pari laughed. Aarush looked at me with astonishment. "How did you not anticipate that, Grady?"

"Oh, and you knew the crab was going to attack my thumb? What are you, a crab whisperer?"

"Indeed," Aarush answered. "The claws are his defensive mechanism. It was only a matter of time before he got tired of your game and used them. You don't have to be a crab expert to know that. It's a matter of knowing the nature of your opponent and giving yourself the advantage of understanding how they will react. It's simple, Grady."

"Yeah, real simple." I stood and brushed off the sand. The school uniforms were amazing material. Nothing stuck to them. I swear, I could wear one for two weeks and you'd never know it wasn't freshly cleaned. Not that I would, I mean. I could if I wanted to.

"Let's go." Aarush gathered his books.

Pari's tablet had rolled down a small dune, the result of my sand-sifting, fencing the crab on two sides.

"I'll get it," I said. I was responsible after all. I reached down to grab the tablet, and a booted foot stepped onto the computer. I looked up to see Elwood leering at me. He ground his foot, tearing the protective cover of the computer. "Stop!" I tried to pull it out from under Elwood's sole. It was as if he were made of granite, he was that heavy. I rose and met him eye to eye. I hadn't seen him much. After one too many disruptions, he had been pulled out of our gym class.

"Do you know what I'm thinking, Grady?" Elwood sneered. His skin had a grayish quality, as if he never saw sunshine. I ignored him and continued to pull the tablet.

It wouldn't budge. "Didn't you listen to Autism Man? Put yourself in my head and you'll know how to anticipate my next move."

"I can't. There's no room in there with all the rocks between your ears." Maybe not the best answer, I decided when I saw his face go all stony.

Elwood's fingers grabbed my wrist in a punishing grip. It was like being squeezed by a vice. I struggled against his hold. My body filled with rage, when I felt Elwood slip.

Aarush stood behind him, his knee bent forward into Elwood's leg, which gave out, collapsing underneath him. He fell, landing with a thud on the soft sand, freeing the computer. I picked it up.

"Thanks for distracting him, Grady," Aarush said happily. "You must have anticipated Elwood was so intent, he wouldn't notice me."

I didn't answer. I looked down at Elwood, my lips thinning in anger. I saw only one thing now. My crab lay squashed. It had been under the tablet.

I was so angry, I couldn't see straight. I wished I could feel that power again in my chest and arms. I tried to inhale deeply but ended up hacking away.

I stalked through the halls, furious I hadn't punched Elwood in the face. I paused by the obelisk and stared up at the neatly lettered quatrain on the stone. The room was empty, and my harsh breathing echoed in the chamber. I looked up at the message. *Failure is good.*

I had failed today, miserably. I felt guilty about the

dead crab—not that it was a pet or anything, but the sheer cold-heartedness of Elwood bothered me.

I sighed gustily, feeling the familiar tightness in my chest, gasping when Miss Parker eased around the corner of the stone pillar. She studied me, her head tilting quizzically, freezing me to the spot. The ring heated up under my shirt.

"What do you want from me?" I demanded.

"What do you think, Grady?" She didn't deny wanting something, and even stranger, she called me by my first name for the second time that day. I watched her with the same wariness as one observes a snake. She walked around me, stopping so we were eye to eye. I was taller than her now. "You don't believe in yourself," she said in a fierce whisper.

"You don't know that," I rasped back.

"You have no idea how much I know."

"Why do you hate me?"

"Sometimes what we see is only a reflection of our own thoughts and insecurities."

Well, that made no sense. She walked away. I spun to watch her, confusion overwhelming me. Miss Parker was smiling.

I related the conversation to Pari, Aarush, and the rest of my friends at dinner.

"Interesting," Aarush commented. "It's not about what they are projecting so much as what your own mind is imposing on them."

"In other words," Pari interjected between bites of vegetarian chili, "you think that she dislikes you, so that's what you see."

"Perhaps, because you believe she is not fond of you, you

communicate that attitude to her and it reflects back towards you," Lydia added.

Oh, enough already. Sometimes a fish is a fish. Miss Parker never liked me. "Wait a second," I said. "From day one, she was cold to me."

"Maybe she was responding to what vibes you were giving her," Bailey added, her brow raised.

Great. Now all of a sudden it's my fault.

"Maybe it is," Lydia said, patting my arm. I hadn't realized I'd spoken out loud again. I was sure I had this time. "You're bristling. I can feel your anger. Perhaps your reaction to her is based on something else?"

Maybe it is, I thought, keeping my mouth shut. If the ring grew hotter each time Miss Parker passed, was it trying to warn me? Could it have made me defensive? Crap, I was back to giving the ring superpowers. I was supposed to be the one getting those.

Valencia Templeton entered the cafeteria. Her presence always put a damper on conversation. I didn't especially like her either. Her demeanor was so cold, they made Miss Parker appear downright warm and fuzzy.

I touched my ring. Strangely, it was stone cold. I rested my hand on my chest. I felt hatred for Elwood over the beach incident, and my ring didn't heat up once. Maybe I did have it all wrong. I bit my lip. Was the ring warning me, or was it all in my head?

The bell rang, indicating it was time to move to our next classes. I watched Valencia make her way across the room. She motioned to Elwood who stood, dutifully following her out of the cafeteria.

Aarush and I volunteered to clean up the chem lab once a week. I didn't mind. It brought back memories of working there together during middle school.

Aarush and I organized the supplies. Aarush's idea of tidiness was putting things on the shelves in alphabetical order. Who was I to quibble? I found it restful, and Aarush would explain what all the tools were. Oh, I know a beaker from a flask. It gave Aarush and me time to play with the Bunsen burners and other assorted glassware.

"What do you think your power is going to be, Aarush?" I asked in what I thought was an offhand manner.

"Not sure yet, Grady. I think I am here to learn my weaknesses. Once I acknowledge them, I will know the answer to your question."

I wanted to say something. I wanted to be strong. Fierce and strong. He made me sound petty and juvenile.

"Yeah," I responded. "That sounds about right."

"Yes. All this failure is like...stepping stones to success," Aarush said.

I mulled the idea over, then asked. "So you are saying you need failure to achieve your dreams?"

Aarush arched a brow. "I thought it was obvious. Why else would failure be good? It's a necessary component to making us smarter and stronger." He picked up a tray of test tubes and went to the sink. "I'll wash?" The teacher, Mr. Neaman, had asked us to make sure things were cleaned.

"Sure," I responded, feeling somewhat lighter. Maybe I wasn't such a failure? "You start. I'll get it after I finish putting away this junk."

I reached for a bunch of stuff spread across the stone top of the workstation. I saw the blood before I even felt the sting of the cut. "*Ow!*" I grabbed my hand and saw a neat slice across my finger.

Aarush rushed over with a wet towel. I have to say it was a lot of blood for one little digit. He grabbed my hand and dragged me to the sink, where he ran the cut under cold water.

"Did you get any chemicals on it?" he asked in that calm way. "Grady, did you touch anything?"

"What? No. What did I touch?"

Aarush left my hand under running water. He went to the station and slid the razor blade off the desk. "This. You have to be more observant," he said.

"Write a quatrain about it," I told him. I pulled my finger out from under the faucet. The skin was puckered from the water, the blood sluggish. Aarush ran to a cabinet and returned with a bandage. He really was a good friend.

"Where are you going?" I asked.

He held a stack of *X-Acto* blades in his hand, blade side exposed and away from his skin. "I am stacking this on this shelf under the letter *X* so you won't carve yourself up anymore."

"Aarush, did you just make a joke?"

"Yes, I did, didn't I?" He laughed, and I joined him in cleaning up the rest of the mess.

CHAPTER 19

A NEW QUATRAIN

I DISLIKED SUBCONSCIOUS STUDIES class. It felt like a cold war had developed between Miss Parker and me. Any of the warm fuzzies had vanished after that day in the hallway by the obelisk. Need a lesson about trusting your instincts? Something was off about that woman. I couldn't figure out what. Either way, thinking about it made me tired. I slept like I'd worked in a coal mine every night.

"Grady." Aarush was shaking me awake one morning. I rose, bleary-eyed. "Come on, you must see it," he urged.

I threw off the covers, yawning. I hadn't slept well...again.

"A new quatrain. There's a new quatrain this morning." Aarush was throwing on clothes.

"What does it say?" I asked, suddenly alert.

"Let's go. I read only the first line. I want to study it."

Aarush was out the door. I thought he was gone, but then I found him waiting for me in the common room, shaking with impatience.

"Come on," I said, and he took off, with me right behind him. We raced through the halls, heedless of the other students. I swear I think Aarush might have even giggled.

The hallways were crowded, the level of excitement measured by the high volume of all the voices. Indeed, there were four new sentences underneath the one about failure. Students milled around the base, copying the new quatrain. Pari and the rest of our friends clustered in a spot and waved us both over.

Somebody bumped into me, hard, shoving me into the crowd gathered before me. The students pushed back with an annoyed curse. The boy directly in front of me elbowed my rib cage.

"Hey!" I shouted, turning around.

There was no one there. I jumped from foot to foot and saw a door close, Elwood Bledsoe's head disappearing into the dark interior. *Ugh. Elwood Bledsoe up to his old tricks*, I thought.

I pulled out my tablet and jockeyed for a position to read the words. I couldn't see them over the mob. Pari dictated the new sentences.

"Do not pass judgment on another's choices. You must understand their options first. Judging a person doesn't define them. It tells others exactly who you are."

Hundreds of students repeated the new statements. I felt my ring heat up. I didn't have to look to know that Miss Parker was watching me.

We entered the cafeteria, our babbling at a fever pitch. Our group sat together, debating the new quatrain.

"It's self-explanatory," Bailey stated.

"It's the same concept that you can judge a person by who they are, by looking at the company they keep," I said, dismissing the quatrain. "It's nothing profound."

"No, it doesn't say that," Bailey responded. "You have it all wrong, Grady. The quatrain is quite clear. You have to learn about people's backgrounds, their lives, to understand what makes them make their decisions."

Pari nodded her head. "Bailey is right. The way you judge someone's actions tells everyone exactly who you are."

"That makes no sense." Shaquille was sitting next to me. I jumped five feet into the air.

"Shaquille, man. Make a little noise when you sit next to a person. You scared the—"

"You see, you're doing it right now." Aarush pointed to me with his stylus. "You are finding fault with the way Shaquille moves around rather than accepting that the problem is yours."

I looked from Shaquille to Aarush blankly.

"Shaquille is not acting out of character," Aarush said simply.

"Neither am I," I said defensively.

Aarush inclined his head and replied, "Maybe you should both examine why you do things the way you do."

"Well," I said in a huff because it was the only response that came to my feeble defense.

"This is going to require me to have to rethink every perception I have," Forrest said.

Forrest was also an empath, but unlike his sister who could

see things, he heard things in people's voices, the way they spoke. Well, I thought, if the empaths were having to rethink all their perceptions, where did that leave the rest of us?

Forrest never said much. I didn't ask him to explain. I nodded in agreement so I wouldn't look as stupid as I felt.

I didn't think it was possible, but I realized I liked quatrain two less than I used to like quatrain one. This stuff was hard on the brain.

"If it were easy, don't you think everybody would do it?" Bailey demanded. I had that strange feeling she was tramping through my thoughts again.

CHAPTER 20

PERCEPTION DECEPTION

*T*HE SCHOOL WAS strangely subdued, most students exchanging excited whispers about the new quatrain. The teachers walked around as if they'd given us the answers to the universe, their expressions smug. I even saw Dr. Templeton roaming the corridors, smiling and nodding like the emperor of the realm.

I walked through the halls, deep in thought. The quatrains were a disappointment, to say the least. I didn't know what I expected from the school. Maybe their idea of a superhero didn't jibe with what I had in mind. If I wasn't going to learn to leap from building to building or lift cars, maybe it wasn't the right fit for me.

I know Aarush was happy. Most people wouldn't see it, but I could tell. He was deep in his studies, enjoying the lessons like they were new revelations. Most of it seemed like it was going right over my head.

I stuffed my hand into my pants pocket to run my fingers on the reassuring feel of my inhaler and felt a strip of paper. Still walking, I pulled it out. It was a ribbon of white paper torn off a sheet with a sentence typed on it. I paused in the hallway and ducked into a corner to look at it.

It lay curled in my palm. I straightened it out and read, "Do not pass judgment on another's choices." *Ah, quatrain two.* I smirked. I turned it over and realized there was more on the other side. "Meet me tonight—the chem lab—midnight.

I walked toward a trash can, stopping when I remembered Elwood's retreating figure. I balled my fist, the strip of paper in the center, and stuffed it into my pocket.

The day passed at an agonizing crawl. Dinner, and finally lights went out precisely at nine p.m.

I could hear Aarush fumble with his book, reading in a small pool of light. He was obsessing about the new quatrain all afternoon and into the evening. If I had to hear one more time about the simple brilliance of it, I would scream.

I was afraid to tell him about the note. Aarush would first try to talk me out of going, and then when he couldn't he would insist on going *with* me. I couldn't worry about him getting hurt. No, I was sure I had to do this on my own.

I waited in bed for his breathing to deepen. Moonlight painted bright stripes on the dark walls of our bedroom. It was a full moon tonight.

I pulled off my pajamas and slid into my uniform, grabbed my rescue inhaler, and stuffed it into my pocket. I took out the strip of paper and looked at the instructions before placing it back into my pocket. As I bent down to put on my sneakers, my asthma inhaler dropped onto the floor with a loud thump. I cursed softly, scooped it up, then darted a glance at my sleeping friend. It was time to go. I booked out of the room.

The halls were deserted. There was a strange kind of echo when I walked in the empty corridors. I picked up speed and climbed the three-story staircase to the science area. It was located toward the top of the building in one of the northern-most towers.

I opened the fire door to look down the darkened hallway. There were no lights on. I ran to the chemistry lab and opened the door slowly. It was pitch dark in the room. I banged into a chair, causing a loud racket.

"Are you sure about this, Miss Templeton?" I heard Elwood say with a bored voice. The lights snapped on, and I was staring at Valencia Templeton, Elwood Bledsoe, and Lucas Reinholt. Elwood looked taller, more formidable. Lucas looked equally formidable.

Elwood moved toward me, his stance aggressive, and I backed away. Elwood's laugh seemed a little forced to me. I opened my mouth to mention it but paused when Valencia held up her hand. She shook her head. We both stood still. With a long red-clad leg she shoved a chair in my direction.

"Have a seat, Grady."

"Really?" Elwood turned to her, his face reddening. "Do we really want—?"

Valencia smiled and walked past him. "Quiet, Elwood. He came. He's here. This could be a good start. He must have liked tasting superior power."

My mind instantly raced back to that strange day in the

hallway when I felt energy surge through me. *I hadn't imagined it! It was her?*

She watched, examining me as if I was some sort of oddity. *Well, compared to some of the kids in this place, maybe I am.* "You showed great courage to come here. Just what we are looking for, right?"

I sat down, feeling edgy and uncomfortable. *Courage?* Maybe more like stupidity. I bit my bottom lip. *What was I thinking to follow some hair-brained note in the middle of the night?*

"Are you happy here?" Valencia leaned down and looked at me eye to eye. "Do you think the school has lived up to its promises?"

I swallowed convulsively and pulled my gaze away.

"That won't work with me, my boy." Her long red nail touched my cheek and forced me to look at her. "Are you happy with the course of studies?" she repeated.

I raised an eyebrow. "It's not what I was expecting."

Valencia walked to the other side of the room and started pacing. "Yes, Grady, it's not what you were expecting. Many of us are not satisfied."

Elwood planted his feet in a wide stance, crossed his arms over his bulging chest, and nodded in agreement. Lucas mirrored his movements. They looked like bookends.

"You see, when the Codex was discovered, a curriculum was created."

"By whom?" I asked.

Valencia looked at me sharply and answered quickly, "It doesn't matter."

I shrugged. "I'm not even sure of the value of the Codex."

"I told you you're wasting your time," Elwood sneered.

"The Codex is the secret to powers beyond your imagination."

"'Do not pass judgment on another's choices. You must understand their options first. Judging a person doesn't define them. It tells others exactly who you are,'" I quoted. "And let's not forget the irreverent 'failure is good' quatrain. I'm thinking it's all a bunch of crap."

"Sacrilege," Valencia said, mocking me and shaking her head. "You don't understand it because it hasn't been utilized the right way. They are boring you to death."

I couldn't argue with her there.

"The Codex was meant to be used, embraced, followed. My father ..." She made a disgusted sound, turning her head away. "He doesn't want to *abuse* the Codex." She said the word *abuse* with disdain, but before I could remark on it, she went on, "He wants it studied first." She paused and added almost in an undertone, "He's afraid of it."

"Why?" I asked quickly.

Valencia didn't answer, but she did look troubled. She stared at the floor lost in some old memory. Finally, she gave a good long shudder that did nothing for my confidence in the Codex.

I waited until she took a deep breath and asked, "What's wrong with it?"

"He's losing you." She went on as though she hadn't heard me. "He's lost hundreds of potential specimens...all gone because he spent so much time dissecting unnecessarily. Join us, Grady." She was leaning over me again, both her hands holding the armrest, imprisoning me. "We need the Codex. Join us tonight as I take it and use it the way your father intended."

The room went silent, narrowing to the two of us. She was so close. I could see every pore in her skin. *Wait...what?* I came out of my stupor.

"What? Whose father?" I asked, my voice cracking. Was she talking about my father, or did she have a screw loose?

"Miss Templeton...Valencia...there is no time. If he doesn't agree, we can't let him go," the ever-helpful Elwood offered, interrupting me.

Elwood rummaged in a metal cabinet and returned with a coil of nylon rope. He dropped a cord around my chest. I attempted to rise, but he slammed me into the seat. His hands were like blocks of stone. In a manner of seconds my wrists were bound to the armrests.

"Show him, Elwood," said Miss Templeton. "Show him what the Codex has taught you."

Elwood went in front of me and posed like he was a body-builder. I nodded as if I were bored, stopping when I realized his skin color was changing. I watched as the surface of his body turned gray, the skin taking on the consistency of granite, or maybe, it was basalt. I couldn't tell the difference.

Elwood laughed. His face looked angular, carved from stone. He clomped around the room, surprisingly agile for a walking statue.

"What the...?"

"Yes." Valencia stood tall. "Now, watch Lucas."

Lucas closed his eyes, and his body turned into quicksilver...or *water?* There was a small puddle at his feet. His skin shone like metal. Well, most of it did. One arm remained stubbornly human-looking. I watched his face concentrating, but the flesh refused to change.

"Concentrate, Lucas," Elwood ordered. "Remember quatrain one. *Failure is good.*"

Here we go again with the failure business, I thought, rolling my eyes.

"I'm trying." Lucas's voice sounded thin, like it was being squeezed out from a small place.

"Oh, enough, Lucas." Valencia sounded impatient.

"How did they do that?" My voice was nothing more than a squeak.

Even without the full morphing, it was pretty awesome. But I was pretty sure I didn't want what Valencia was offering. There had to be a catch, and it couldn't be good. I was still ruminating on the *father* part of our conversation.

She leaned close and whispered in my ear, "I can teach you things you never believed were possible. You will be a god among mortals, like the ancient Greeks." Her voice was rising.

I stopped listening when the restraints were put on. While my mind struggled with the mention of my father, I was more concerned about what I thought was Valencia's disintegrating mental health. Tying up students didn't make for a good lesson plan. They clamped my hands together with a zip tie.

The ring on my chest pulsed to life. She backed away as if it burned her, the expression on her face filled with...fear?

"You don't believe me?" she shrieked. "There is no time for me to prove myself to you. My father has become drunk on his own power. He won't share the Codex the way it was meant to be. 'Do not pass judgment on *my* choices!'" She was shouting. "You must understand the options first. You are judging me on my father's perceptions!"

I didn't know what she was talking about. She must have realized that because next she spat. "He's still under Parker's influence." She was raving. *Wait*, I thought. *Fathers again.* Did she mean *her father* or *my father*?

"I would like you to clarify—" I started, but she was screaming now.

"This means nothing to him! We are wasting our time!" She leaned closer. "This is my time. The Codex will be mine."

She drew herself up to her considerable height and swept herself from the room. She snapped those long fingers, and a ball of fire appeared on the granite lab countertop.

"Finish what I started." She spun, and to my astonishment, she vanished from the room.

Elwood and Lucas were casually ripping pages from a book, creating a ring of fire around my chair. Lucas broke a chair and stuffed papers under the wood like a campfire. Smoke stung my eyes. My jaw must have dropped. Wait... they were going to *roast* me?

"Elwood...what is going on?" I demanded. "This can't be for real."

Elwood's grayish muscles flexed impressively. "You could have learned how to do that," he said.

"Why would I want to?" I shot back, sweat pouring down my face.

He put his hand into the flames, a wicked grin on his face. "I'm impervious. And that's from only half the Codex. This is just the beginning." He looked down at me and clicked his tongue. "Well, the beginning for some of us. For others, it's the end."

"You're not leaving me here, Elwood!" I shouted. "Elwood! Lucas! Where are you going?"

He stomped to the door and turned before he left. "You

still haven't figured it out, Whilliboy? We are going to steal the Codex."

"The monolith?"

"No, you idiot. The book, hidden in Templeton's vault, under the school." He looked at me as if I were a slug. "It's wasted on people like you." He slammed the door, and the glass shattered like a waterfall on the floor.

The room grew hot, the heat from the fire scorching me. It was getting hard to breathe. The flames surrounded me. I struggled against the bonds holding me to the seat. I rocked the chair hard. It teetered, then fell with a jarring crash. I tried to fill my lungs with good air; they felt squashed, constricted. My hands were growing numb.

I was on the floor, my face inches from the searing flames. I coughed, the smoke thick above me, the floor hot below me. Twisting my wrists, I felt my lungs heave and couldn't pull air into my chest.

Where are the smoke alarms in this place? Someone is going to take this up with the local fire department. Wait! There is no fire department! I knew then I was doomed. No fire department, no cavalry to rescue me. Where were the *freakin'* alarms? What kind of place was this?

I had nothing—nothing except the first quatrain.

I started reciting it as I struggled against the bonds holding me. "*Do not fear failure. Failure makes us stronger. Failure makes us smarter. Failure is good. Do not fear failure. Failure makes us stronger. Failure makes us smarter. Failure is good.*"

The wood from the chair crackled and burned.

I lay on the floor, watching the clouds of smoke rise above me, hoping it would set off the smoke alarm. I was frozen in fear. *I am going to die unless I start moving.*

Well, I was proving I was pretty good at one thing at Templeton Academy. Too bad I excelled at failure. I rested my head against the floor and felt tears pricking my eyes. I was failing miserably. Tears clouded my vision. *Don't fear failure!* I wanted to shout.

Aarush's words came rushing back to me. *Use failure as a tool, a stepping stone.* A tool. Use failure as a tool. When you fail at one thing, try another.

Using my knees, I pushed my body toward the teacher's desk. I couldn't get far, and the growing fire was in the way. *Think!* I ordered myself. *Think!*

The heat from the flames seared the air near my head. This wasn't working. I twisted my neck, looking for anything to help me.

The supply shelves stood against the wall on the other side of the room, shelves that Aarush and I had stocked yesterday. Sweat poured down my face. My palms dripped. The cut on my finger burned from the dampness. Balling my hands into fists, I felt the injury I'd gotten earlier split. Warm blood coated my skin. *My cut opened up*, I thought stupidly, and then the X-acto-blades came into my head. Where had Aarush put them? I looked up at the shelving. They were in the *X* section on the shelf. Maybe he put them in the *R* section for razor, I couldn't remember!

I rocked myself, forcing the chair to roll over awkwardly. I landed with a bone-jarring crash, my head banging hard on the floor. I think I saw stars for a minute, but I knew time was critical. I forced myself to focus, rocked myself again, and rolled another foot. The room was getting hotter. Someone had to hear what was going on. The question was would I be toast before they got here?

I strained against the bonds on my chest and the ties binding my wrists, the chair making choppy progress across the room. Finally, I slammed into the shelving, and supplies rained down on me. The pointy razor clattered to the floor next to my hand, the sharp blade sliding into position. I grabbed the handle of the blade awkwardly.

It slid from my hand, the blood making it hard to hold. I stretched my fingers, but the razor evaded my grasp. My two fingers could not maneuver onto the blade to pick it up. I was going to smother in a minute from the smoke. *Think. Failure is good. Think how to overcome this failure.* I slid my finger on the dusty floor, impaling my pointer finger on the opened blade. I gasped from the pain and got a lungful of smoke.

My sore finger split open. It didn't matter. I gripped the handle and eased it from my flesh. I maneuvered the blade under the plastic tie and sawed like crazy. I cut the bindings, repeating the quatrain over and over again. Feelings rushed into my limbs as soon as they were freed. I worked the ropes imprisoning my feet.

When I got up, the door of the room burst open. Aarush was holding a fire extinguisher, spraying retardant onto the flames. The white powder arrested the growing fire until all that was left was smoke and charred bits of paper on the floor. Aarush was showering with the fire extinguisher a little too enthusiastically. The fire was out. "Enough." I held up my hand. "You killed it."

"Are you okay? he asked, his glasses askew. He was wearing a pajama shirt with his uniform bottoms.

"Valencia," I gasped. "She's going to steal the Codex."

"The stone monument?" Aarush looked up quizzically.

He said the same thing as me. That made me feel good.

"No, the actual book."

"That's crazy. Why would she do something like that?"

I coughed for a bit, then answered, "She's nuts. We've got to warn Dr. Templeton."

We ran toward the staircase. "There's no time. We have to stop them," I said. We raced down the steps, our feet making hollow sounds in the empty stairwell. My finger dripped blood, leaving a slippery trail. "How did you find me?"

"You dropped a strip of paper on the floor saying to meet someone here. When I heard you leave, I found it and followed you. Why does she want to steal the Codex?"

"Because she's pure evil," a female voice said at the bottom of the steps.

Miss Parker stood at the last landing, her face grim. I skidded to a halt. She reached out to steady me, but I flinched.

She sniffed the air. "Was there a fire?"

"Yeah, and no alarms," I said. "Boy, are you guys in trouble."

"Of course there are alarms. She must have tampered with them."

Aarush nodded in agreement. "That's not the only thing she's tampered with."

Miss Parker lowered her hand. "Quickly! Tell me what you know."

We stood staring at each other, and I growled, "Why should I tell you anything?" I had a healthy distrust of Miss Parker.

"Grady says she's after the Codex," the ever-trusting Aarush blurted.

"Aarush, stop!" I turned to her. "How do I know you're not after it too?"

"You don't." She touched my temple, where a bruise was

blooming courtesy of my fall. My skin tingled. "I guess this is where you'll have to trust your instincts."

"The last time I trusted my instincts with you, I had my hands wrapped around someone else's neck. Besides, I don't even know what the Codex is," I shouted, panting. I dug into my pocket and pulled out the spray. I inhaled deeply. It caused a fit of coughing.

"It's a book. A secret book. Your father found it, and now we have to stop her. Whoever has that book will rule the world."

Again my father! I looked up at Miss Parker, the blood draining from my face. I staggered. "Did...did you say...*my father?*" My hand was throbbing now.

"There's no time for that now, Grady," she answered.

Oh sure, there's never time for that! I wanted to yell, but I knew she was right.

"We have to get Dr. Templeton," Aarush interrupted.

I was still processing her mentioning my father.

"Come on!" she shouted. Miss Parker took off. Aarush followed me as we ran.

CHAPTER 21

WTH

MISS PARKER DID indeed know her way around the school. Using a special key, she was able to get us into a part of the building I had never seen. We went down past the level of Dr. Templeton's office and entered a lounge area.

"Sit there," she ordered, gesturing toward a trio of leather couches. I sat down and felt myself sink into the deep cushions.

Miss Parker returned a minute later with a cloth and some spray. She took my hand, and not gently either, I have to say. She cleaned the blood and then sprayed a liquid on my finger. A film covered my wound, changing into skin instantly.

Aarush watched with great interest. "I've heard about this. Is it synthetic?"

Miss Parker shook her head. "No." She held my hand in the air to dry. "It's actually Grady's spray. I requested it when I saw him. It's made of his DNA."

"My DNA?" I looked at my hand. Skin was growing over the cut. "Cool."

"We each have one," she informed us as if having a personal can of regenerated tissue available was normal.

"Don't you remember the DNA samples they took?" Aarush asked.

"Well, in anticipation of next year's studies and the possible injuries, we created individual repair kits for each of the students."

I would have kept staring at it but was distracted by Dr. Templeton's entrance. He was holding a book under his arm. *The Book.* It was old, like one of those manuscripts you'd see in an action movie, with thick, warped pages and a rusty clasp holding it shut.

"I didn't see you call anyone," I said watching them. Still, Templeton was here, and apparently so was the book.

"You couldn't have seen me," Miss Parker answered cryptically, still busy with my hand.

"Yes, Grady, she does it up here." Aarush pointed to his head. "Dr. Templeton, Valencia has gone crazy. She's stealing the Codex."

"Impossible," he said, his face pale. "As you can see, it's right here."

I sat up. *Is he talking to me? Maybe they are all crazy.*

"Grady?" Miss Parker looked at me. "Tell Dr. Templeton everything."

They joined us on the sofa. Dr. Templeton rested the heavy book on his knees.

"I didn't actually see a book, but Dr. Templeton...I mean Valencia...said she had it. They tried to kill me."

"She wouldn't do that, my boy. Valencia may be high-spirited—"

Miss Parker stood up, outraged. "High-spirited!" she shouted. "Clifford, she almost killed this boy! She's coveted the Codex for years!"

He tapped the dusty cover with his palm. "But she has nothing, Erin. We have the Codex. It's safe. The boy is safe. Remember quatrain two: *Never judge because of the choices— unless you know their options. Judging a person doesn't define who they are. It defines who you are.*"

"Enough, Clifford! You are always making excuses for her. Elwood Bledsoe is completely in her thrall."

"He was there tonight? With her?" he asked me, his gaze direct and piercing.

I nodded. "And Lucas Reinholt. They changed. Elwood became hard, like he was made of stone, and Lucas turned into water or some sort of liquid, I think." I wanted to add I always thought that kid was a drip but figured it was not a good time for humor.

Dr. Templeton looked lost for a second.

"Clifford," said Miss Parker, "she's advanced them to morphing. She's dangerous. She must have a copy of the Codex."

"Too complicated, the nuances. One has to work with the real thing. You know that, Erin. She's merely flexing her wings."

Miss Parker made an impatient sound. "Shall we consider quatrain three, then?" she asked, her eyes bright with tears.

Aarush perked up. "I'd like to know what it is."

"Enough." Templeton stood. He walked over to Miss Parker. There was a history here, of that I was sure. "Erin." He placed his hands on her shoulders. "She'll wear herself out and come back. We mustn't let this break us apart. We are so close to finishing the term. One hundred forty-seven students made it through." He smiled. "More than we could have ever hoped for."

I did the quick math, but before I could answer, Aarush responded, "That means fifty-eight Weribus are still here. We beat them," he added with pride.

"There is no competition here," Dr. Templeton addressed him. "You've been working next to each other the entire semester."

Aarush sat down abruptly. "How can that be possible?" He looked up at the doctor, his glasses sliding down his nose. "Don't tell me a parallel universe?"

Dr. Templeton smiled indulgently. "You've found us out, my boy. But that is for next year when you'll meet your classmates and learn to work with them."

"Enough!" Miss Parker shouted. "Valencia has to be stopped." She turned to look at Dr. Templeton. It was as if we weren't in the room.

Personally, I was still bothered by all this talk about my father, not to mention nobody seemed to care that Valencia had tried to barbeque me. Now add in some kind of atom-splitting or something. It was too much.

"She tried to kill Grady," Miss Parker whispered. "She set a fire."

"Erin. I didn't hear an alarm. I'm sure there is some sort of explanation. He has a longstanding feud with the Bledsoe boy. Maybe she used the power of suggestion." He raised his eyebrows.

"Dr. Templeton! He smells like smoke!"

While I watched Miss Parker and Dr. Templeton, Aarush

moved to the other couch. I turned to see him touch the book with reverence. We both looked back at the adults, who were busy arguing. Miss Parker said something about the Patels.

Aarush's head was down, and I heard the sound of his turning pages. "Grady," he whispered. "Grady …"

I looked at him. "What?"

"The book. Look at the book."

I glanced down. The Codex was splayed open on his knees. Both sides of the pages were blank. I turned the page, then riffled through the rest. They were all blank.

The adults must have overheard because when I looked up, they were staring at us, their faces bleached of color.

"The Codex …" Aarush said.

"No!" Dr. Templeton looked like the air had been deflated from him.

"Valencia has it," said Miss Parker. "Where is she, Clifford?"

The ground took this time to shake and open a large fissure across the floor. Miss Parker cried out. Aarush and I jumped up. "It's an earthquake!" I yelled.

"She's activating the volcano," Miss Parker exclaimed.

"Volcano?" Aarush repeated. "There are no volcanoes here."

Dr. Temepleton shook his head. "We created one in case we had to destroy the island."

Destroy the island? Who were these people?

"Evacuate the building. I know where she is," Miss Parker said grimly.

I followed her toward the door. She held out a hand. "Where are you going?" she yelled.

"I think you'll need help."

She opened her mouth to say *no*, of course.

"Miss Parker," I said over the roar of another earthquake, "allow me to follow my instincts."

It was a great moment between us, but I have to say, Miss Parker ruined it for me. She shook her head sadly and replied, "Not going to happen. Help get the students out of the school."

I blinked and she was gone. She vanished, leaving me wondering how I was supposed to accomplish her order when I could see only half of the students.

CHAPTER 22

FOLLOWING MY INSTINCTS

DR. TEMPLETON HIT an intercom, and the voice on the other end came to groggy life. "Gwennie, Samuel, Code Five. Summon the ships. We must evacuate the island."

Nobody answered. A siren blared. "Alert the students." Dr. Templeton wobbled on his feet. I went to steady him, but he stood tall, and I could see strength flood into his limbs. He took off for the door.

Aarush and I rushed through the corridors to the dorm area. Aarush ran to his room.

"Where are you going?" I demanded as he took off.

"I need a magic marker," Aarush said.

"Oh," I responded as if that explained everything.

We split up. The doctor ran into the Weribus side while I pounded on the doors of the Kashinka housing. I wasn't sure how he intended to alert people in an alternate universe, but what do I know?

Pari emerged, rubbing her face.

"We have to evacuate," I told her. "Grab Lydia, Kelsea, and Bailey and get out. They summoned a ship."

I ran to the next dorm door and repeated the message. The students were fast. We had rehearsed for these kinds of emergencies, never thinking the procedure would ever be used.

Aarush and I met outside in the center hall. The floor rocked as another explosion burst outside. I saw a crowd emerge, all wearing blue bracelets. "How did you...you know...get to them?" I asked incredulously.

"Oh, it was easy. I wrote a note on the wall of their rec room." He held up his magic marker; the tip was crushed. "Once they read it, I guess the teacher was able to move them in sync with us."

"That explains a lot," I said sarcastically.

"Well, when we have an hour or two, I'll tell you how I think it works."

"Never mind." I motioned to the group. "Go with them." I pushed Aarush toward the students and teachers filing out. I headed in the other direction.

"Grady? Where are you going?" Aarush called.

Without thinking, I responded, "I've got to help her."

"You've picked a great time to discover confidence. Let the grown-ups handle this."

"Aarush, you're turning into a regular comedian," I laughed. I couldn't understand, but I knew I had to help Miss Parker. I had so many questions.

"We will do this together," Aarush said firmly.

I opened my mouth to tell him no, then snapped it shut. There was no arguing with Aarush when he had an idea.

We raced to the door, darting between students, and zipped down the gangway to stand in the marshy sand. The night sky was lit up by belching fire from the volcano behind the school. Aarush and I took off following the tangled path. I heard footsteps pounding behind me and spun. Pari ran into me, followed by Lydia, Shaquille, Bailey, and Forrest.

"This is not a school trip!" I yelled. "Go back!"

Forrest pulled his sister to leave, but she stood firm. He shook her head. "I have a bad feeling, Lyddie."

"I don't," Lydia shot back. "We help them. Lead the way, Grady."

Our desert island took this time to turn into a tropical rainforest. The sky opened up and it poured.

The rain spit down on us as we stumbled from the paved road toward the rocky path. "Go back!" I shouted to my friends. "We have to help Miss Parker!"

Bailey shook her head. "Miss Parker?"

Aarush opened his mouth, but I cut him off. "Long story. She's okay, really and needs the help."

"You can't do this alone." Bailey's blonde hair was plastered to her scalp. "None of us has skills yet."

"True," Pari agreed. "But we have heart. Let's go."

Lydia moaned, her hands grasping her skull. "They've got her! Miss Parker! I can feel her anger... and fear. Can you hear anything, Forrest?"

Her brother tilted his head and looked toward the mountain, his eyes distant. "It's hollow sounding and coming from there. Miss Parker is trapped...there!" He pointed toward the volcano. The way up was a dense mess of bushes, the ground, a tangled web of knotted roots and vines. This was not going to be a walk in the park.

I spun, almost slipping in the mud. "How do you know that?

"*Duh*. We're empaths. We feel things. There's no time for this, Grady."

Bailey shoved me out of the way, moving determinedly toward the other end of the island.

The rain was coming down. I moved sideways, only to find Shaquille next to me. "Don't waste minutes. Let's go," he urged.

I stopped in the downpour, my feet sinking into the sand. "It's dangerous."

Aarush put his hand on my shoulder. "Then we'll all face it together."

Pari climbed up the incline. "Come on."

The ring burned on my chest. I turned to look at Scarface Mountain, its peak was hidden by a cluster of clouds.

Forrest pointed to the summit. "Up there. We have to get there."

We took off. The rain stung our faces but stopped as abruptly as it started. Much as I want to say the school uniform was able to soak up the downpour, we were so wet, I felt clammy under the material.

My chest tightened with anxiety, and I reached for my asthma inhaler. I closed my eyes for a second, breathing deeply, trying to control my nerves by using Miss Garcia's calming exercises. The wheeze subsided.

I heard Aarush panting as he pulled himself up the roots, my nails breaking as I gripped the vines to claw my way to the top. There appeared to be flat, sandy surfaces between the roots. I stepped on the muddy soil only to lose my footing as the sand sucked at my feet.

"Watch out! The ground is not solid," I called.

Forrest looked skyward and shouted, "*Oh no.*" He was holding on with both hands to a branch from a clump of bushes as we trudged up the rock-strewn path. "Guys…look up."

The screech of something very large echoed above us. I glanced through the thick leaves, my eyes going wide. "Aarush, how is that even possible…?"

"*Hmmm,*" came Aarush's reply. "DNA?"

Two pterodactyls circled overhead, their huge wingspans flapping as they dipped to observe us. They were enormous. We must have looked like dinner to them.

"Do you think they're real?" Pari asked. We stood peering through the trees. "Maybe they're an illusion like Miss Parker's octopus."

"Well, I don't want to test that theory," Bailey said. I saw her back stiffen along with the curse she uttered.

"What is it?" I asked.

"We've got company," Bailey replied.

Lucas Reinholt stood boldly on the ground above us, blocking our way. He appeared taller, more filled out. His skin had a strange luminosity, a silver quality, as if he were made of fluid. I watched his face turn steely as he took us in. He crooked his finger, inviting us to join him.

Bailey grunted and raced up the incline, the screeching pterodactyls forgotten. She reached Lucas. She reared back a fist and surged forward, attacking him.

I heard Aarush gasp in awe as Lucas's body bent backward, avoiding Bailey's blow. Lucas's fluid body disappeared from the spot, reformed whole and dangerous nearby, steering clear of her punch. He pushed Bailey, and she tumbled down the side of the hill. Shaquille was there in an instant and stopped her descent. Winded, she got on all fours and clawed her way up the hilly terrain.

I leaped onto an outcropping of dirt and rocks, Aarush next to me. I pushed the heels of my hands forward. They connected with Lucas, going right through his body. I heard him laughing.

"Where is Miss Parker?" I demanded.

Lucas made a swooshing sound, like a tide coming in to shore. Sidestepping me, he evaded my attack as neatly as he'd done with Bailey's.

"Grady!" Pari yelled. "Watch out!"

With the force of a hurricane, water hit me squarely in my chest, knocking the wind from me. I rolled down, roots and branches smacking my face until I felt Shaquille's small body blocking my fall.

"How'd you get here so fast?" I asked groggily. I saw Bailey cresting the landing again, only to be pushed down by Lucas's superior strength. Shaquille was gone an instant later.

Aarush was calmly observing Lucas and dodging the assault. He almost seemed as if he were doing a dance. Aarush's face constantly turned upward. He was watching for something. *Was he attempting to call the giant pterodactyls for help?* Not one of his best ideas, I wanted to shout.

I opened my mouth to yell. Lucas was throwing Forrest and his sister, Lydia, over the side of the outcropping now. Pari was hanging onto a branch. I saw her dangle her feet over, gain purchase, swing twice, and finally land on the ledge.

She and Aarush cornered Lucas. I saw Aarush raise his face to the sky, followed by a glance at Pari with satisfaction.

She nodded with a grim smile, and the two of them moved toward Lucas in unison.

"Aarush!" I screamed. They were going to be annihilated. I forced my leaden legs to climb, but the wet soil sucked at me, pulling me into its mushy embrace.

Aarush kept glancing toward the horizon. Then I saw it. Rocks and debris exploded from the volcano. It soared high and was now traveling down to earth.

"Over there!" Aarush shouted to Pari pointing to the center of the cliff we were on. I slogged up the mountain and reached the fight, boxing in Lucas. He lunged for me. I ducked to the right and, with a glance to where Aarush pointed, did a little shuffle in that direction.

"Come get me, you drowned rat!" I called.

Lucas leaped for me, and his hands weighed down my chest. He was throttling me, his fingers pressed against my windpipe, the breath seizing in my chest.

"Left, Grady. Move left," Aarush called.

Lucas's hands were heavy and wet. I felt water flooding my throat. Choking, my airway compressed, I pulled him along, moving as far left as I could drag him and his water-logged body.

The sound of screaming like a missile headed for earth, rang out from above us. We both looked up at the same time. Lucas's watery body tensed, and his hands dropped. I jumped backward, landing ten feet away, flat on my back. The hot lava rock hit Lucas, causing the fluid in his cells to sizzle and crackle as his temperature rose. The water that comprised him boiled. I sat slack-jawed as he was reduced to hissing steam, evaporating a second later.

I sprawled onto the hard ground, exhausted. Aarush and the others joined me.

"Horrible," Pari said with a shudder. "I feel bad about Lucas."

Nobody responded.

"Clearly, Valencia Templeton has accelerated their studies." Aarush collapsed next to me. "You okay?"

I nodded. "You?"

He rose and studied the sweeping side of the volcano. "We'd better get going."

"How did you know it was going to blow?"

Aarush stamped his foot. "I felt the vibrations under my feet."

We continued our climb. It could have been hours. The clouds surrounded us, and my skin pebbled from the cold. Leaves slashed us, their razor-sharp fronds slicing our tender skin. We crowded into a clearing near the top and stopped. It was as far as we could go. The ground was soft under our feet. I looked at the cone of the volcano. I had no idea how we were going to get into that thing.

Bailey stared at the summit. "Holy, shemoly. What is this thing?"

Pari stood next to her. "It's too small to be a volcano."

Forrest laid his ear against the wall of the cliff. "It sounds man-made," he said.

"That's what Miss Parker indicated," Aarush stated. "She said they created it as a defense mechanism."

"Let me take another listen." Forrest edged toward a clearing, then yelled, his feet sinking into the ground. He waved his hands wildly and looked to be shrinking by the minute. With a start, I realized he was sinking!

"Quicksand!" he yelled.

"Don't move!" Aarush shouted. "Be still! The more you move, the quicker you will sink into quicksand!"

That Aarush, I marveled, is a vault of information.

Shaquille was there in an instant. Both Aarush and I reached over the sandpit toward Forrest. Our hands couldn't reach him. Lydia pushed her way through us. I had to hold her back from falling into the quagmire. Forrest bobbed, sinking lower with each moment.

"We need something to pull him out," Shaquille said.

Lydia disappeared. A minute later, we heard her shouting above us. She had sprinted up a palm tree and was untangling a long vine from the trunk.

"Look out!" she called. I watched her take a deep breath. Hanging on the vine, she swung toward her brother, her arm outstretched. "Forrest!" she shouted.

We all ducked. Lydia flew through the air, gripped Forrest by his outstretched hand, and plucked him from the quicksand. He popped out like a cork from a champagne bottle. We all cheered but quieted when he heard them crash into a thicket of trees on the other side.

Lydia was out cold, Forrest on top of her. We scrambled to their sprawled bodies.

Forrest got to his feet shakily. I steadied him as he looked down at his sister. "Lydie?"

Her head rolled against the tree. Pari was on the ground, lifting Lydia's eyelid. "She's okay. Bumped her head, I think."

"I have to get her back," Forrest said. He tried to carry her, but couldn't on the rocky terrain.

"Shaquille, you and Forrest carry her back. We'll go on," Bailey said.

The mountaintop belched a plume of thick, black smoke. I heard Bailey mutter, "You'd better get moving. This thing looks like it's going to blow." The land rocked. Bailey pushed her hair out of her eyes. "Let's get moving."

Forrest and Shaquille propped their shoulders against Lydia and started their return. "Good luck," Shaquille called, his face grim.

We inched around the clearing. The ground got narrower as we neared the edge of the cliff. Everything smelled like burnt rubber. The ground shook, and small rocks rained down on us.

Pari and Bailey stood together. Bailey made a cup with her hands for Pari to step on to climb upwards.

The volcano roared. Pari shouted. I watched in horror as the ground cracked, creating a jagged opening that separated us from the girls. They teetered over the edge, then slipped in a gash through the ground. I heard their screams echoing back. There was a grinding sound, and the ground closed up.

"Why did I let them come?" I screamed. "Pari!"

Aarush fell on his hands and knees to examine the raw cut in the earth. "It *is* man-made."

I kneeled. "I'm not sure about this."

"I am." Aarush grabbed a stick and scraped at the dirt. The sound changed when he hit metal.

"Let me see." I pushed away the pile of earth and felt a metal wall, jumping away when I touched hot steel. "The whole thing is artificial. There has to be a way into here."

The entire mountain shook, sending us tumbling down the cliff in a tangle of branches, tree limbs, and an occasional puddle of steaming rocks. My foot got stuck and Aarush pulled it out of the sneaker.

Something hit me with the force of a Mack truck. I went down the incline like a cannonball. I could hear Aarush's grunts as he slid down the rocky hill into a small pond of water.

You remember it all began with my coming to awareness with a great hulking humanoid hewn from stone hanging over me laughing. You must have guessed who it was by now. I heard Aarush groan.

"You okay, Aarush?"

I heard a weak response. "Yes."

"The others?"

"Gone, Whill! They are gone forever!" a hateful voice roared.

"Elwood," I said, looking up at the brute above me. "What happened to you?"

Elwood laughed, that maniacal laughter that's meant to scare rather than share a joke. I found his sense of humor pathetic but thought it prudent not to point that out with his foot crushing the air from my chest.

"Just as you have honed your skills, so have I."

Skills? I thought wildly. *Skills*. All I've done is wrestle with the meaning of a useless bunch of poetry. This year was a waste. A total waste. I came to Templeton to change my life and found myself in the same spot as before—under Elwood's proverbial heel.

"Wanna arm wrestle?" He laughed.

I peered up at him. He looked as if he were carved from the granite that made up the island. I raised a hand and touched his leg. I was right earlier. He was stone. How was this possible?

"You wasted your time chasing after stupid statements while I learned practical applications with a professor who shared rather than hoarded her information." Elwood flexed his muscles. "Valencia is a good teacher."

We stopped talking. I heard a splash as Aarush waded through the stream, making his way to dry land.

"Aarush!" I called.

"Forget him, Grady," said Elwood. "He's damaged goods. Don't you see? I'll give you one last chance. Join Valencia. Forget about the school. It's a distraction." He ground his heel into my chest, making me feel the loose rocks bite into the skin of my back.

"*Ow.* Cut. It. Out. Elwood." I struggled against the pressure of his foot, but I was caught like an insect. Behind us, Scarface Mountain lit up like a Fourth of July fireworks display. All I wanted to do was get up and see if the others were okay. Boulder Boy was absorbed at the pyrotechnics display.

I glanced to my left. Aarush was making his way steadily toward me, his face determined. He was repeating something softly. Gandhi. He was reciting what he had told me about being strong. It wasn't a quatrain, but it would do just fine. My mind rushed back to what he'd said. "*Strength does not come from physical capacity. It comes from an indomitable will. You can do this if you believe.*"

This would be as good a time as any for me to become a believer. I had to find my friends and Miss Parker. I closed my eyes, taking a deep breath. I concentrated on the oxygen bubbling throughout my bloodstream, invigorating each of my cells.

I felt the air being crushed out of me. Elwood must have been pressing harder. I let my mind roam over my entire body one bone at a time. I think I might have stopped breathing. I felt so removed from myself, I slipped into a sleeplike state. I honestly don't remember much.

Something happened. It started in the center of my chest where the ring rested against my breastbone. It heated up, and the warmth spread from my chest down my arms. I flexed my hands, feeling a tingling that grew in intensity. My muscles twitched as if they had a mind of their own.

I thought about my journey to get to this place, Aarush talking about the simple physics of arm wrestling, cryptic asymmetry, the illusion of strength due to size, Gandhi, the power coming from within, and failure being good. Failure makes us stronger. Failure works because we come back ready to try and try again. Quatrain two resounded in my head loud and clear.

I looked at Elwood and really saw him. I had to stop judging his strength on what I was seeing and realize I only had to worry about me, where I knew *my* strength came from. Of this I was sure. I had to define my strength not on what I thought Elwood might be. The memory of our arm-wrestling rushed back with sudden clarity. *Strength does not come from physical capacity; it comes from an indomitable will.*

I rose up like a rocket, my hand fisted, aiming for Elwood's rock-hewn face. I pounded him on the chin and for a minute felt nothing until the pain radiated up to my armpit. *"Ow!"* He was solid rock, impenetrable, dense.

Elwood picked me up by the neck and shook me like a rag doll. He hung me over the cliff. "I'd like to say it's been fun, but I'm tired of playing games."

"Games?" I heard Aarush's voice. "I like games."

"No, Aarush!"

"Rock, paper, scissors….Rock, paper, scissors."

"What are you talking about, you numbnut? You'd better run, Rooshy, 'cause you're next," Elwood said with a confident laugh.

I heard Elwood's chuckle as I hung suspended over the gorge. I saw Aarush coming up from behind. He was shirtless, his uniform flapping in the breeze.

"What are you doing?" I choked out. "Go....Aarush, run!"

"Rock, paper, scissors....Rock, paper, scissors. ..." Aarush was sending me a message, but all I heard was his monotonous voice, and I couldn't control the sinking feeling my friend was going to be murdered.

Aarush swung his shirt up, hooking it over Elwood's head, effectively blinding him. Elwood twisted around and dropped me on the ground instead of off the cliff. His clumsy fingers couldn't grip the shirt material to pull it off. He howled in frustration.

"Paper wins," Aarush said. "Well, technically not paper, but my shirt will do." I could tell Aarush was pleased with himself. He looked at me. "It has nothing to do with size or strength, Grady. Remember?"

I dodged around Elwood's hulking body. He had his arms outstretched like Frankenstein's monster.

"You have to look for weaknesses. His fingers have no feeling," Aarush told me. "They can't make fine motor movements."

"*Shhh*," I warned. "Be quiet. Let's get out of here."

Aarush shook his head and replied, "Not yet. Here I am. Come get me, you petrified lunk."

Elwood roared blindly, trying to locate us.

"Over here, doofus. Leave no stone unturned." Aarush was watching Elwood make his clumsy way over. "I think you've hit rock bottom, blockhead."

I ran over to Aarush and grabbed his thin arms. This was no time for him to test his stand-up routine. Aarush disengaged my hands with determination in his face. I shook him then. "Are you suicidal?"

"Come and get me, stonehead," he called.

Elwood managed to tear off the shirt, which flew away like a streamer. He lunged for Aarush and me. Aarush pushed me out of the way. Elwood landed with a splash in the quicksand that had almost swallowed Forrest.

"No!" Elwood screamed, flailing his arms. "Help me!"

I wiped the sweat from my forehead, leaving a dark streak. "Good thinking, Aarush."

"Yes," he said. "Let's go, now."

I looked at Aarush and opened my mouth to say we couldn't leave Elwood to die when he gave me a warning with an almost imperceptible nod of his head. "Come on, Grady. Let's get moving."

"No!" Elwood screamed. He dipped his mouth, filling it with quicksand. He coughed and sputtered for a minute, then pleaded, "I can help you find the others. There's a way in."

Aarush's eyebrows rose so far up, I might have laughed. His lips tipped at one corner in what I knew was an Aarush smile.

"Where? How?" I leaned over toward Elwood.

"Help me, Grady." Elwood held out one hand, pleading for me to take it.

I reached out. Aarush slapped my hand away. "Don't help him, Grady. He'll be fine," he said, looking at our former roommate, "if he sits still."

Elwood slipped lower into the muddy sand. Soon it covered his chin.

"You're between a rock and a soft place, Elwood," I said and sat back on my heels. "You'll be okay if you stop struggling. How do we get in?"

He motioned to the rock wall. "You'll need me to move the boulder in front of the entrance." He swayed buoyantly, sputtering when he got a mouthful of quicksand. "Help me and I'll take you to them."

I stood up and looked at the stone blocking a cave-like entrance. *How did I miss that?*

"You need me," he called, his voice on the edge of hysteria.

I looked at Aarush, who responded with a definite negative shake of his head. I nodded. "I don't think so. We can do this on our own. Just pretend you're floating, Elwood. We'll be back as soon as we find Miss Parker."

CHAPTER 23

THROUGH THE WORMHOLE

WE LEFT ELWOOD spitting and cursing but imprisoned in the quicksand and headed to the blocked entrance.

Aarush examined the seam in the rock. He pressed against the stone. It didn't budge.

"What do we do now?" I asked.

Aarush continued pushing with his shoulder, his face red from the effort.

I looked around for an idea. We were in a jungle, nothing here but a bunch of bushes and us. I thought about Pari, my heart beating wildly in my chest. I had to find a way to her. I bunched my fist in frustration, striking it against the wall of greenery behind me. Stalks of bamboo echoed hollowly back at us. I leaned against several of the trees, my lips pursed in thought.

Aarush lifted his face, and scratched his head. "We need

something to place underneath the boulder to move it. Something cylindrical. That's how they moved the big blocks for the pyramids. They placed logs underneath the heavy rocks, and they were able to push…Hey, Grady, where are you going?"

I didn't wait. I climbed up a group of straight shoots of bamboo, forcing it to bend and finally splitting them at the base.

"Ah, yes. The bamboo. Nicely done." Aarush grabbed a few of the broken shafts, twisting the fibers until they tore.

"Forget about that," I said. "Start digging space under the rock so we can squeeze shafts between the rock and soil."

Aarush cupped his hands and dug like a dog while I broke off a half-dozen stalks. The bamboo was hard and fibrous. Without a knife, it was nearly impossible to rip a stalk off its base. Gritting my teeth, I didn't think about the difficulty. My mind merely saw the pile of small logs growing, and that was all I needed to motivate me to break the bamboo off. My hands bled. I was stabbed by a sharpened spike, but adrenaline kept me from noticing or even feeling it. Sweat dripping from my forehead; we stuffed the stalks under the rock until it looked like we had a bamboo mat underneath it.

Elwood's feeble cries filled the clearing, but we ignored him.

The rock jiggled, then rolled on the bamboo as if the stalks were on a conveyor belt. Aarush and I cheered with excitement and pushed the boulder a short distance, making a space large enough for us to squeeze through.

Aarush didn't wait. He leaped before me. I heard his yell of surprise, his voice growing distant as if he were falling. I squeezed through the small space, and my foot landed on something slippery. It wrenched my leg, and I fell hard on my butt. I slid downward as if on an amusement park ride.

"Aarush!" I screamed, but it came out in a thin wail. The darkness smothered me. It felt like I was going down an endless tunnel. I landed with a thump and careened into a soft body that moaned when I slammed into it.

"Aarush?"

Aarush sat up, holding his head. "I went down headfirst." I could see blood shining on his face under his nose. "What do you think this place is?" I asked.

"No idea." Aarush rose shakily to his feet.

I wasn't too steady either. I got up, and turning around, I realized we were in some sort of tunnel. Holding onto the carved walls, we walked downward. We could hear the roar of the volcano as we got closer.

The passageway opened to a laboratory. We stopped short of entering. Valencia Templeton was at a control panel, her gaze rapt. Behind her, Miss Parker was in a large cube, suspended in midair. In separate boxes were Pari and Bailey. There were no bars.

"Electromagnetic force field," Aarush squinted. "My dad's been working on something like this for the government. It's what he's been using to keep my room floating over the living room."

"What?"

"Yes, Grady. My father is using magnetic power to make the rooms float in—"

I turned to look at him. "I thought your dad makes games for video systems."

He shrugged. "Oh, that's just a cover."

I wanted to question him further, but this was not the

time or place for that. "Okay, so how do we get them out?" I asked in a whisper.

Aarush rubbed a cut on his cheek. "We have to pull the plug?"

I looked at him. "You're kidding."

He looked at me with those serious brown eyes.

"You're not kidding?" I felt the adrenaline leave as my body got shaky.

"No. We have to locate the power ..." His voice trailed off as he scanned the room. "Right there." He pointed to a huge box.

"Great. How do you expect us to turn off the power?"

Aarush looked at me and then glanced at Valencia. "I will need just a few minutes."

I nodded. I knew what I had to do; I had to distract Valencia. We crouched by an pile of boulders, watching and waiting for an opportunity.

Valencia Templeton had changed drastically. Her hair wasn't neatly confined to a ponytail. It was like a wild red halo around her face. Her jaw had hardened like Elwood's, but not from rock; hers had determination. Her amber eyes now appeared to be blazing yellow; they glowed intensely.

"She looks crazy," I whispered.

Aarush nodded in agreement.

Miss Parker threw herself against the force field. It crackled and hummed, holding her captive with its energy. She slid to the floor, wiped out from the jolt of whatever powered that thing.

"Valencia, let us out," Miss Parker called weakly.

Valencia ignored her. She was busy adjusting buttons on her control panel.

"At least let the children go," Miss Parker implored.

"At least let the children go," Valencia mimicked. "It's gone too far for that, Erin. I've told you all once already. You can either join me or die."

Miss Parker got to her knees. "This is insane, Valencia. Why are you doing this?"

Valencia stormed to the cube holding them. She held up her hands, her thumb and forefinger touching. "Watch this, children."

Valencia stretched her two fingers apart. An electric current ran between them. "Look, Erin. Look what I can do." She pointed to the group of boulders where both Aarush and I were hiding, then snapped her fingers and pointed. The rocks grew hot.

Aarush pushed me back. We scrambled behind a wall as the stones exploded. We must have been exposed for a second because Pari's eyes locked on mine as we retreated to the shadows. She knew I was there. Pari leaned over and whispered something to Bailey. I saw Pari's gaze sweep the cavern.

"You've read the whole Codex?" Miss Parker asked.

Valencia inclined her head. "Read, tested, and absorbed."

"Your father hasn't given permission yet." Miss Parker leaned weakly against the cube's wall. "Where is the Codex.?"

"You'll never find it, Erin," Valencia laughed. She shrugged indifferently. "My father is old and feeble. He's afraid of the power. He'd rather spend his time playing principal than using our gifts. Join me, Erin."

"Remember what it did to Brad and Susan! The knowledge destroyed them!"

My mouth dropped open. Brad and Susan were my parents! I mean, what was the possibility of two couples with the same name?

Valencia shrugged. "They were not capable of handling the Codex."

Miss Parker looked down, her expression sad. "Yes, and that's why your father decided we shall all learn it slowly, carefully."

"Stay and play your school games with him, Erin." She turned to the girls. "Bailey, Pari, come with me."

"I'll join you," Baily called out. "Let me out of this contraption."

Valencia laughed, a wild, crazy laugh. I knew then she was nuts. She raised a finger to the box. I saw Bailey look directly at me with a barely imperceptible nod.

"On my command, we rush her," I said. Aarush dipped his head.

Valencia raised her fingers, snapped them, and an electrical charge exploded from them directed at the cube. She used hand movements to bring the device down to the floor.

"Now," I said softly. Both Aarush and I ran from our spot and smashed into Valencia, causing her aim to go wide and hit the control panel. The controls fizzled, then crackled with a shower of sparks. The cube hung drunkenly to one side, the force field snapping as if short-circuited.

Valencia went down flat on her back. Her heels lashed out, catching me on the shoulder and ripped my uniform. So much for being indestructible.

Aarush struggled with Valencia's hands, keeping her fingers from touching. She grappled with him, then shoved him off. He landed with a thud, his head connecting with the edge of a console. His eyes slid shut. My chest constricted with worry, but I had to subdue Valencia before I could see if Aarush was alright.

Valencia got to her feet. I grabbed her and dragged her back down. I heard her ankle crack. She moaned, managed to twist out of my grasp, and snap her fingers.

I heard Bailey yell, "Grady, watch out!"

I smelled burning bacon and realized it was me. My uniformed arm was on fire.

I dropped and rolled. It didn't work! Something in the uniform was aggravating the fire.

"Blow it out, Grady! You can do it!" Miss Parker called.

"Don't tell him that. It will fan the flames!" Pari wailed.

"No, Grady. Trust me." Miss Parker's voice cut through all the noise.

I hopped to my feet, blowing ineffectually at the flames. Sweat poured down my face.

"Blow harder, like you are the north wind!" cried Miss Parker.

I tapped the flames with my hand, burning the skin on my palm. I was going to die, or at the very least be burned to a crisp.

"Come on, Grady! You can do this!" Bailey shouted. "You have to believe in yourself."

I tried to block out the commotion raging around me. Mere seconds passed, but everything crystalized in a clear message in my brain.

The quatrains appeared, floating in three-dimensional bright colors. *Do not fear failure. Failure makes us stronger. Failure makes us smarter. Failure is good.*

Aarush's voice filled my ears. "Strength does not come from physical capacity. It comes from an indomitable will."

Miss Garcia's lessons reverberated within me. "Reality is a product of your inner voice. If you want to alter it, change what you say to yourself."

Crabs with misshapen claws marched inside my brain. "Just because someone is bigger, they have the illusion of more strength. You have the same amount of power. All you have to do is use your brain."

Lastly, my own inner voice drowned out all the others. *Thoughts become things. ...*

I took a deep breath that felt like it came from Antarctica and blew. A breeze as cold as the north wind whistled from my lips. I opened my eyes to see the fire extinguished on my arm and Valencia's face dusted with frost. She had dragged herself to the control console and was fighting to rise.

There was the screech of something large and scary, followed by the flap of leather wings. Shattered glass rained down on us as bus-sized pterodactyl swept in from the opening of the volcano. I reached forward and yanked a dazed Aarush as the flying dinosaur glided down, snatched Valencia with its talons, and pulled her up through the broken roof. They flew upward and Valencia's screams became fainter.

"Who did that?" Miss Parker demanded.

Bailey leaped down from her defunct cube and said, "Me."

Simultaneously Pari shouted, "I did!" She was bouncing on the shell of her cube. "Aarush, move that closer." She pointed to a console on wheels. "I think I can jump onto it."

Miss Parker chuckled weakly. She was dangling with one arm from her cube. "It was all of us. How we all thought of the same thing at once is a miracle."

"I disagree. You all thought about what was bigger than Valencia and—," Aarush started.

"Never mind that!" I yelled. "She's getting away!"

"Maybe she'll be lunch," Miss Parker responded.

"For imaginary creatures?" I said.

"Thoughts become things," Pari said. She stood next to me. "You were very brave."

"They were real?" I asked.

"They are now," answered Miss Parker. "The Codex has to be treated with respect. Your parents didn't understand that."

Ah, yes, my parents. "What are you talking about?"

A door burst open. Dr. Templeton walked through.

"The upshot is ..." he said, "your father discovered the Codex and brought it to me."

"How ...?" I stuttered.

Dr. Templeton raised his arm to stop me from speaking. "I was his professor at college. He and your mother found it. I warned them it had to be studied. If not fully comprehended, the knowledge of the Codex is a frightening thing."

"It's only dangerous if you don't understand the extent of what it can do," Miss Parker explained. "I'm sorry about Valencia. We did not recover the Codex." Dr. Templeton sighed. Above us, the sounds of a helicopter echoed. "That will be your father, Aarush," Dr. Templeton said.

Aarush nodded.

Was I the only one who didn't understand what was going on?

Dr. Templeton herded us toward a ramp and led us out. "I'm sorry I couldn't get here sooner. I had to evacuate the school."

The island looked shriveled. The exploded volcano, a hollow shell, the lush greenery, wasted and smoking. The sun was setting in the West on both the island and our stay there.

"Elwood!" I yelled.

Dr. Templeton pointed to two specks in the distance. "Another pterodactyl plucked him from the pit he was in, and there they go."

"Apparently they won't be on the menu," Bailey added.

"If thoughts become things, I'm inclined to believe Valencia figured out a way to redirect their instincts," Dr. Templeton said softly. He stroked his chin and said with regret, "I always felt she was too smart for her own good."

"Pity," Miss Parker replied.

"I want to know more about my parents!" I rounded on Dr. Templeton with fury. "Are you telling me you all knew them? And," I said, turning to Aarush, "why is your father rescuing us?"

"I own Dream Weaver Industries," Dr. Templeton said calmly. "Aarush's parents work for me."

"Did you know?" I asked Aarush.

"No," Aarush quietly. I thought he looked hurt. "I thought he worked for the government. I would have told you."

I swallowed the lump in my throat. "I know. That still doesn't answer my questions about my parents."

"You will have to redefine your past, and that can't happen in a few minutes. I will help you with that," Miss Parker said. I looked at her and for the first time saw something other than hostility in her face. "You are just seeing me in a new light, Grady. It was there the whole time. Your mother was my best friend. I have so much to tell you."

"When do we start?"

"Not for some time," Dr. Templeton said. "We have to find a new location for the school."

Miss Parker nodded grimly. "We did not recover the Codex."

The chopper landed on a small clearing. The rotating blades stirred the thick air. Aarush's mother bounded out of the helicopter and ran to embrace her son. She pulled me into her hug, along with Bailey and Pari. "Let's get you kids home," she said.

Home, I wondered. *Where is that now?* I had begun to think of school as my home, but it was gone. Leo and Joni— what did they know? I looked at Miss Parker.

"I know you have a lot of questions. I will answer them all in time, I promise. For now, your uncle will fill you in."

My uncle? "Leo?" I asked, my voice a mere whisper.

Mrs. Dr. Patel pulled my unresisting body toward the chopper. I must have been in some sort of shock because it never registered on my dazed mind that I was going to be very high up in the sky soon.

I dug in my heels, pulling my arm out of Aarush's mother's grasp. I ran to Miss Parker. "What does my uncle know?" I demanded.

"Some of it. It's his story to tell you. Go home, Grady. I will see you soon enough and fill in the rest."

The subject was closed. She turned to talk to Dr. Templeton.

I could see from her set face and the warmth of the stone near my chest. It was talking to me; I knew it. Don't ask how, but I just knew it. I heard the words in my head. Part of me wanted to be as far as possible from everybody. I wanted to examine everything, from my discoveries about my parents and their secret life to the weird communications I was getting from the ring.

They loaded us onto the gleaming black helicopter, *Dream Weaver Enterprises* emblazoned on the side. We lifted off and circled away, the defunct volcano looking hollow and devoid of life, the school half-covered with smoking lava.

"You'll find out everything, Grady. Sophomore year

is always the one for revelations!" I heard Aarush yell over the din.

I looked down to see Miss Parker standing next to Dr. Templeton. She looked up, shielding her eyes from the bright glare of the sun. Then she waved.

"See you in September," I whispered.

"You're going back?" Pari asked.

I didn't answer. Instead, all my attention was on Templeton and Miss Parker, watching them until they looked like nothing more than black dots on the smoking island.

Pari turned to her aunt. "Aren't they getting out?"

"There's another helicopter coming for them. Don't worry about Dr. Templeton."

Aarush moved closer to me. "Look, Grady, you're not even afraid."

I shook myself out of my stupor and realized I was hundreds of feet above a solid mass of water in nothing more than a glorified mosquito.

"You did learn something in that school," said Aarush.

I swallowed, words clogging my throat.

Bailey tapped my arm. "Are you coming back?"

"Are you?" I asked.

She looked at Pari, Aarush, and me. "You bet. You?"

I looked down at the rushing waves beneath me. My fear was gone. Frankly, I had no idea where it had gone and was more than okay with that. All that was then replaced by a yearning. I had so much I needed to discover. I looked at the concerned faces of Pari and Aarush and nodded. "I have to go back."

The helicopter banked toward Miami and the setting sun. First, I wanted to talk to Leo and find out what he did know. Then I had to go back to discover what happened to Valencia, Elwood, and the Codex. I needed to find out what Miss Parker knew about my parents. And most importantly, I wanted to know what quatrain three was. I was ready to learn.

EPILOGUE

I ARRIVED HOME THE same way I left, with the clothes on my back, my asthma inhaler, and my father's peculiar ring.

I stared at my reflection in Mema's hall mirror. I appeared the same, just somewhat older. Yet everything in my world had shifted as if some seismic event had occurred.

The house was empty. No dishes were in the sink; the fridge had an abundance of food. I felt as if I were in a parallel universe.

I walked from room to room, touching the furniture, picking up a picture, trying to see what was different. When Mema had died, our home had turned into a house—cold, uninviting. Over the course of the year, it had become a home again. Had I slipped through a portal into another universe, to some strange dimension? Had the year at Templeton never happened? Had Mema and Grandpa not died? And it was all a bad dream?

I ran into Mema and Pops's room. It was different. One wall was painted a pale purple. The bedspread was new, with some gray geometric design. I swung open the closet door to find it filled with Leo's and...Joni's wardrobe. What was going on?

I heard a throat clearing. My heart jumped into my own throat.

"We were going to tell you."

I spun. Joni stood in the doorway, her hair a soft natural brown, her face jewelry gone. She looked older.

"You live here now?" I asked.

"Leo and I got engaged while you were away." She walked toward me and put her arm around my back.

"You didn't say anything." I swallowed hard, processing the information. I felt left out.

"We wanted to share the news with you in person." Joni looked at me earnestly.

I must have stiffened because she squeezed my shoulders, "Ask him now, Leo." She had such a sweet smile on her face it was hard to stay mad.

"It was kinda sudden," Leo said. Joni cuffed him on the shoulder and he laughed. "Well, it was."

Leo's expression forced a bubble of laughter to escape my lips. Leo looked nervous. "We... I mean, me- It would mean a lot to me if you'd be my best man."

"Leo missed you so much," she said simply, then added. "He missed having a family. Will you let me be part of yours?"

I grinned back at her and without thinking responded, "I thought you already were."

Leo ruffled my hair, his expression relieved.

"I have a lot of questions," I said, but I have to admit my voice felt thick.

Joni smiled. "I bet you do."

"Not about what you think," I said. "I'm glad you're together." I kissed her cheek. "Welcome to the family, Aunt."

She hugged me. The ring on my chest warmed, I looked down at Leo's hand noticing for the first time he was wearing an identical ring that was pulsing with a life of its own.

"You said it was my birthright."

I didn't have to say more. Leo walked me toward the sofa. We sat down, and he looked me right in the eye.

"You come from a long line of special people, Grady. It's time you found out about it."

And so it began.

AUTHOR'S NOTE

I HOPE YOU ENJOYED *Grady Whill and the Templeton Codex.* This book developed from a conversation about kids with special needs. My sons and I kicked around an idea about superheroes that face more than crime issues, but the simple challenges of everyday life. And so Aarush was born!

I have lived with learning disabilities my entire life. The simple task of tying a shoelace, math problems, and telling time did not come easily to me. Yet, I worked hard with patient teachers who never let these deficits get in the way of my confidence. I went on to build a huge business and write over sixty award-winning books.

Both my son and granddaughter overcame great obstacles as well to learn what others think are mundane tasks. We had to work hard to compensate for that which comes to other people naturally. I have immense respect for parents, teachers, and students who work tirelessly through those challenges.

People who are different struggle with many things besides education. Sometimes friendships are difficult. They are overlooked and not included. Bullies find them easy targets. All people have so much to offer. This world has a lot to learn about valuing others.

I decided to give Grady asthma. Both of my sons have struggled with severe allergies and asthma. They were thrilled to cheer on a fellow asthmatic to victory.

In order to achieve anything you need a team. I have the best support system in the world.

Miranda Reads, Erin Glen, and Michele Hudson's beta reading give encouragement and help me sew up those pesky plot holes. Their keen understanding of what I'm trying to do often goes unspoken between us. They get it. *Yeah,* guys. I love Aarush too. Jane, Robin, and Molly are the best cheering squad I could have.

I'd like to thank Chrissy Hobbs from Indie Publishing Group, whose patience and professionalism make editing appear both easy and seamless. Also, special thanks to my friend Grady Harp, who generously lent me his delightful first name.

My extended family, Stuart and the rest. Thanks for your support.

My daughters-in-law, Sharon and Jennifer keep me on my toes and relevant. I would be lost without you. Alexander, Hallie, Cayla, and Zachary are my motivation. I'll do anything to get you guys to read! Kevin, you taught me how to tie my shoes fifty years ago and never gave up on me. My sons, Michael and Eric, have shown me that reinvention is the mother of success. I couldn't work with better partners.

Lastly to my parents and David. Without you, it would never have been worth it.

Carole P. Roman

Oyster Bay Cove 2022

AUTHOR BIO

Carole P. Roman is the award-winning author of over fifty children's books. Whether it's pirates, princesses, and spies, or discovering the world around us, her books have enchanted educators, parents, and her diverse audience of children.

Carole has co-authored two self-help books. Navigating Indieworld: A Beginners Guide to Self-Publishing and Marketing with Julie A. Gerber, and Marketing Indieworld with both Julie A. Gerber and Angela Hausman. She published Mindfulness for Kids with J. Robin Albertson-Wren. The Big Book of Silly Jokes for Kids: 800+ Jokes! has reached the number one best-selling book on all of Amazon.

She writes adult fiction under the name Brit Lunden and is currently helping to create an anthology of the mythical town of Bulwark, Georgia with a group of indie authors. She lives on Long Island near her children and grandchildren.

Her series includes:

Captain No Beard

If You Were Me and Lived in- Cultural

If You Were Me and Lived in- Historical

Nursery series

Oh Susannah- Early Reader and coloring book

Mindfulness for Kids with co-author J. Robin Albertson-Wren

The Big Book of Silly Jokes for Kids; 800 plus Jokes!

Spies, Code Talkers, and Secret Agents
A World War 2 Book for Kids

Navigating Indieworld- with co-author Julie A. Gerber

Marketing Indieworld-
with co-authors Angela Hausman and Julie A. Gerber

Adult Fiction under the pen name Brit Lunden

Bulwark

The Knowing- Book 1- A Bulwark Anthology

The Devil and Dayna Dalton- Book 9-A Bulwark Anthology